World's End
By

G. Scovill

World's End

Copyright © 2017 by G. Scovill

Cover photo by GDKPhotography

The opinions expressed in this manuscript are solely the opinions of the author and do not represent the opinions or thoughts of the publisher. The author represents and warrants that s/he either owns or has the legal right to publish all material in this book.

First published in 2017

All Rights Reserved. This book may not be reproduced, transmitted, or stored in whole or in part by any means, including graphic, electronic, or mechanical without the express written consent of the publisher except in the case of brief quotations embodied in critical articles and reviews.

PRINTED IN THE UNITED STATES OF AMERICA

Chapter 1

October 21st, 5:55 p.m.

Dawson made his way out of his office toward the front door of the shop. With any luck at all he could close a few minutes early and head for home. It had been an exhausting day and he was done with it. Right now all he wanted was to go home, pour himself a stiff one and kick back in the recliner. He was about to lock the shop door when his cellphone rang. He sighed as he looked at the caller I.D. He slipped the lock on the door and answered the phone as he pulled the shades on the door.

"Hello, Janie." He said as politely as he could. Jane VanOrder was his ex-wife. Usually their conversations were polite and even cordial. Sometimes, however, they were not. The problem was he never knew until he answered the phone which it was going to be. Jane was bi-polar and her mood swings were unpredictable, instantaneous, and sometimes hazardous to those around her.

"Did you make your alimony payment yet?" she snapped.

Dawson sighed, "Yes, Janie, I did. It should be in your account by now. I moved it electronically last night."

"You are late!"

"Only by a technicality: I paid you on the day it was due, just after banking hours. It isn't my fault people don't pay their bills on time."

"I don't care about other people. I have expenses I have to cover." She snapped as though a few hours would make a difference.

Dawson sighed again. "Janie, it is a loop. People don't pay me, I can't pay you, and you can't pay your bills. Although I doubt the Piedmont Power is going to shut off your lights because you paid your bill on the 21st rather than the 20th."

"That isn't the point! It was late! I hate being late!" she snapped. "You don't get that."

"I'll tell you what...if they charge you a late fee for being one day behind let me know and I'll cover it."

"It isn't about the money!"

"Then I don't understand why we are having this discussion."

"I was late because you were late!"

Dawson sighed. This wasn't going anywhere and he knew Janie had fixated. "I'm sorry." He said in resignation. "I'll try to plan better in the future so it doesn't happen again."

"Thank you." She said and then added sweetly. "Can you come over tonight?"

"Come over?"

"Yeah...I'm lonely and need you to....well you know."

Dawson rolled his eyes. Obviously her mood had swung and now she was craving intimacy. Janie had divorced him because she wanted her freedom. She felt she was missing life and at thirty three years old she was almost past her prime, as she described it. The problem was that once she had her freedom she discovered the world wasn't what she thought it would be. She wasn't able to have a boyfriend of any significance. Her mood swings were more than they could handle, or wanted to handle, and soon bailed out on her. Dawson had married her when she was twenty one and she was still fairly normal and as her mood swings got worse over the years he had been able to adjust to them because they didn't just suddenly get worse overnight. Guys going into new a new relationship with her quickly discovered they weren't equipped to deal with her emotional instability. The result was a very long string of one night stands and two week long "forever" romances that ended in heartbreak for her.

The problem was that while Dawson had discovered he still loved Janie, he was living a much less stress filled life without her. He didn't want her back. Janie, on the other hand had come to realize she wanted him back. She wanted desperately to fix what she'd broken. As far as Dawson was concerned their relationship, like Humpty Dumpty, was beyond fixing no matter who tried what. Janie, however, refused to accept that.

"I don't think so, Janie. I have some things I need to do."

"I'm something you need to do." She purred seductively. "I'll even let you tie me up if you want."

"Janie, I..."

"Please?" She interrupted him. "Pretty please? I'll swallow. You know I hate that but I'll do it for you tonight if you'll come over." She continued to purr. "I just need you tonight. You can do anything you want to me all night long; and I really do mean you can do anything you want. Absolutely anything – even things I've never let you do before. I'll be your slave completely and entirely."

'Yeah, sure you will. Right up until your mood changes' Dawson thought to himself. To be honest, he was tempted. The one thing about Janie that *was* consistent was that she was fantastic in bed no matter what her mood. On the other hand he didn't want to give her any hope that their relationship could be repaired.

"I'll think about it." He lied. "I really will."

"I'll be naked when you get here." She said knowing he was tempted.

"I said I'll think about it. I have some important things I have to do first. I wasn't planning on coming to your place so I made a couple of commitments I have to honor. When they are covered, I'll come over." He was lying but he also knew she'd keep at it until her mood either shifted again or he gave in completely.

"I'll accept that." She cooed, "Just don't keep me waiting too long."

"I'll try to not do that." He said "I have to go. Like I said I have some things I have to do."

"OK. See you later, lover." She purred and then hung up.

Dawson sighed as he stared at the phone in his hand. He shook his head and then put the phone into his pocket. He wasn't going over to Janie's but he knew it was going to be a long night.

October 21st, 11:00 p.m.

"Open the hatch." Hassan Anvari ordered his First Mate. His First Mate passed the order along. It had been a long voyage. They had left port of Chabahar two weeks earlier in Iran as had her sister ships. Each had different destinations; all had the same purpose. His ship had taken a rather circuitous route to get where it was at this moment. The last week of the voyage had been sailed with the ship transponders turned off and she had spent the larger part of the voyage outside normal shipping lanes.

His ship was not a ship of war. It was a freighter. However, this voyage would be her last and she would never reach her declared destination. Her official declared destination was nowhere close to her current location which was, according to his sealed orders, her real destination. So now she sat well outside the territorial waters of the United States; a silent, waiting predator preparing to strike.

If things had gone according to plan her sister ships were now in their designated places and all were making the same preparations Anvari was making. By now those crews, like his own crew, had made their final prayers and performed their rituals. Now they were busy about their final tasks; tasks that would bring them martyrdom and entry into heaven by striking where no one could strike and bringing their great enemy to its knees. If the plan succeeded, the West would fall and Islam and Iran in particular, would pick up the pieces.

"Prepare for launch." he ordered after getting the message that the hatch was open. In moments over the normal noise of the ship he could hear the sounds of the hydraulics raising the missile into launch position. It would take a few minutes to get it into final position and all systems checked. Then countdown would begin. The missile was not huge, but neither was it a standard shipborne missile. The freighter had been refitted and reinforced but the ship would not likely survive the missile's launch. It was most likely that blast of ignition would set in motion the destruction of the very launch platform that sent it skyward. The ship would sink with all hands on board and disappear from existence taking with it all evidence of what nation initiated the strike.

Anvari was prepared for this. He'd spent his whole life preparing for this. To die striking at the heart of the enemies of Allah would be the ultimate sacrifice and would earn him the ultimate reward. He wasn't even nervous as most men would be if they knew their death was immanent and under his own control. Actually, he was excited. He was about to do a great thing.

"Missile positioned." His First Mate said in a businesslike manner.

"Very good. Right on time. Begin final preparations and checks."

"Yes, Sir!"

Anvari glanced down at the picture of his wife and two children he'd placed on the counter in front of him. He loved Behtan with all his heart. He and she had been fortunate in that they had married for love and not for family or for politics, or for any other reason couples often married in Iran. Leaving her was the only hard part of the mission. However, he felt he was giving his children a better world so such a loss was minor. He was lost in thought and so lost track of time.

"Preparations and checks complete." His First Mate said, interrupting his reveries.

"Good. Good. Start the countdown." He glanced at the clock. "Fifteen minutes."

The First Mate nodded. "Yes, Sir!"

It was all out of his hands now. The computers had been programmed such that once the countdown was initiated it was irreversible and the launch was automatic. It was a failsafe against captains having last moment second thoughts and aborting the launch.

"Countdown started" the First Mate reported.

"Good. Good. Well, Ahmad, it has been an honor."

"For me as well." The First Mate said. They then turned and looked out the window at the missile clearly visible standing in the hold yet sticking out well above the deck. Neither man said anything as they stood there watching. Occasionally one would glance at the other members of the bridge crew busily manning their stations.

"Captain! We have two radar contacts. They appear to be United States naval vessels and they are heading toward us!" the radar crewman shouted.

"Calm yourself." Anvari said without alarm, and while never taking his eyes off the missile. "They cannot get here before we have launched. They are of no consequence." He then turned to his First Mate. "Have them raise the Panamanian flag." He said. "They may send a helicopter to check on us. We cannot hide the missile but we can hide our identity and perhaps confuse them for a moment or two."

"Yes, sir!" Ahmad said sharply and passed along the order.

Minutes passed and neither man spoke. As the time for launch drew nearer the bridge grew quieter.

"Helicopter approaching!" the radar tech announced calmly.

"Let him come." Anvari said evenly. "He will see nothing but the end."

Anvari could see the small speck on the horizon growing larger. He smiled ruefully. 'So much technology and yet you cannot stop me.' He thought to himself. In a few minutes he could make out the helicopter completely though it was still a distance off. He was certain that the pilot was reporting the missile.

Suddenly the hold began to fill with smoke and the ship began to shudder. There was a deafening roar as the missiles engines came to life and began to push against the launch platform. Anvari could hear the ship straining against the push of the missile engines. The missile began to shudder and then slowly rise up out of the hold. It gained speed as it climbed upward. The ship hull protested and screamed as if in agony, then it buckled as had been predicted. Water began to rush in through the fractures as the missile cleared the deck. It climbed higher and higher speeding up as it headed towards its destiny. The ship hull gave way and the ship began to break in half.

As his ship began to slip beneath the waves Anvari could see the pilot of the helicopter clearly. His face was etched with confusion and with concern.

"The fool!" Anvari spat. "He has no idea I've destroyed his world. He thinks he can save us." Anvari gave a quick glance around his bridge. His crew members had secured themselves by lines to their stations guaranteeing they would go down with the ship and not survive to be interrogated. He knew the rest of the crew throughout the ship had done likewise. He walked to his formal station and attached the line secured to the station to his belt.

Ten minutes later the ship slipped completely beneath the waves and was gone. At about the same time the warhead on the missile exploded high above the continental United States. The nuclear blast resulted in a massive Electro Magnetic Pulse. The lights in the United States and Canada went out, just as they were going out in Europe, Russia, and China as the missiles from Anvari's ship's sisters did their job.

The world as the vast majority of the population had known it had ended. In that momentary flash of light high in the sky the balance of power had shifted. The supposed superpowers were now deprived of their computers and their electronics and most of their high tech weapons systems. Suddenly Australia and Brazil found themselves to be the new superpowers with Iran as their adversary. Israel remained viable but weakened without her allies. It was only a matter of time before the rest Arab world seized on the opportunity Iran had given them. Iran would not need to attack Israel directly. They could expend resources elsewhere. And they would. The invasion of Australia and India had already begun even as Anvari had launched his missile. Iran's allies had started their offensive against China.

As planned, computer systems failed, airliners crashed, hospitals lost records and patients died as support systems failed, economies collapsed, and governments eventually fell apart as their countries fragmented and slid into chaos over the next few days. The world was within their grasp, or so they thought.

Ultimately the plan would fail, but at this point they did not know that. The troops Iran landed in Australia, for example, would largely become victims of the outback whose harshness and dangers they'd underestimated. Those that remained were no match for the RAAF. This gave Australia the ability to come to the aid of England and to the United States. Not all Arab countries rallied to the cause either. A dominant Iran was the last thing they wanted. As a result the Middle East became a conflagration of war unlike anything anyone had ever imagined.

Chapter 2

Dawson carefully moved the curtain aside to peer out his window. It hadn't taken long for civilization to end. He was amazed at how quickly a once civilized people devolved into unruly mobs of looters, rapists, and murderers. It had only taken three or four short days, actually. It was now a world without the rule of law and life was quickly becoming the living example of Thomas Hobbs' description of life in a bygone era: "Nasty, brutish, and short."

The house across the street was still smoldering. He and his neighbors had been involved in a firefight the night before with a large gang that invaded the neighborhood looking for food, and women. They had successfully driven the gang off, but the Merlin's had lost their home. The gang had left their dead behind along with two of their badly wounded. Apparently they thought the neighborhood would be kind to them and abide by some kind of P.O.W. rule and tend them. Tom Kilbourne had taken care of them with two rounds from his 1911 handgun.

Dawson went out onto his porch letting his rifle sling carry his rifle. He surveyed the neighborhood. It was beginning to look like a refugee caravan. The raid the night before had unnerved most of his neighbors. They were leaving for relative's homes in other towns or out in the country. Some, those whose cars were unaffected by the EMP drove off. Others carried their belongings in whatever conveyance they could scrounge and were walking out. Dawson couldn't blame them. His only concern was that they were setting themselves up to become victims. Most of them would end up dead along the highway somewhere, raped and robbed. They hadn't planned for evacuation in terms of doing it safely. They were just running away. Running away with no plan and in panic would get them killed or worse.

"You OK?" Tom Kilbourne asked as he approached Dawson's house. As usual he was carrying his mug of coffee.

"Yeah. You?"

"Passable. Passable." Tom responded.

"You heading out?"

"Yeah. Just waiting for my brother and his family to get here. Then we are going to the rally point for my prepper team. Once we are all together we'll convoy out to our retreat."

"Your cars are still working, then?"

"Yeah. They were shut off when the blast hit them. Didn't hurt them at all."

"Mine too. Got lucky that day."

They were silent for a moment just looking up and down the street in what had become a reflexive defense mode.

"Glad you aren't going alone." Dawson said after a few moments, picking up the conversation.

"What about you? You're going to your hidey hole?" Tom asked after he'd taken a sip of coffee.

"Yeah. Soon. Still haven't heard from Janie. I'm waiting on her in case she changes her mind. I can't call her so I don't know what's on her mind."

"You'll probably have to go get her. Not sure I'd want her trying to cross town alone anyway."

"That was what I was thinking."

"Well, stow your stuff securely. Take the carbine with you and your sidearm." Tom said with a grin. He knew Dawson was as prepared and savvy as he was.

"Great advice. Thanks!" Dawson said with a grin. "I don't know why I didn't think of that!"

Dawson and Tom came alert as a car turned the corner onto their street. Tom's hand went for his pistol, while Dawson slipped his rifle into a ready position. Tom then relaxed.

"It's OK. That's Danny's car. Guess we will be leaving soon."

"Take care, Tom. I hope you make it."

"You too Dawson. It was good knowing you." With that Tom turned and headed for his house. Dawson went back into his. He waited around for another hour and then took his AR-15 and his Sig P220 and got into the car. He backed out of his garage and pulled out onto the street. He hit the garage door opener out of habit and then laughed at himself. The electric company computers were dead so, as a result, the electrical power everyone took for granted no longer existed. He pulled back into the drive and closed the door manually. Then he made his way across town to find Janie.

The drive across town was both uneventful and heartbreaking. Looters had destroyed the downtown district. Dead bodies were lying in the streets. He could see smoke rising above the skyline from residential areas where homes were on fire. Trash and debris was strewn everywhere. No one walked the sidewalks either downtown or in neighborhoods.

He pulled into Janie's neighborhood and passed a car on fire. Two homes were burning as well. No one was attempting to put them out. As he drew close to Jane's house he could see bodies lying on the lawn in front of one her neighbor's houses. Two of them were naked and even from the street he could tell they'd been raped. With a deep sense of foreboding he pulled up in front of Janie's house. As he got out of his car he could not help but notice the profound silence of the neighborhood. No kids were making noise, no dogs barked. It was just silent.

He approached Janie's door and was dismayed to find it open. Old habits, long stored away, kicked in and long embedded training guided him. He sliced the pie, with his rifle at the ready, to check to see if the room beyond it was clear and then entered carefully visually assessing the room: the placement of furniture, the way belongings were strewn around the room, suspicious open doors, and so on. The living room was destroyed. It had been ransacked. He carefully cleared every room on the ground floor and was relieved to find it empty. However, the absence of Janie was troubling.

He made his way carefully up the stairs with his AR at the ready. Once in the upstairs hallway he cleared the guest bedrooms first and then moved to Janie's bedroom. The door was wide open and he approached carefully. Once he was at the doorway he could see Janie's body lying naked in the middle of the room. She'd been beaten, raped and then strangled. It was hard to tell if there had been a struggle or not. Whoever did it ransacked everything so any sign of a struggle or of the numbers of people involved were erased.

Dawson sat on the floor next to Janie's body for a long while. He couldn't bring himself to cry although something deep inside him said he should. He just couldn't find the emotional energy to do it. After a while he got up, covered her body with a blanket from the bed, and went downstairs. He then went out the front door and crossed the lawn to Janie's neighbor's house.

He knew the Jensen family a little bit. They'd met on a couple of occasions when he'd had to come to see Janie for one reason or another. Deep down he knew what he was going to find at their house but if on the odd chance he found anything different we was prepared to offer them a way out if they wanted it. The front door, like Janie's was wide open. He doubted he'd find anything different.

When he entered the house he found Allen Jensen and his son Kyle dead in the living room with bullet wounds to the back of the head with their hands tied behind their backs. They'd been executed. He searched the house completely and did not find Ashley, Allen's wife, or Kelley and Tanya their 15 and 17 year old daughters. It was obvious they'd been taken by whoever killed Allen and Kyle. By now, he suspected they were dead somewhere across town or wishing they were dead. It was entirely possible they had been taken as sex slaves by whatever gang took them and if that was the case their deaths were certain but on hold until their captors tired of them.

Sighing in frustration Dawson went back to his car. He had no way of rescuing the Jensen women and he'd been too late to help Janie.

"Help me!!" a young female voice called out in desperation.

Dawson whirled around and brought his rifle up. The person calling for help was running toward him. It was clearly a very young girl and she was running toward him in sheer terror. Dawson lowered his rifle and the girl ran into his arms sobbing.

"Shhh...shhh...It is alright." He said soothingly. "No one is going to hurt you."

"They killed daddy." She sobbed "And they took mommy!"

"Who were they?" Dawson asked gently.

"I don't know. There was a lot of them and they took mommy!"

"It is OK, sweetie. You are safe with me."

"I hid from them when I heard mommy screaming and then I heard gunshots and then mommy screamed some more and then they took her away! I saw them dragging her down the sidewalk to their cars." She started sobbing again and buried her face against Dawson's chest.

"Do you have any relatives here in town?" Dawson asked.

She shook her head as she continued to cry hard. Dawson hugged her gently and then sighed.

"What is your name, sweetie."

"Addison." She said as took a stuttering breath. "Miller."

"How old are you?"

"T..T..Twelve" she said still stuttering.

"My name is Dawson, Addison. Take me to your house and I'll see if there is anything I can do."

Addison led him to her house. Dawson made her stay on the porch while he went back inside. Addison's father was dead on the living room floor just as Allen and Kyle were: hands tied behind his back and a bullet wound to the back of the head. The family's German Shepherd laid dead next to him. Dawson guessed the dog went first when the gang first barged into the house. It was obviously the same crew at work. He did a quick search of the house and found nothing and no one.

"Well sweetie," Dawson said to Addison when he came back out onto the porch. "You can't stay here. It is too dangerous. If you want you can come with me or I can take you somewhere else – a friend's house maybe?"

"Can you take me to my friend Millie's house?"

"I can do that." Dawson said. "Where does she live?"

"Down the block." Addison said.

Dawson swallowed hard. If Millie and her family lived in the same neighborhood he could guess what he was going to find when they got there. He took Addison to his car and followed her directions to Millie's house. His suspicions were borne out when they pulled up to the house.

"Stay here in the car, Addison." Dawson could see the family dog lying dead in the front yard and the front door was wide open.

Dawson got out and went into the house. Millie's father and older brothers were dead in the living room just as the others had been. Her baby brother was dead in his room. Her mother and Millie were both missing. He went back out and got into the car.

"I can't leave you here, Addison. No one is home. If you want you can go with me and I'll take you somewhere safe."

She didn't say anything but nodded her head. Dawson felt sorry for her. Her whole world had come crashing down. She'd had to suddenly deal with way too much death for such a young person.

Once they were safely back at his house Dawson made up a bed for Addison on the couch and fixed her something to eat. She picked at her food but did finally eat something. Occasionally she would cry a little but in general she managed to hold it together. Dawson kept an eye out the window for anything out of the ordinary. There were far fewer neighbors now and those that remained were untrustworthy if it came to defending the neighborhood. It wasn't that they were cowards so much as it was a case that they were unprepared, unarmed, or incapable physically. They were mere sheep waiting for the wolves come and take them. As much as he hated to admit it, he would have to leave for his retreat the next day. Staying here was no longer viable.

He tried not to think about what was likely happening to Addison's friend and her mother as he packed his SUV that night. The same was true for Ashley Jensen and her daughters.

"They all had red triangle tattoos." Addison said when he came into the living room to pick up something he'd forgotten but wanted to pack. Dawson was surprised by her speaking. Last he knew she had been asleep.

"Red triangle tattoos?" Dawson asked. "Are you sure?"

"Yes." she said in a very certain voice.

"OK, sweetie that is good to know. Thank you. Now go to sleep. If you wake up and I'm not here don't panic. I'll be back for you. I promise. I may have to run pick up some things but I won't be gone very long."

"OK." Addison said as she yawned widely. "I'll wait."

Dawson sat down on the couch and watched her fall asleep. He contemplated the new dilemma he was confronted with. The red triangle tattoo was the mark of the Diablos gang. He'd run into them on occasion at job sites. They'd never been any trouble to him but it was clear they could have been. The gang was your classic 'hood gang' into pushing drugs and causing mayhem in turf wars with other similar gangs. Their rules were street rules which meant they had none. Dawson was never too worried though. He could handle them and so could his employees. They were clearly dangerous people, however, to anyone else.

He was torn as to what to do. He really didn't know the Jensen's. He'd only met them a couple of times and they'd seemed like nice people. He didn't know Millie's friend's family at all. Something inside him told him he should just walk away. He couldn't save everyone. The odds were against him if he tried to rescue them alone against the whole gang. Perhaps Addison was all he should worry about. On the other hand, another part of him told him that just sitting by and doing nothing was unacceptable. It wasn't in his nature.

He sighed as he stood up. He was going on a fool's errand and one that could leave Addison in as bad of shape as she was before he brought her to his home. Yet, he'd run fool's errands before. It had been his job.

When he'd first met Janie he'd just come home from overseas. His boss was a private contractor with a government contract. They did things that couldn't be put on record books or have money trails attached to them. Getting in and out alive wasn't always easy, but they'd always done it and they always did their job. His team had never left a man behind. Some people would have called them mercenaries. The truth was they weren't that at all. They just served their country in ways the military could not and did things the rules of war would not have allowed. This fool's errand wasn't his first, but it was – he hoped – his last.

He went to the SUV and retrieved his M1A and four magazines for it. The magazines were already loaded so he didn't have to prepare them. After a moment's thought he took another case out of the car as well. He opened it up and removed the suppressor from the case. He looked ruefully at the Federal stamp he'd had to purchase in order buy the suppressor. It seemed a little silly now that he'd had actually purchase a permit to buy something that in other countries was considered simply good manners.

He screwed the suppressor to the muzzle of the rifle. He put the rifle into the back of his car and backed out of the garage. The car really wasn't his first choice for doing what he was thinking of doing but he didn't want to unpack the SUV. He shut the garage door and got back into the car and backed out into the street.

He knew where the gang had their headquarters located. It wasn't far from a job site his security company had worked on once. He had to admit to himself that he really had no plan on what to do when he got there. It occurred to him that impromptu was probably not a good plan, but it wouldn't be the first time he'd had to improvise a plan, or even create one, on the move. On the other hand what choice did he have? He didn't know the exact layout of the headquarters. He did know it was an old construction company warehouse with an enclosed outdoor storage area where the former owners had parked large equipment and company trucks. Beyond that he knew nothing. He could assume that inside the building it was largely open with maybe a break room and an office space somewhere. He doubted there would be second floor. However, he didn't know where the Jensen's would be held. Impromptu was the only option, even if it was a bad one.

He didn't drive to the exact address. Instead he went to an old warehouse which was located about 250 yards from the Diablos' headquarters. From there he figured he should be able to at least see into the parking area of the headquarters and perhaps get a better view of the layout if he could find a vantage point on the second floor or even on the roof. If he was lucky enough he might be able to see into the warehouse itself.

He got out of the car and, after quickly checking the area to make sure it was secure, he opened a warehouse door and drove the car inside. After closing the door to prevent discovery he made his way up the stairs to the second floor. From the second floor he could hear screaming coming from the direction of the Diablos headquarters. Unfortunately he couldn't find a window that would open so he broke one out.

    The vantage point was very good. He could see clearly into the compound and what he saw sickened him. The compound fences were made of corrugated steel sheets making viewing or attacking from the street difficult. There were two gates: one out the left side of the compound and one out the right. The one on the left emptied directly into the street. There was a group of about twenty five guys in the middle of the compound. They were laughing and drinking. There was a large cage holding several women along the left fence of the compound. Along the right fence were two rows of X shaped crosses or St. James crosses, enough for twelve women. Several women and young girls were already hanging on the crosses, including a girl who looked to be Addison's age judging by her apparent height and the clear fact that she was just hitting puberty. He scanned them with his binoculars to see if they were being crucified or just restrained. They hung limply as though drugged but did move their heads occasionally. They all appeared to have been tied to their cross and not nailed to them. All of them had been branded with a triangle shaped branding iron and it looked like perhaps the brands had been inked as well, making them red and marking the woman as Diablos property. The guys in the group appeared to be alternating between mocking the women on the crosses and the women in the cage. He recognized one of the women on a cross as Ashley Jensen.

    In the middle of compound was a large fire which was obviously for heating the branding iron and provide light in the growing darkness. There was also a mattress near the fire. As he watched a woman was dragged off the mattress and dragged to a vacant cross where several gang members secured to it without being gentle at all. One of the gang members then took the branding iron and branded her right inner thigh and then sprayed something into the wound. The group appeared to delight in the branding as howls of laughter mixed with her screams of pain as she was branded.

The gang members then went back to the cage and dragged another girl out of the cage to mattress. He recognized her as one of the Jensen girls. She resisted as much as she could and Dawson could hear her screaming in fear. When they got her to the mattress they ripped her clothes off in spite of her resistance. Once she was naked she was thrown down on the mattress and before she could move two gang members jumped on her to hold her down. A third gang member approached her with a syringe and wrapped a band around her arm and then after a moment injected something into her arm. She seemed to go limp and the gang members got off her. It then became clear they intended to rape her.

Dawson unslung his M1A and readied it. Using his front sight as a range finder he estimated the distance between him and the compound. It was a little over 250 yards. He took aim at the Diablos member who had just gotten between the Jensen girl's legs. He was unzipping his jeans when Dawson's round him in the chest. He looked around in confusion and then toppled sideways.

Dawson had no way of knowing if the M1A could be heard at 250 yards with the suppressor on it. He doubted it could be heard over the sounds of the fire and other sounds in the compound. However he could not be sure. As a result he worked quickly. He took aim at another gang member and squeezed trigger. He too jerked as the .308 bullet hit him squarely in the chest. Dawson quickly chose another target and squeezed off the round. A third member dropped clutching his stomach and screaming in agony.

By now the gang members had begun to retreat inside the warehouse. Dawson took a shot at a running gangster and missed. It was his only shot at the fleeing gang members. He knew they would now be trying to locate him so he stayed motionless knowing that the growing darkness would help shield him as the gang member's vision past light of the giant bonfire they'd lit would be greatly impaired.

Suddenly the lights came on inside and outside the headquarters. Obviously they had generator and they hadn't had enough foresight to disable the automatic timer most warehouse lights are on. His gaze soon fell, however, on something deep inside the warehouse. When the construction company had abandoned the warehouse they'd left behind several oxygen and acetylene tanks. Dawson knew that if he shot them, they would not likely blow up. They could however potentially become missiles as the compressed gas escaped, provided that the tanks still had compressed gas in them.

He took aim at one of the oxygen tanks and fired. On impact the tank took off across the floor of the warehouse in a jagged, fishtailing, haphazard course like a balloon with air escaping it. Apparently it hit someone after it flew out of his line of sight because he could hear someone screaming in agony. He fired another round into another tank and it did nothing. Dawson then waited for a moment to see what would happen in the warehouse. He kept his rifle trained on the tanks, however, in case someone shut the lights off.

After a short moment the lights did go off. He smiled. Now they had no way of knowing if the tanks were coming at them. He fired again. If he hit anything it would be sheer luck but bullets flying around would keep their heads down. On the other hand he didn't need to hit a cylinder directly. Any puncture would send it flying or at least make it sound like it was going to go. He could not see in the darkness if the tank took off or not but he did eventually see it as it blew though the side of the building and then spun crazily around in the street outside. He heard cursing and screaming coming from inside the building. He fired again and either missed any of the darkness enshrouded tanks or the one he hit didn't blow. There was more excited shouting and some pain filled screaming came from inside the warehouse.

Suddenly the exit doors to the warehouse flew open and he could see figures abandoning in the building, fleeing into the darkness. Some came back out into the compound while others ran off down the street. Street gangs like the Diablos weren't exactly prepared with any kind of defensive strategy.   Self-preservation took over and they ran. He had no doubt however, that they would regroup, strategize, and try to find him. His time was limited. Those in the compound tried to take shelter behind stacks of pallets and oil drums. Dawson could see them in the light of the bonfire whenever they poked their heads out to look around.

He waited as patiently as he could, knowing he had limited time. It paid off. One of the hiding gang members made a break for the gate that led out into the street. Dawson dropped him half way to the gate. A second gang member tried to run to the girl on the mattress apparently thinking to use her as a shield for his escape. Dawson's bullet hit him as he started to kneel down to grab the girl. He fell over on top of her. She didn't move. The three of four remaining gangsters ran back into the darkness of the warehouse. Dawson fired a probing shot, aimed for the general vicinity where he remembered the tanks being located and then fired again. The gang members ran out the exit door into the street and disappeared into the darkness. Whether he'd actually hit a tank or not he did not know. Either way, hit or miss, the gang members had taken off.

He quickly went down to his car and drove it out of the warehouse to the gate of the compound. The gate was open so he was able to drive straight into the compound. He wasn't foolish enough to believe for a moment that the gang had gone very far. He guessed they'd gone only a block at most and were probably regrouping to return to the compound while others fanned out to find him. As he got out of the car he could hear the agonized screams of the wounded gang members inside the warehouse begging for help.

Dawson took a couple shots into the warehouse, not intending to hit anything but to keep up the illusion that the compound was still under sniper attack, or if his car had been observed driving into the compound to make it appear that the danger wasn't over. He did see one gang member crawling toward him. His legs were broken. He started cursing at Dawson. Dawson pulled his sidearm and killed him.

He quickly opened the back doors of the car and then went to the cage. He shot the lock off and opened the door. He looked at the four occupants.

"You can come with me or run for your lives. No guarantees either way." He said crisply. "If you come with me, I'll need help to cut them down." He said as he quickly pointed at the women on the crosses."

"I'll help you." One of them said. He recognized her as one of the Jensen girls.

The others just sat paralyzed as they huddled in the corner of the cage. Dawson nodded at the girl.

"Grab your sister off that mattress. There's a knife in the front seat. Grab it!"

She nodded and ran to the girl on the mattress. She rolled the dead man off her and dragged her sister to the car. While she struggled to get her into the car Dawson ran across the short distance to the crosses. He cut the little girl down first and let her collapse down over his shoulder. He then ran to the car and gave her to the Jensen girl who has finally gotten her sister into the car. He went back for Ashley Jensen and did the same for her.

"Do you know that little girl?" he asked when he'd carried Ashley back to the car.

"No." was the short answer.

"Do you know which one is her mother?"

"Yeah. She's dead. They raped her first thing and then killed her for resisting them. I thought the little girl was going to go crazy."

"Do you know a Mrs. Miller?"

"Yes. She's dead too."

"You know any of the others?"

"Yeah. A couple." She pointed to couple of teenagers hanging on the crosses. "Those two."

"Their mothers here too?"

She shook her head. "No. Just them."

Dawson ran to the crosses and cut one of the girls down and carried her over his shoulder back to the car. Then he returned for the other. As he returned to the car with the second girl a bullet whined past his ear.

"Get in the car!" he yelled urgently. "Get down!"

The Jensen girl slammed the back door and jumped into the front passenger side seat. Dawson fired his sidearm in the general direction the bullet had come from and kept running. He got to the driver's side door and dumped the teenager into the car. He then fired another couple of rounds out the gate way and then into the warehouse. While he did this the Jensen girl struggled to pull her friend into the passenger seat with her.

Dawson cast a quick glance at the women still hanging on crosses and the three women still huddled in the cage. There was nothing he could do for them. He had run out of time. He jumped into the car and ended up sitting on the nearly unconscious teenager's lower legs and feet. He threw the car into reverse and did a quick turnaround, his tires throwing gravel as he hit the accelerator. He handed his sidearm to the girl in the passenger seat.

"If you see someone: throw lead their way. Keep them dodging." He had no hope she'd actually hit something given that she was running on adrenaline, was scared to death, probably had no clue how to shoot, and the vehicle would be moving quickly. His hope was that she could at least come close enough to keep them hesitant until he got down the block. He gunned the accelerator and the car sped through the gateway throwing gravel in its wake. As they sped off down the street a bullet shattered the rear window and another hit the trunk.

Once they were a couple blocks away, Dawson breathed easier and slowed down and took the pistol back from the girl in the passenger seat. He'd been lucky. Very lucky. It had been a fool's mission. To have rescued six of the kidnapped women was a miracle. He should have been killed.

"Which Jensen girl are you" he asked. "I met you all a couple times but I'm horrible sometimes with names and faces sometimes."

"Tanya." The girl said as she looked over the seat at the pile of nearly unconscious women in the backseat. Concern and worry was etched into her face.

"What did they shoot them up with?" Dawson asked.

"I don't know. I know they were talking about turning us into heroin addicts to control us and make us slaves. They taunted us about turning us into to crack whores and heroin sluts and about how we'd fuck a dog for a fix when they were done with us. The first one they dragged out of the cage was that little girl's mother. They must not have given her much because she fought them the whole time they were raping her. After that they must have upped the dosage. My mom was next and she just kind of became a zombie before they raped her and she didn't scream much at all when they branded her."

She got real quiet for a long time. Dawson glanced at her as she held her friend in her arms. She looked lost and scared.

"Where are we going?" she asked suddenly. There was worry in her voice. Dawson surmised she thought that perhaps she'd jumped from the frying pan into the fire.

"My house. Where you go after that depends on a number of things, I guess. Either way I'm bugging out tomorrow." He said simply.

"My dad and brother are dead, aren't they?"

Dawson nodded.

"I thought so. As they were dragging mom and my sister and me away I thought I heard gunshots." Dawson could tell from her voice that she'd started to cry. He didn't need to look.

"I'm sorry." Dawson said sincerely.

She nodded and was clearly trying not to cry any more as the whole day suddenly crashed in on her. It was ultimately too much for her. She started to sob heavily and uncontrollably. "I was so scared." She said between sobs. Dawson started to reach over to console her but stopped himself. After all she'd been through being touched was probably not something she would welcome or appreciate.

"You are safe now." He said in a comforting tone. "No one is going to hurt you or your family anymore."

Once they were safely back at Dawson's house Tanya helped him unload the car. Getting the women into the house would have been a huge chore for him to have accomplished alone. He then pulled his gear out of the car and repacked the SUV. Then he went inside. Tanya had taken the liberty of going through his dresser and closet and had found at some t-shirts or sport shirts to cover the women's at least partially and give them some sense of modesty when they came around. They were all laid side by side on the floor in the living room covered with blankets from Dawson's linen closet. Tanya had collapsed into the recliner and was falling asleep. Dawson went into his bedroom and did the same.

The next morning Dawson got up and went into the living room. He was greeted by the sight of Addison sitting on the floor cradling her friend's body in her lap. She was crying softly.

"She died." Addison said as she looked up at Dawson once she was aware that he was in the room.

Dawson knelt down and checked the girl for a pulse. There was none. He got up and retrieved his travel shaving mirror from the cabinet in the bathroom and held it to the girl's face. Finally he put the mirror down.

"I'm sorry, sweetie. I really am. I tried to save her. I guess what they did to her was too much for her little body."

Addison nodded her head but kept crying softly not taking her eyes off her friend.

"My mom?" she asked suddenly looking up at Dawson. She was only now realizing her mother wasn't in the group he'd brought home.

"She wasn't there." Dawson said in a half truth. "I don't know what they did with her. I looked for her but she wasn't there."

"She's probably dead too." Addison said flatly. "Now I am all alone."

"No, you aren't. I will take care of you from now on." Dawson said.

He sat with Addison for a while longer and then got up and went into the garage. He pulled a tarp down off of the rack he used to store them on and laid it out in the backyard. Then he went inside the house and gently took Millie from Addison. He carried her outside and laid her on the tarp and wrapped her up in it. Once she was tightly wrapped up in the tarp he got some rope out of the garage and tied the tarp in place around her body. He then spent the rest of the morning digging a grave for the girl. Once he got down about four or five feet he carefully lowered the little girl's body into it and then filled in the grave. He fashioned a cross out of pressurized wood and set it into the ground.

By the time he'd finished the women inside the house were coming down from their high and he found most of them curled up against the wall in near fetal positions. Tanya was comforting them as best she could, assuring them that they were safe and that nothing was going to hurt them now. It was clear to Dawson packing them up and moving them today was not going to be a workable plan. He would have to wait for tomorrow.

"Thank you for rescuing us." A female voice said from behind him as he drank a cup of coffee and looked out the window at the small grave in his backyard. He turned to see who had spoken. It was Ashley Jensen.

"I couldn't leave you there." He said in simple explanation.

"Why?" Ashley asked, "Anyone else would have."

"I guess I'm not anyone else."

"I'm glad you aren't. Thank you."

Dawson shrugged.

"They were cruel to us." She continued as though needing to get things off her chest. "After I saw them kill that little girl's mother for resisting them, I'd have let the whole gang fuck me without the heroin. I was so scared. When they branded me I was so high I didn't care. I didn't care they were going to rape my daughters. I didn't care that they'd told me they were going to sell us to the highest bidder at a slave auction. I'd have let them do anything to me." Dawson could tell she was trying hard to control herself and not cry.

"Well, a bunch of them are dead now." Dawson said quietly.

"Not enough of them. But it will have to do." She said bitterly. She paused for a moment and then continued in a tone of voice that said she knew she probably did not want the answer to the question she was asking. "What about the others?"

"I couldn't save them." Dawson said with regret in his voice. "There wasn't enough time."

"I see." Ashley said simply and with as much regret in her voice as Dawson had felt when he'd left them behind.

"Did you know them?"

She nodded, "Yes. Most of them. We were all neighbors. I at least knew them on sight if not more personally." She shuddered. "I don't want to think about what they are going through right now. The gang isn't going to be pleased you took us. They'll likely take it out on them."

"Yeah. Probably. I wish I'd had more time."

Ashley nodded. "Me too, but it is what it is." Then she continued hesitantly. "What about…Janie?"

"Dead. I found her just before Addison found me."

"I'm sorry. I know you two were divorced but she did care about you."

"In her own way, I guess." Dawson said with a shrug.

"Where are you going to take us?" she asked after an awkward pause in the conversation.

"That is kind of up to you. I'm heading out to my retreat. It is about a twelve hour drive from here in the old days. No idea how long it will take now. I'm going to have to siphon gas out of abandoned vehicles along the way too. The SUV is full now, but that won't last and I'm pretty sure I'm not going to find any functional gas stations along the way.

"Do you have someplace to go? I might be able to drop you off." he asked.

She shook her head 'no'. "No. Nowhere. This was all Jack and I had. We have no family left on either side. It was just us against the world."

"What about the other girls?"

"Annie and Cassie? I don't know, honestly. Their families weren't close with us. They were just Tanya's friends. I really don't know their backgrounds much."

Dawson nodded. "Well, I guess after supper tonight we'll need to talk things out. I really don't have space for a huge entourage, but I can't leave you all here either."

"I'm sure we will be alright. I mean, if you will let us stay here, that is."

"Not wise. We drove off a gang the day before yesterday. When I saw how your neighborhood got hit I kind of guessed it was the same crew. It wasn't. They or someone else like the crew that hit your neighborhood will be back here sooner or later. After a few weeks the gangs like the Diablos will give way to more professional gangs – former vets and cops – and there's no guarantee they'll have the public interest in mind either. Either way, the people who are left in this neighborhood are just sheep waiting for slaughter. They won't rise up to defend the neighborhood any more than they did the day before yesterday. You'd likely end up right where you were last night.

"Beyond that food stores here will run out pretty quickly. You'd have no way to replenish them even if you raided the abandoned houses in the area."

"I suppose you are right." Ashley said in resignation. "I just don't know what to do. I can't go back to where Jack and Billy died. I just...couldn't." her voice trailed off in sorrow.

"Well, even if you wanted to go back it wouldn't be a good idea for the same reasons staying here wouldn't be a good idea. We can talk about it as a group tonight. As it stands right now, I'll likely be taking Addison with me. She's all alone. That is all I know for certain."

Ashley nodded. "OK. We'll talk after dinner."

That evening after dinner had been served up and eaten the group sat in the living room to discuss options.

"We don't have many options here, to be honest." Dawson said bluntly. "We can't stay here. If we do it is only a matter of time before the neighborhood gets raided again by one gang or another. They may only come looking for drugs or food or valuables they can use for barter. They may come looking for women like the gang did that hit your neighborhood. Either way, I would not recommend staying here.

"There are some families in the neighborhood with kids your age." He said directly to Cassie and Annie, "but they didn't help fight the last time the neighborhood was attacked so I'm going to guess they are incapable of it. Which means they are dead and don't know it yet and their women are...well....and they don't know that yet either.

"Now, I'm heading out tomorrow. My retreat is about twelve hours drive from here – on a good day. I don't really have room for you all, but if you need to come with me you are welcome. We'll figure it out when we get there.

"Now Annie and Cassie, I haven't asked before but I'll ask now. Do you have someone you can go to: Family, grandparents, uncles, aunts?"

"I have an aunt in Barrow." Cassie said.

"OK. Good. Barrow is right on the way. Do you want to go there?"

"My...Dad...and my aunt...hated each other. We maybe can stop and ask, though."

"OK. We will ask, but you are welcome to stay with the group."

"Annie?"

"My grandparents are in Pall's Fork. But they are elderly and not well. I have an Uncle in Pall's Fork too."

Dawson sighed in frustration. "Pall's Fork is the opposite way we are going. Do you want to try to get there on your own or come with us?"

"I'll come with you if I can." She said uncertainly. "I don't know how I'd get to Pall's Fork alone."

"OK. Settled then. It will be tight and it will require all of us to work hard. I have the feeling the world will get a whole lot worse before it gets better. The things we've seen in the last few days are probably going to be nothing compared to what is likely coming. A lot of people are going to die. However, if we stick together we should make it fine."

Later that evening he took the SUV down the street to a neighbor's house and hooked on to their small cargo trailer. They'd left it behind when they'd evacuated. He knew they would not be back for it. Once he had it back at his house he transferred most of the cargo in the SUV to the trailer to free up room for the added passengers. Even at that the SUV would be cramped.

"I'll keep watch tonight." Dawson told Ashley as the others settled down for the night. "Tomorrow we will take off. I'll get us out to I-18 and turn the driving over to you so I can get some sleep. All you have to do is stay on 18 until we get to Barrow. If I wake up before we get to Barrow I'll take over driving. I should be good for the rest of the trip if I can get a few hours of sleep."

Ashley nodded, "OK. That sounds good."

The next morning they loaded up and took off. The SUV was crowded to say the least but no one complained. All anyone cared about was getting away from the city and finding refuge. As they pulled onto the entrance ramp to the interstate Dawson stared in amazement. The highway was a slalom course of wrecked vehicles and dead bodies. It was obvious that criminals had used the highway as a hunting ground and likely would continue to do so. Getting any sleep was not likely.

He pulled to the side of the highway entrance ramp and mulled his options. The highway was the most convenient route. It appeared, however, to be more dangerous. Side roads would be slower, but probably safer. Even at that though there would likely be roadblocks and highwaymen to contend with on occasion. He didn't like that option either. He finally decided to chance the interstate and not sleep. He got his AK-47 out of the trailer and put his M1A away. He also got out a couple of ammo cans to make sure he had plenty of ammo. He put them into the car at Tanya's feet in the back seat.

"Now," he said to Tanya. "Your job is to keep these magazines full. Addison, if I drop a mag you grab it and hand it to Tanya in the backseat. I hope we don't need to reload or even use this, but we need to have a plan just in case we encounter trouble.

"Most of all, no one panic! Panic will kill you faster than a bullet. If we hit trouble, stay calm and do what I tell you. It may be against your nature but stay calm.

"Ashley, you keep driving if we hit trouble. Find a way around, through, over, or under, I don't care what you have to do. Just don't get stuck and don't crash into something. You must stay calm no matter what. OK?"

Ashley looked very nervous but nodded her head. The rest of the occupants did as well.

"Alright. Let's hit the road."

The drive was arduous. Ashley had to drive down the median on several occasions to avoid blockages and, in one case, a trap. Dawson had had to fire several rounds to cover the SUV's passage but they'd made it past. Late that night, far later than it should have been, they arrived at Cassie's aunt's house in Barrow.

"No one get out of the car!" Dawson said firmly. "They aren't expecting us, it is late, and I don't want anyone to get shot by someone with a nervous trigger finger. Cassie, move over by the window and start yelling at the house. Tell them who you are, call them by name. Keep at it until we get a response."

Cassie got over next to the window and rolled it down. She started yelling at the house, calling her aunt and uncle by name, asking to be allowed to come inside."

Eventually someone came out onto the porch with a rifle already aimed at the car. Dawson found that amusing in a sad way. If they had indeed been raiders using Cassie as a decoy – which wasn't out of the realm of possibility – he'd have been dead before he could have fired on the car.

"Cassie?" he yelled. "Is that you?"

"Yes! It's me, Uncle Don. It's your sister's daughter."

"Where's your mother?" he yelled back.

"Dead!" Cassie yelled back at him. "Can I come up to the porch and talk to you?"

"Come on!" he yelled. "And if anyone in that car thinks they can pull something funny, just be aware there are two more rifles trained on you from inside."

Cassie got out of the car and walked carefully to the porch holding her hands out to her sides showing she was unarmed.

Dawson couldn't tell what was being said between them. Her uncle seemed rather animated in his gestures and did not seem too offer much in the way of a friendly reception. The conversation did not seem to be going well. Finally Cassie threw up her hands in resignation and walked back to the car.

"I can't stay, but Uncle Don says we can stay tonight and tomorrow. Then we have to go."

Everyone all got out of the car and made our way toward the house. Out of nowhere several women appeared and ushered the girls and Ashley into the house. They all seemed genuinely worried and caring. Dawson paused as he got up next to Cassie's uncle.

"We will talk in the morning." He said crisply before Dawson could speak and then turned and stalked into the house. Dawson followed him inside.

"There's not much room." Cassie's uncle said bluntly. "Find a spot somewhere and bed down." Then he turned and climbed the stairs to the second floor apparently to go to bed. Dawson ended up sleeping sitting up in a corner of the living room.

The sun was well up when he awoke. He slowly stood and worked the kinks out of his back and walked out onto the porch. Cassie's uncle sat in one of two rockers on the porch as though waiting for Dawson to appear. Dawson sat down in the other rocker.

"I suppose I should thank you for saving my niece." He said crisply.

"Well, I have to be honest I wasn't there for her. I just threw her in with the rest."

"No matter. You saved her. I thank you for that."

Dawson didn't say anything. He had the feeling that Cassie's uncle had something more to say.

"It ain't that I don't want her here." He said finally. "Her mother and I didn't get along but I don't blame the girl for that. If things were different I'd take her in in a heartbeat. The fact is I don't think we will make it through the winter as it is. I've got all four of my children home right now. They came with their spouses and my six grandkids. Hannah and I have food set aside but not enough for this sized crew. We have fourteen more mouths to feed than we planned on for winter. We will be near starving by the time spring comes if not actually starving. Some of us may not make through the winter as it is. If I bring Cassie into the mix there will be deaths for certain. I just can't do it.

"Stay today. Get rested. Best of luck to you. That is all I can offer you." He said with a tinge of regret in his voice. "I'm sorry."

Don's wife, Hannah, spent the day fussing over the girl's brands. She cleaned them out as best she could and put antibiotic on the wounds. While she was treating Ashley's she wrinkled her nose in disgust.

"Infected already." She said. "Honey, you have to work hard on keeping this clean. What did they brand you with anyway? Some rusty piece of steel?"

"I really don't remember. Probably a piece of re-rod they'd found. I wasn't very lucid when they did it but I was the first one they branded." Ashley said dismally.

Hannah nodded grimly and indicated the burn with her head as she stood up. "It probably wasn't clean even if it was sterile despite the heat. Probably left rust behind in the burn. Be careful with it. I don't like the look of it." She then walked over to the teenagers and forced the girls to let her examine their brands more closely. She seemed satisfied with what she found.

The next day they loaded up the SUV after refueling from stores Cassie's uncle had collected. He apologized to Dawson again for turning Cassie away as he helped Dawson refuel. Dawson got the impression that the fuel for the SUV was his guilt offering. As everyone was getting back into the car he gave Cassie a hug and wished her the best. Then they pulled out and headed for the retreat.

Chapter 3

The seasonal road that led to Dawson's cabin was long and winding. He'd chosen the cabin because of that. He didn't want to be close to anyone. He had few neighbors; only one was within a quarter mile of him. The Johnson family had a small farmstead in the valley just down from his retreat. He planned on trading furs and things with them for produce and grains. He had another neighbor, the Harrisons, who lived only a little further from him only in the other direction. They also ran a small farm and had been set up for complete off grid living.

He liked both families. He especially like the Harrison's however. Caroline Harrison fit his ideal of a perfect woman. She had the figure and the grace of personality that just seemed to make her irresistible to Dawson. A couple of years before Dawson had come to the cabin to get away from it all for an extended period after Janie left him and filed for divorce. He and Caroline had had an affair that had been hot and steamy. The affair lasted nearly a year. Caroline broke it off when she realized she had fallen in love with Dawson but was afraid of losing her kids if she got a divorce. Whether her husband Bryan ever knew or suspected the affair Dawson never knew.

The Johnson's were cordial whenever he'd stopped by. Ed Johnson and he had gotten to be pretty good friends and hunting buddies. Off and on they'd engage in a friendly shooting competition. Dawson knew that he could count on Ed and the boys if he needed them. All in all he felt pretty secure where he was.

The SUV pulled to a stop at the front door of the cabin and everyone piled out.

"Well, here it is!" Dawson said as cheerily as he could. "It ain't much but it will have to do."

They all went inside and began the process of settling in. After dinner that night Dawson gathered everyone together to lay out a game plan for life in the cabin.

"Now, we will need to think of defenses first. The river behind us will pretty much prevent anyone from coming at us from that way. The rapids are too fast and too deep for fording. They may not look it but they are. Take that as a warning, by the way! Do not try to swim back there. You'll be gone in a heartbeat.

"We will need to set up defenses along the front and the sides of the cabin. Split rail fence will work pretty well to break up anyone trying to come at us straight on and will give them very little cover. What we want to do is push them out onto the driveway if they want to come at us. The fences will create a choke point at the driveway. The rails are already stored in the barn. I intended to have built the fences by now anyway. All we have to do is put them together.

"Can't they just tear down the fence or climb over it?" Ashley asked.

"They could tear it apart if it was just a normal split rail. We will wire and nail it together. It won't come apart easily and if they try to do so under fire they will have to expose themselves to do it. The same would be true if they tried to climb over it. I expect some will try. We just have 'encourage' them to not do that.

"Now, I spent a lot of money on making the cabin as bullet resistant as possible. We should have pretty good protection as long as we aren't in an extended conflict. Still, like any other kind of protection it has its limits so don't get stupid and expose yourselves if something goes wrong. The idea here is to keep the bad guys coming at us from the front where the best protection is.

"This of course means you all will have to become familiar with firearms. I can't defend the place alone. I have several rifles stashed here along with the ones I brought with me. I have more ammunition than the U.S. Government probably would have been comfortable with me having. We should have enough to defend what we got.

"Any questions? Good! We start tomorrow with the building and training."

That night sleeping arrangements needed to be settled. Annie and Cassie got the double bed in the guest room. Kelly and Tanya got the hide-a-bed. Addison got the recliner, which for her was nearly a regular bed.

"I guess that means you and I sleep together?" Ashley said tentatively.

"I guess so. We'll just have to be adults about it. Under normal circumstances it would raise eyebrows, I'll grant you that. Now, however, I don't think anyone knows what normal is right now."

That night as they lay in bed Ashley giggled as Dawson was about to drift off to sleep.

"Huh?" Dawson said sleepily. "What's so funny?"

"It just seems odd to be sleeping nearly naked next to a nearly naked man who isn't trying to get between my legs." She said as she giggled again.

"I can try if you want." He said drowsily without rousing much.

"That isn't fair." Ashley said still giggling. "I can't really say no without it sounding like I am ungrateful for all you've done."

"That's alright." Dawson said, "To be honest, I'm too tired to even think about getting an erection let alone actually having sex with you."

Ashley picked herself up a little and kissed Dawson on the cheek. "Thank you." She said softly.

Then she laid back down and drifted off to sleep with him.

The next morning after breakfast he gathered the ladies out on the front lawn. He handed each of them a rifle from the locker. The teens were all given an AR-15, Ashley was given the AK. He gave Addison a Hi-Point Carbine in 45 ACP. He'd bought that as a plinking gun and not for defense but given Addison's small stature it was the only real choice for her. They spent the rest of the morning becoming comfortable with their weapons and then target practicing to become comfortable with sighting and firing. He planned on daily target practice for the next week in order to make them very familiar with their firearms as well as improve their accuracy. Dawson harbored no illusions about their accuracy or their real ability to hit anything under stress. All he could really realistically hope for was that they would keep any attackers off guard and hesitant while occasionally actually hitting something.

About mid-morning, however, Ashley put her rifle away and sat down in a rocking chair on the porch. Dawson walked over to check on her. He noticed she looked pale.

"Are you alright?" he asked.

"Yeah. I'm just...tired." She said as though picking her last word carefully.

"Tired?"

She nodded. "Yeah...and my leg hurts."

"Let me see." Dawson said in an authoritative tone.

Ashley nodded and stood up. She slid her shorts down to expose the brand which had been place high on her inner thigh. Then she sat down and spread her legs so Dawson could see the wound clearly. What he saw concerned him. Cassie's aunt had cleaned it as best she could and put antibiotic on it but it was now bright red and he could see pus oozing from it.

"How long has it been doing that?" he asked.

"I noticed it this morning." She said. "It is bad, isn't it?"

"I won't lie. Yeah. It looks bad." Then he paused for moment trying to mentally go through his medical supplies hoping he had something stored away that might help. "I've got some sulfa powder that I can put on it. Maybe that will help. The wound is still pretty open so maybe it will. Sit tight!"

He got up and went inside and opened the medical locker. It didn't take him long to find the powder and return to Ashley. He sprinkled the powder liberally on the wound.

"Now, leave the shorts off. I don't want anything coming in contact with that wound. Other than the cellophane I'm going to put over it in a minute, that is. We have to make sure you don't get more bacteria of any kind from any source get into the wound."

"I can't just run around in my underwear!" Ashley said in protest.

"I don't care if you have to run around naked! Don't let anything come in contact with that burn! This is looking pretty serious." Dawson said sharply. "This afternoon while we start work on the fence you stay in the house! I don't care what you do, just protect that burn!"

He then went inside and came back with cellophane wrap and wrapped her thigh in it.

"That probably will feel odd." He said when he was done "and it probably won't want to stay put so don't walk around much."

She nodded "OK."

He sat down on the porch step and turned to look out at the girls who had continued to target practice in the front yard.

"Gotta build the target range I'd planned on building." He said aloud but more to himself than to Ashley.

"You seem to have a plan for everything." Ashley said.

"Well, not really. I bought this place about five years ago. I have always kind of been a prepper. This place made sense to me at the time. So I rebuilt the walls and made them harder for bullets to penetrate. You can't tell it by looking but I did. I set aside all the ammo I could get my hands on and a few extra rifles. I did the same thing with food that came with very long shelf life to it – MREs, and so on. I put in that pitcher pump in the kitchen to guarantee water when I needed it. I put in the basement so I could have more storage for everything as well as have room for the reloading equipment. Basically I was preparing for a natural disaster on a huge scale. I never anticipated what really happened though. The world today is way beyond what I'd imagined."

"So you created a fort!" Ashley said with a laugh. "Little boys build cardboard forts so they can grow up to be adults and build real forts."

"I suppose so." He said with a grin.

"I'm glad you did." She was said and then grew quiet. "We are so lucky to be here." She added after a long pause.

"I'm glad you are here too. I'm not much of a people person, but having someone around to talk to does keep you from going crazy. Well, guess I need to go do some coaching out there. I can see some problems developing." With that he got out and Ashley watched him as he went out to the firing line and began to individually coach the girls on proper shooting techniques.

Over the next couple of days Dawson and the girls finished the split rail fence and put in two other lines of barricades and obstacles further out from the fence. Just a few yards in front of the fence they'd put in a couple of strands of barbed wire fencing just in case anyone should scale the split rail fence. The intent wasn't to keep people out, but to slow them down and make them think twice about not using the driveway to approach the house. The side fences were made even more daunting. Ashley sat on the porch 'supervising."

"That leg isn't getting any better." Dawson said as Ashley and he sat on the front porch.

She sighed. "No. It isn't."'

"Tomorrow I'll take you over to the Johnson place. Della was a nurse in the E.R. She may have something to help it."

Ashley nodded.

The next Ashley and the girls climbed into the car and Dawson drove them down the road to the Johnson farm.

"You know, as things are going now," Dawson said in a musing tone, "A year from now cars will be a thing of the past. There won't be any gasoline to run them. Farming will go back to horse teams and common transportation will be a bicycle, horseback, or walking. Life will be very much different for a long time, I think, beginning in the not so distant future."

They pulled into the driveway and drove up to the front of the Johnson house. Dawson liked this farm. The front, back, and side yards were huge and well cared for but not overly so. The back yard doubled as staging area for tractors and wagons and other equipment during haying season or harvest. The farmhouse was an old classic two story farmhouse with a sprawling first floor. The upstairs contained several bedrooms – enough for a very large family which made sense given when the house was built. Large families were the norm back then and almost necessary for a large farm to operate properly. The main barn was huge as well, and painted the traditional bright red. The barn was as old as the house and had the old hay loft and then atop the roof a square spire rose up with a weather vane atop it. The venting in the spire vented heat out of the hay loft and kept weather out while doing so. A milking parlor came off the side of the main barn and was large enough that back in the day when it was fulling operational it could handle about fifteen cows at a time. Behind the house was a series of barns used for equipment storage and the farm shop used for making repairs to equipment. Two sixty foot tall steel domed silos stood near the barns. It was obvious from the weeds growing around the bases that they'd not been used in several years.

One of the Johnson boys came out on the porch with a hunting rifle at the ready to check them out.

Dawson got out of the car. "Hello, Caleb! Long time no see!"

"Dawson!" Caleb answered. "We didn't know you'd come to the cabin or we'd have come to visit!" Caleb was clearly glad to see Dawson. "Mom! Dawson's here!" he yelled through the front door. In moments Della Johnson made her appearance all flustered and excited. Dawson noticed she looked like she had more gray hair than he remembered, but then she was in her mid-forties so that wasn't unexpected.

"Dawson!" she said as she rushed to greet him. "Welcome home!"

Dawson chuckled. For Della her place was home to everyone. "It is nice to be home, Della. It really is." At that point the girls and Ashley got out of the car knowing it was safe and no one was going to start shooting at them. Dawson introduced them all, waiting to introduce Ashley last of all.

"...And this is Ashley. She's the reason we came to visit. We have a medical problem."

"Medical problem?" Della asked suddenly sounding professional.

"Yeah. Let's go inside so you can see for yourself."

Once inside in the kitchen Ashley dropped her shorts and Della gasped when she saw the angry burn on her thigh.

"Who the hell did this?" she demanded.

Ashley explained the whole story beginning with her kidnapping. She told Della about the rape and the branding and the heroin.

"Oh..my...God!" Della gasped when the story was done. "They did that to all of you?"

"Half of them." Dawson said. "I got to them before they could touch Tanya. Kelley got the heroin but nothing else."

"What about the little one?" Della asked looking at Addison in worry.

"No. No one got near her. I'd taken her to my place long before the rescue."

"Ok." Della said taking charge of the situation. "Ellen! Keep the boys out of the house! Send Caleb for your father!" She looked at Dawson for a moment and then said, "You can stay. You aren't seeing anything you haven't seen. Now, any of you that got branded, drop your pants! I want to see those burns and I want to see your arms where they shot you up."

Annie and Cassie took off their pants and let Della examine their burns and then their arms. Della nodded in satisfaction. "Keep them clean: lots of soap and water. Keep dirt and foreign matter away from them. They look like they are fine now, but they could still go south on you. It is going to take a long time before those nasty things heal up." Then she turned to Ashley and sighed. "We have work to do.

"Tell me what you remember about the branding and what happened afterwards! I know you were high but anything you remember may give me an idea what to do here."

Ashley looked troubled. "I don't remember much that is clear." She said softly.

"Just tell me what you remember no matter how fuzzy." Della said comfortingly.

Ashley looked at Dawson who nodded his encouragement. Then she took a deep breath.

"I was in the cage. They'd already taken one woman and raped her. She fought them too much after they'd doped her so they killed her. I think it was so they could make the rest of us more compliant, maybe? Anyway...They grabbed me next and dragged me to the mattress. There were five or six of them on me. They ripped my clothes off and threw me down on the mattress. That was when the one with the needle drugged me. Then they took turns raping me. I...." her voice faltered.

"It is OK, Ashley." Della said comfortingly, "Take your time."

"I vaguely remember them finishing and laughing at me. Then they dragged me to the cross and tied me up. I remember one guy kept putting his hands on my thighs while he held me up so I could be tied to the cross. He made a comment about having just peed all over his hands – or at least I think he did. I was high, I could have misheard him. I remember them pulling the branding iron out of the fire. It glowed bright red. It looked like they'd made it themselves. It was just some kind of bent iron with patterns on it. Reinforcement rod, maybe? I don't know. When they branded me they laughed because I didn't scream much. I really don't remember feeling it at all." She looked at Dawson in shame.

"It is alright." Della said comfortingly. "You were the victim and you aren't responsible. Now let's see what we can do about this.

"Dawson and the rest of you go on relax in the living room or on the porch. I need to be able to work in here."

Dawson went out onto the porch while the girls all went into the living room with Ellen. Just as he was closing the door behind him, Ed Johnson came up the walk.

"Dawson!" Ed called happily. "Good to see you!"

"Hey, Ed!" Dawson answered. "What's new?"

"Oh you know...nothing much...world as we knew it came to an end. Nothing to write home about."

"Well, Geez. I was hoping to hear something exciting." Dawson said in a deadpan.

"Nope. Nothing here." Ed deadpanned back.

They then sat down on the porch step.

"How long you been home?" Ed asked.

"Couple of days. Brought some rescues with me so I had to get them settled."

"Ah! Not alone then."

"No, not for now anyway. I don't know what I'm going to do though. I'm really not set up to handle the extras. On the other hand I don't want to farm them out like they were free kittens or something."

"You ain't seen Caroline yet then?"

"No...not...yet."

"Damn shame." Ed said ambiguously.

"What do you mean?"

"I mean you should have never let her go. Her husband is an arrogant ass and she deserves better."

"It really wasn't my choice, Ed."

"Still...it's a damn shame. Hell, I almost outed the two of you just to force the issue with that jerk of a husband she's got."

"That probably would not have been a good thing."

"Probably not. That's why I didn't do it. I may not like him, but I do think the world of Caroline."

Dawson snorted a laugh, "The whole world thinks the world of Caroline."

Ed nodded in agreement. "Kinda hard not to like her. That's for sure."

About then Della came out on the porch and sat down next to Ed.

"I want to keep Ashley, Annie and Cassie here for a few weeks. I think Annie and Cassie are fine with their burns but they got raped and could be pregnant. I want to monitor that. Ashley...well...I think she is in trouble. I think sepsis is setting in pretty quickly. That guy may not have been kidding about pissing on his hands."

Dawson took a deep breath and nodded. "I didn't mean to shove my problems off on you." He said apologetically.

"I am a nurse. It is what I do. Besides, right now I am the closest thing to a doctor for miles around. I guess that makes my house the hospital. I need you and Ed to run into Carrollton and get some supplies for me though."

"Hon," Ed said gently, "I'm pretty sure the drugstore isn't open."

Della looked at him icily. "I need antibiotics. Break into the store and pick them up if there are any left on the shelves. I'll take prescription or OTC – whatever they got left. I need it."

Carrollton hadn't ever been a particularly good town. It had originated as a cattle town and then silver had been discovered in the foot hills around it. The influx of miners, profiteers, cowboys and saloons had made for a bad mix and Carrollton had gained a reputation as a wild and fairly lawless place. That reputation, though muted by time, never seemed far from the Carrollton's modern day reality. Carrollton had had the largest police force in the quad county area and they were largely kept busy.

Dawson thought it rather instructive that Carrollton had been home to three brothels, four topless bars, and one adult bookstore, but only two churches. The brothels were completely illegal but operated freely and openly while the police force chased after bigger fish and turned a blind eye to their presence. The local high school seemed to specialize in football, basketball, and pregnant teenage girls. He also surmised that Carrollton was the only town on the face of the earth where a man could have felony conviction for embezzlement and still get appointed city treasurer. Yet, it had happened.

Ed brought his car to a halt at the blockade in the road at the city limit. An overweight man in mismatched camouflage and wearing an ugly scowl on his face approached the car with his rifle slung over his shoulder while two other men kept their rifles trained on the car and its occupants. Ed rolled down his window as the man approached.

"Afternoon!" Ed said pleasantly.

"Is it?" the man said gruffly. "What's your business?"

"Just came to town shopping for supplies." Ed said still trying to sound pleasant.

"Ain't nothin' open. Wastin' your time. Go home."

"I wish I could be we need antibiotics. We got a woman back at the farm who has a badly infected leg. The nurse says she's critical."

"That a fact?" the man seemingly less enthused than he had been.

"It is." Ed said.

"And how is that Carrollton's problem?"

"It isn't. We were sent by the nurse. She was hoping you'd have extra. We are prepared to barter for it, of course. We don't want charity."

"What you got for barter?"

"I would think that would be between us and the druggist." Ed said still trying to sound pleasant.

"She died. She and three quarters of the town."

"Three quarters?" Ed asked incredulously.

"No lie. Those who needed electrical power to keep their medicines good went first. Then the riots killed more. Then there was a turf war. Finally us guys in the Carrollton militia took over and put an end to the violence. There it stands.

"But you ain't answered my question: what you got to barter with?"

"Well, I think we may have reached an impasse here then. I don't know you and you don't know me. For all I know once you find out what I have you may just decide to 'confiscate' it. Then where would I be? I'd have no medicine and no means to obtain it."

The scowling man studied Ed and Dawson for a long time.

"Alright. Go straight down Main Street. You'll find the doctor's office on your right. Maybe one of them will help you out. Maybe not. Don't know. Don't care. Thinking of causing trouble, think twice. We got militia watching the office." He then signaled to the men behind the barricade and it was opened wide enough for Ed's car to pass through.

"Well, that went well." Ed said as he drove slowly down Main Street.

"Yeah." Dawson said. "We didn't bring anything to barter with though. You know that right?"

Ed grinned. "One problem at a time, my friend. One problem at a time."

He pulled to a stop in front of the doctor's office and they got out and went inside. A Carrollton militia member looked at them menacingly as they walked in but didn't say anything.

"Excuse me." Dawson said to the receptionist. "We need medicine. We were told to speak to the doctor."

"Which doctor?" she asked in a very unpleasant tone.

"I guess I thought there was only one." Dawson said.

"We have three here now. Which were you told to see?"

"The guard at the gate said 'doctor' he didn't say which one." Dawson said.

The receptionist sighed heavily. "Fine. I'll tell Doctor Newsome you are here. Wait right here."

She got up and disappeared into another room. She returned a few minutes later.

"Doctor Newsome will see you in his office. Go through those doors, turn right. The hall goes straight to his office. His name is on the door."

"Thank you." Dawson said and he and Ed walked through the doors the receptionist pointed at. The walked down the hall until they came to a door with "Dr. Newsome' on it.

Dawson chuckled. "Looks like Doctor Newsome works out of broom closet. Look at this door!"

Ed laughed, "Not to mention his name was painted on the door by a third grader. I get the impression this Doctor Newsome isn't popular around here."

The two men walked into the doctor's office and it soon became apparent that the doctor's office had indeed at some time been a storage room. Now, however, there was a desk and a couple of chairs in the room along with some steel rack bookcases. A young man sat behind the desk and he looked up as Dawson and Ed walked in.

"How may I help you?" he asked politely. "Emma said something about medicines?"

"Yes." Dawson said, "We have a badly injured woman back at the farm. Ed's wife is a nurse and she said if we don't get some antibiotics the woman may die."

"I see. May I ask what the nature of the injury is?"

Dawson gave a brief description of the burn and how it occurred. Doctor Newsome listened attentively.

"Well, unfortunately with the injury being what sounds like a third degree burn I really don't know what antibiotic she needs or even if it would be effective. She could have a bacterial infection of some kind: staph or strep infection is most likely. However, if sepsis has started as your nurse indicated the situation is more serious. It would be best if you brought her into the clinic here so we can treat her, if treatment is possible."

"If possible?"

"Yes. Unfortunately in the last couple of weeks medicine has been set back seventy five years. We no longer have tools we used to have in terms availability, supply, and efficacy. I suspect by the time things settle down we'll be set back a hundred years and will be relying on near folk medicine."

"So....?"

"So, I need to see the patient."

"I doubt she will want to come into Carrollton." Ed said. "Carrollton is a long way from anything she knows and she's been through hell to get this far."

"I see. Well, in that case I will have to come to her. The problem is getting past my jailors."

"Jailors?" Dawson asked.

"In a matter of speaking. I am not from Carrollton. I was driving across the country on my way to New York when my car suddenly died. I walked into Carrollton to get assistance and discovered the world had died right along with my car. Once they found out I was a doctor...well...here I am still."

"So you can't leave?" Dawson asked.

"Well, I don't know about 'can't' so much as 'actively encouraged to remain through constant monitoring and intimidation.'"

"That can't make for good doctor/patient relations." Ed said.

'For the most part the people here are good people. They are rough around the edges – sometimes sharply so – but they are good people. It is the militia that cause the trouble now-days."

"So if we could get you out of town, you'd treat Ashley?"

"Of course. Provided I have the necessary tools."

"Well, doc, gather up what you need. If I can't get medicine I'll get the doctor." Dawson said.

It took Doctor Newsome about fifteen minutes to gather what he thought he might need.

"Now, gentlemen, how do you propose to get me out of town?" he asked.

"Well, doc, I'll need a small bag and a bottle of penicillin or something like that. We'll put you in the back seat of the car on the floor board and cover you up with a blanket and some old clothes. We will likely get stopped at the gate by Mr. Friendly. We'll show him the bag with the pills in it and he'll likely be satisfied. Once we are out of sight of town you can sit up and enjoy the ride."

Doctor Newsome nodded. "Very well. Let me gather what you need."

He came back in a few minutes and handed Dawson a small white bag with a bottle of Tetracycline in it. They then walked out of the office. The guard at the door eyed them suspiciously as they walked toward the exit.

"Just be a moment. I need to check a patient in the car. It sounds like abdominal distention and I want to make sure she isn't contagious so you stay put. If I need you I'll come and get you. I don't want you to take something home to your children."

The guard nodded and looked apprehensive.

Once they were out at the car Doctor Newsome quickly got inside and hunkered down on the floor. Ed covered him with a blanket and a pair of coveralls he kept in the car. Then they got in and drove off.

"What was that you told the guard about?"

"I said she might have cramps." Doctor Newsome said with a laugh. "The lout barely has a high school education. He had no idea what I was saying."

"Well… here's Mr. Friendly. Let's hope this works."

The man they referred to walked up to the side of the car and Ed rolled his window down.

"Success!" he said happily as he shook the bag.

"Let me see it!" the man said grumpily. He took the bag and removed the bottle and looked at the label. "Teter..cycle..in? Never heard of it."

"It is an antibiotic. It good for treating later stages of well…" Ed pointed down to his groin, "in women."

Mr. Friendly dropped the bottle back into the bag and handed it back to Ed. "What'd you give for it?"

"Box of .308 ammo."

"A whole box?" then he laughed. "You got took."

"Perhaps. However, I think my wife is worth it even if I did."

"Well, if she's got something and you didn't give it to her I'd let her die if I was you."

"Well, I suppose. However we live out in the country and sometimes we have raiders you don't get in town. Things happen."

Mr. Friendly nodded. "Yeah. Probably. Alright. Get outta town. Don't come back unless you have something to trade. No more doctor visits."

"Hopefully we won't need one." Ed said as he started to roll the car ahead. The gate opened and he drove on through.

After they'd driven about a mile Ed told Doctor Newsome he could get up.

"Well played, Mr. Johnson." Doctor Newsome said when he'd gotten situated in the back seat.

"Call me Ed. Everyone else does."

"Very well. You can call me Arnie. All my friends do."

The next hour and a half was spent just talking about the last two weeks and changes they'd experienced and what they feared for the future. They pulled into Ed's driveway just about sunset.

They got out and went into the house. "Brought the doctor with me!" Ed called out when he'd walked into the kitchen. Della came out and greeted them and then offered them a cup of coffee. While they drank their coffee she went and got Ashley.

When Ashley came into the room Doctor Newsome had her drop her shorts and sit up on the table so he could examine the burn.

"I debrided the wound as best I could with what I had available." Della said. "There was some rusty flakes of metal and some gravel in the wound."

"Excellent. Did you notice any necrotic tissue and cut it away?"

"No. I did not. However, had I found any I don't think I am qualified to remove it."

"Mrs. Johnson…times have changed." Doctor Newsome said without looking up from Ashley's burn while examining it very closely. "We are now in the era of field medicine. You must do what you must to for the life of the patient."

"Yes, doctor." Della said in a differential voice. "I had not looked at it that way."

"We are plunged back into an era of hot water, soap and the antibiotics of World War 2." He said in a musing tone as he probed her burn with his finger. "For example, latex gloves: soon to be no longer available. We are back to scrubbing and alcohol. I shudder to think what surgery might become although chloroform is easy enough to make, I guess.

"Well, Mrs. Jensen do you want the good news or the bad news first."

"Good?" Ashley said tentatively.

"Well the good is that thanks for your nurses' good care we may have a shot at this. The bad is that you have indeed begun to get blood poisoning. I have antibiotics but I doubt I have enough now that I see the wound. We will give it our best shot and perhaps – given that we are catching this early we can stop it.

"Now I'm going to start with an injectable form of penicillin. It is not the preferred treatment now-days but it is what we have. That is assuming, of course, you are not allergic to penicillin."

"No. I am not." Ashley said, "But I am really afraid of needles."

"Ah, well…we shall have to have a stiff upper lip then, I guess. No way around it." Doctor Newsome said faking a British accent which made Ashley laugh.

He produced a bottle from his bag of supplies and a syringe. He drew some liquid out of the bottle and then turned to Ashley. "Now, my dear, I would think it would be most helpful to you if you were to describe for me, in very great detail that picture on the wall over there."

Ashley turned and looked at the picture on the wall. She began to describe it in minute detail. Doctor Newsome let her continue for a very long time and somewhere in the midst of it all administered the shot. Ashley never felt it.

"There all done!" he said long after he'd actually finished.

Ashley looked around. "I never felt anything." She said in amazement.

"Of course not. I gave the shot to myself. I don't want what you got." Doctor Newsome said in a teasing manner.

"Doctor," Della said, "We have two other girls who were branded and raped. Would you like to examine them as well?"

"Yes, actually I would when I am done with Mrs. Jensen here. If you gentlemen will excuse us we will need privacy now. Things are going to be 'delicate' for the next hour or so.

"Mrs. Johnson I will need you to assist."

"Yes, doctor." She said professionally.

An hour later Dawson and Ed were called back into the kitchen. The whole crew was gathered in the kitchen including Addison.

"Well...it would appear that everything is good. I assume that you are assuming parental responsibility for the Annie and Cassie?" He looked at Dawson expectantly.

"I guess I am now that you bring it up. I never thought about it that way."

"Excellent. They are minor children and need parental permission for medical treatment."

"That would include Addison as well, I presume?" I asked.

"Under the circumstances, yes. Of course."

"What treatment do they require?" Dawson asked with growing apprehension.

"At the moment it would appear they need none. However, burns like that take a long time to heal. Additionally we cannot rule certain STDs at this point. Treatment may be required for those if they develop. Hopefully we need not worry about HPV or Herpes or, God forbid, AIDS but we must be watchful.

"Now I am keeping Mrs. Jensen here in our little hospital but you may take your daughters home. I will check on them periodically, however."

"My daughters?" Dawson said.

"Well…yes. They are. You've adopted them, no?"

"Well, no. We've never been to court or anything."

Doctor Newsome laughed. "It no longer works that way. Just as in medicine so in the legal system. We are thrown back in time. I would guess the closest actual court of law is several thousand miles away and God only knows what that system of justice is. No, now we just make do and then sort it out when the world settles down – if it does.

"So ladies, you may, by the power vested in me by my medical degree now properly refer to Mr. VanOrder as 'Dad'."

The girls all giggled at Doctor Newsome's silliness.

"OK, daughters: let's go home."

"Yes, daddy." They all chimed in while still giggling.

The three girls started for the door. Tanya and Kelly stayed where they stood. Dawson gave them a questioning look.

"We'd like to stay with mom." Tanya said. It was clear she was nervous about her mother's health.

"No problem. I'll check back tomorrow."

Chapter 4

October 30th 1:30 p.m.

"Hello, Caroline." Dawson said as he stood on the Harrison's front porch. He stood silently waiting, visually taking in the woman before him. Her brown eyes, long, near waist length, brown hair and slender petite figure entranced him. They always had.

"Dawson!" Caroline said happily. She nearly jumped into his arms and held him tightly. Dawson hugged her back with equal fervor. "I've missed you so much." She whispered in his ear as they embraced.

"I've missed you too." He whispered back. They embraced longer than what would probably be socially acceptable; neither wanting to let go of the other. It was, therefore, not unexpected when they kissed. Dawson's hand ran down her back and he squeezed her backside. She did not protest.

When they finally stopped kissing Caroline said, "Bryan and the boys just left for Carrollton. Bryan wanted to visit his brother."

Dawson looked at her with questioning eyes. Caroline nodded her head demurely and took his hand. Dawson knew where the bedroom was. He'd been there many times, she didn't need to lead him but he let her do so. Once in the bedroom they kissed again with heated passion and undressed each other as they did so. Once they were both naked they continued to kiss until they seemed to just fall together on the bed.

"I've missed you so much it hurt sometimes." Caroline said after they'd made love and she was curled up next to Dawson with her head on his chest.

"I've missed you too." Dawson said.

"It's been a year!" she said softly but bitterly. "A whole year since you...I...left."

"I know. I didn't want to make things any harder on you than they already were."

She kissed his chest, "I made a mistake back then." She said softly. "Bryan has been...unbearable."

Dawson gently stroked her back with his fingertips. "I'm sorry." He said sincerely. "Does he know?"

She shook her head without raising it off his chest. "No...I don't think so, anyway. If he does he's never let on."

Dawson didn't say anything he just continued to stroke Caroline's back and side with his fingertips. She let him do that for a long time.

"That feels good." She said softly. "I've always liked it when you did that."

Dawson didn't say anything for a while. Then Caroline moved up and kissed him. He caressed her breast urgently as they kissed and then rolled her onto her back. She spread her legs for him eagerly and hungrily.

"It's been so long." She whispered as they started to make love a second time. "Too long."

"Dawson?" Caroline asked quietly as she lay curled up next to Dawson in the bed.

"Yes?" he answered drowsily.

"Do you forgive me?" she asked without raising her head from his chest.

"For what?"

"For not staying with you."

"Carrie, that wasn't something you needed to be forgiven for. You did what you thought was right."

"I hurt you terribly." She sounded nearly heartbroken.

Dawson didn't say anything he just started stroking back and sides like he always did when they'd made love.

She picked herself up onto her elbow and looked him in the eye.

"Can you take me back?" she asked anxiously.

"What about your family?" Dawson asked not in an unkind tone.

She sighed. "The kids are older now. Not by much, but they are older. They need me less than they did. Bryan is…well…Bryan."

Dawson nodded, "How do you want this to go?"

"I want to be with you. It will take a little time, but I want that. I promise not to change my mind."

"I have daughters now." Dawson said. "You should know that."

"You have daughters?" she asked skeptically.

"Yeah. Two seventeen year olds and a twelve year old."

"What'd you do? Find some chick, have kids and then use some kind of Miracle Grow on them?" she said with a laugh.

"No. Nothing like that. They have no one left." He then told her briefly what had happened.

Caroline looked at him lovingly. "That is part of why I love you." She said. "No one else would have risked his life for people he didn't know at all. At least no one I know." Then she cuddled back down with him and sighed contentedly. They drifted off to sleep.

A couple hours later they both woke up and made love again.

"Bryan should be home soon." Caroline said regretfully.

"I know. I should go. The girls are probably wondering where I am." Dawson said with as much regret.

"I'll come see you in a couple of days." Caroline said. "I want you and it will be easier at your house than here."

Dawson nodded and then kissed her.

"You should go." She said after they'd kissed. "I need to get cleaned up before Bryan gets home."

Dawson sat on his front porch that evening reflecting on the day. He hadn't expected to bed Caroline, but he was glad they were back together. He loved her and missed her. Now he felt complete again. He listened to the sounds of the girls in the cabin. They were taking a bath and he wanted to give them privacy. They might be his daughters and rules of privacy had probably changed along with everything else but he didn't feel comfortable being around three naked teens – especially the two that were fully developed young women.

The next morning he went over to Ed and Della's. Fall was setting in in earnest. He would need to put some venison away for the winter and he wanted to see if Ed needed to do the same thing. Beyond that he wanted to check on Ashley.

He hadn't quite made it to the house when he saw Ed coming out of the barn. He changed direction and went to greet Ed.

"Hey, Ed!" he said when they got close.

"Dawson. How's it goin'? Getting used to having children?" Ed asked with a laugh.

"Getting there." Dawson said with a chuckle. "How's Ashley?" he asked turning serious.

Ed sighed. "You'll have to talk to Doc Arnie. I'm not a medical person."

"Bad?" Dawson asked apprehensively.

Ed nodded, "Yeah."

"Shit." Dawson said in a disappointed tone.

"Let's go up to the house and you can see her for yourself."

As they walked toward the house Ed changed the subject.

"How are we going to handle marriages?"

Dawson stopped walking and turned to look at Ed. The change in subject matter had caught him off guard.

"Caleb and Tanya have started sleeping together. They claim they married each other."

"That was kind of quick." Dawson said. "They've only known each other a few days."

"That is what I said." Ed said in agreement. "They said they knew that but they figured no one knew how much time they had anymore and that long courtships were a thing of the past."

"That sounds like hormones talking, if you ask me." Dawson said cautiously.

"Yeah. I agree. Anyway the fact is they are sleeping together and, well, she could get pregnant. So how do we handle marriages?"

"Did you ask Doc Arnie?"

"Yeah. He just threw up his hands, laughed, and said he only handles adoptions."

"Well that wasn't much help."

"Nope. None at all."

"We could just have them jump the broom I guess. That was an accepted way for the slaves in pre-Civil War times. At least it would be recognition of some kind of commitment. Common Law marriage always seemed to me to be too 'convenient', I guess. No promises, no commitments, kind of thing."

Ed thought about it for a while. "I suppose that would work. We could make them promise each other and then jump the broom. It might seem more official given that there isn't anyone to pronounce them officially married."

Dawson shrugged. "Something to mull over I guess."

"We'd better mull it quick." Ed laughed. "They ain't waiting for us to make decisions."

"I suppose you are right. You got three other boys coming up."

"And a daughter. Not that there's much for her to choose from right now. We ain't allowing incest."

"There's Johnny Myers. They don't live that far away."

"True. Ellen does like him. His dad would be an insufferable father-in-law though. He's as big an ass as Caroline's husband. Speaking of which, you see her yet?"

"Yeah. I dropped by her place yesterday. That's why I didn't swing by and check on Ashley."

Ed studied Dawson for a minute. "Good. Glad you did. Hope it works out this time." He said genuinely as though somehow knowing they'd been in bed together.

They finished walking up to the house in silence and Ed led the way into the house. Doc Arnie was sitting in the kitchen drinking some coffee.

"Hello, Dawson!" he said cheerily. "How's the family?"

"Good, Doc. Good."

"Coffee's fresh. Della just made it."

Dawson poured himself a cup and then gestured to Ed to see if Ed wanted one. Ed declined, so Dawson sat down at the table.

"How's Ashley?" he asked.

Doc Arnie sighed. "Not good. The sepsis isn't responding to treatment. It has only been a few days, but she's far more feverish now which isn't a good sign."

"You think…we are going…."

"To lose her?" Doc Arnie finished the question for him. "We might. It's too soon to say for sure, but I'm afraid we may be heading that way."

"Can I see her?"

"Oh absolutely!" Doc Arnie said emphatically. "It might help boost her spirits, actually."

Dawson took his coffee mug with him and went to Ashley's room and knocked gently on the door then went in.

"Hi, Dawson." She said weakly without rousing much in her bed.

"Hey! There you are!" Dawson said in an affectionate tone.

"I'm here….for now." She added the last part softly as though speaking to herself.

"'For now?'" Dawson repeated.

She nodded her head, "I know what is going on. I'm dying. No one is saying it, but I am."

"Nonsense!" Dawson said emphatically. "You'll beat this infection."

"No…" she said softly. "I don't think so. My leg is burning up and the pus just flows out of it. I'd be surprised if gangrene doesn't set in soon."

"Doc Arnie will take care of that. You'll make it."

"That is what everyone says, but…." Then she looked directly at Dawson. "Adopt my daughters!"

"Huh?" Dawson said in surprise.

"When I'm gone, adopt my daughters. I need to know they will be taken care of" she said pleadingly. "Please?"

"Alright…I'm not sure how adopting a forty year old works, but I will do it for you."

"I'm not joking." She said in protest. "Tanya will likely get married soon but Kelly is only fifteen. She will need someone to care for her for a couple of years. Please promise me you'll do that for me."

Dawson took her hand and gave it a gentle squeeze. "I promise." He said genuinely.

"Thank you. I'll rest easier knowing my babies will have a home."

"Speaking of Tanya I guess she and Caleb want to marry." Dawson said trying to change the subject to something more cheery.

Ashley nodded. "They do. Tanya talked with me about it. They should do it soon…before…."

"What are you saying?"

"Tomorrow. I think they should do it tomorrow so I can see it and enjoy their happy day and not be sick and dying…just alert and dying."

"Ed and I talked about it. We will probably just have them jump a broom or something like that."

"Oh God!" Ashley said laughing weakly. "How corny."

"It is tried and true." Dawson said. "It also has a long historical precedent."

"That much is true, yes." Ashley said. Then she sighed. "I really don't care how they do it. I just need to know my baby is going to be cared for when I am gone."

The next day everyone gathered in Ashley's bedroom. Once they were all together it occurred to them that no one had decided who was to conduct the service or even what the service would look like. The all looked expectantly at Doc Arnie.

"Oh no!" he said raising his hands. "I have no trouble being the adopter-in-chief but I draw the line at priest. I would suggest that the father of the bride conduct the service but there is no father in this case."

"No," Ashley said weakly "but there is someone she owes her life to as much as the man who helped make her. I think Dawson should do it."

Everyone nodded their heads in agreement. Dawson looked at Tanya to see what she thought.

"I'd really like it if you would do it." She said shyly.

Dawson drew a deep breath and then nodded his head.

"Let me go get something first. I just thought of something significant. Come on Ed. I'll need some help."

They left the room and were gone for a long time. When they returned they had some kind of fairly straight tree branch about three inches in diameter. Dawson laid it on the floor between him and the two young people.

"Everyone ready?" he looked around the room, then at Ashley who nodded her head, and then at the couple who smiled at him excitedly.

"Alright...Friends, we've all gathered here to witness Caleb and Tanya promising themselves to each other and taking their first step as husband and wife. They are young. Maybe too young in some people's eyes but then love knows no age or boundary. It is good that they are young. It means they have their whole lives ahead of them and they can experience it together. They have a lifetime to learn about one another, please one another and grow together into one person.

"Caleb... do you take Tanya as your wife, now and forever? Do you promise to love her, take care of her, and honor her as your wife for as long as you live?"

"I do." Caleb said solemnly.

"Tanya, do you take Caleb as your husband, now and forever? Do you promise to love him, take care of him, and honor him as your husband for as long as you live?"

"I do." Tanya said nervously.

"In front of you is a limb from an oak tree." Dawson continued. "Oaks are strong, they are sturdy. You will need to be strong for one another and dependable – like an oak. They are this way for a reason: Oaks grow slowly and carefully and in so doing become strong and sturdy. They are not like Pines that grow quickly and are soft. This is why an Oak can weather storms that break Pine trees. Grow together slowly so your life together will be solid and dependable; able to weather the storms of life – not for those around you – but for you and your future. Now, if this is the life you chose for yourselves and each other, step over the limb and take the first step on your life together."

Caleb and Tanya looked at each other with excited eyes and then they both stepped over the limb.

"So you have begun your life together. May you have joy and happiness all your days. Caleb, you may kiss your bride."

The two newlyweds kissed while everyone cheered, except for Ashley who was crying her eyes out in happiness.

"You need to write that all down. I think we've got our own wedding ceremony there." Doc Arnie said as they sat at the kitchen table drinking coffee. "That was pretty good for impromptu."

Dawson grinned. "My grandfather was a preacher. I kinda picked up some things from him, I guess."

"Well, still, write it down. We are our own community out here. Granted it is only five or six families strung out over a couple of miles, but we are a community. We need some traditions to hold us together."

"Yeah. I suppose that is true."

"You know you'll likely have to come up with another service in a week or so." Doc Arnie said after a long pause.

Dawson shot Doc Arnie a questioning look. Doctor Arnie glanced up the stairs toward Ashley's room but said nothing.

"You think so?" Dawson asked cautiously.

Doc Arnie nodded his head. "Yeah. I'm pretty sure. The infection isn't responding at all to antibiotics. It isn't MERSA as far as I can tell, but it seems just as resistant to everything I've tried."

"Should we take her to Carrollton?"

Doc Arnie snorted. "No. They are no better equipped there than we are here. Actually we are better off than they are in a way. I took some of their best stuff when I left. The only thing we don't have is surgical equipment. We don't have anything along that line."

"Yes we do." Dawson said. "I bought a couple of army surplus surgical sets a few years back. It has forceps, scalpels, clamps, spare blades, sutures and needles. Stainless steel and supposedly 'everything you'll ever need.'"

"Really? That would be a good start if I could have a set."

"Sure. No problem. I'll bring one up for you."

Doc Arnie glanced up the stairs again. "Damn shame." He said softly. "She seems like a fine woman."

Chapter 5

Dawson sat alone at the breakfast table looking out his window. One of the things he'd gotten used to was the fact that teenage girls do not rise early. He, on the other hand, did. Prior to the collapse his employment had required it. Now it was ingrained habit. He sipped his coffee enjoying the calm and quiet before the girls got up. The early November chill had put a coat of frost on the world outside his window. Leaves of yellow and red fell in clouds of color when the wind blew. It was a beautiful morning.

The still of the cabin was disturbed by a young female voice. "Dad, can I talk to you for a minute?"

"Sure, Cassie. What's on your mind?"

Cassie sat down at the table and looked uncomfortable. Finally she spit it out.

"I like Mike." She said.

"Mike? Mike Johnson?"

"Yeah. He likes me too."

"I wasn't aware you were spending time together."

She nodded her head. "We get together when you are out hunting."

"What do you mean: 'get together'?" Dawson asked in a parental tone worried about where the conversation was heading.

She shifted in her chair uncomfortably and did not answer.

"I see." Dawson said. "And what else?"

"We want to get married."

"Cassie... you are only seventeen. Mike is only eighteen."

"So? Tanya was eighteen and Caleb is twenty. We aren't that much younger than them. Besides not long ago I could get married with parental permission, he doesn't need any. I'm asking for your permission." Dawson could tell from the tone of her voice she was set on this."

"Cassie, you've only known each other two weeks." He objected.

"So? Tanya and Caleb knew each other for a shorter length of time."

Dawson sat for a while studying the girl who had been his daughter for only a couple of weeks.

"Cassandra VanOrder you try my patience." He said humorously.

"Wow! I've never heard my new adopted name in full like that." Cassie said in a big grin. "I kind of like it! It would be more perfect, however, if it was Cassandra Johnson."

"Alright." Dawson said in resignation, "If Mike's parents don't object, I guess I can't either. I think you are too young but…." He waved his hand in a futile gesture.

Cassie and Mike were married the next day. The ceremony was held in Ashley's room so she could be a part of it. Once the ceremony was finished everyone quickly filed out of the room because it was obvious that Ashley was fatigued from the excitement. Dawson could also tell from her sallow coloring that she was failing fast because of the infection.

"Dawson?" Ashley said as Dawson followed the crowd out the door.

"Yes?" He asked as he stopped and turned to look at Ashley.

"Can you stay for a while?" she asked. "I…don't want to be alone."

"Sure, Ashley. No problem." Dawson pulled up a chair and sat down next to her bed.

"You'll adopt Kelly, right?" she asked weakly but urgently.

"I promised you I would. So, yes, I will."

She nodded her head and closed her eyes. "I love those girls so much." She said softly. "I wish I could see my grandbabies."

"Ashley…"

"No! No, it's alright. I know what's coming. The infection is taking me." A tear ran down her cheek, but she kept her eyes closed. "I've known since the first, I think."

Dawson sat quietly but said nothing.

"It was a pretty wedding." Ashley said, her voice faltering.

"Cassie was a beautiful bride." Dawson said in agreement.

"Too bad her parents weren't here." She said regretfully. "Cassie would have loved that."

"Yeah."

"I'll miss Kelly's wedding when it happens. It will probably be hard on her." Her voice still filled with regret.

"Ashley…you'll be there."

She slowly shook her head and didn't open her eyes.

"Thank you for saving me and the girls. You are my hero and I will always be grateful for what you did." She said after a few moments of silence. Her voice seemed weaker than before.

Dawson reached out and took Ashley's hand. He gave it a gentle but continual squeeze. She squeezed back as though he were her lifeline to salvation.

"Tell Kelly and Tanya that I'm sorry." She said softly and weakly.

"You have nothing to be sorry for." Dawson said gently.

"It doesn't feel that way." she said with a tremor in her voice.

"Tell my grandbabies that their grandma loved them even before they were born."

"I will. I promise."

"Thank you."

Dawson didn't say anything. He just sat next to her bed, holding her hand. Long minutes passed in silence. Suddenly her eyes flew open.

"Don't leave me." She said weakly but urgently.

"I won't." Dawson said with apprehension and Ashley closed her eyes again.

"I'm so tired." Ashley said after another long silence.

"You should rest."

"I will." She said quietly and weakly. Dawson noticed that her breathing was slowing. "It is so beautiful." She said quietly and suddenly. "So very beautiful."

Dawson didn't say anything. Rather he choked back tears and held her hand more firmly. Gradually her grip on his hand relaxed, but he still held on as though he could keep her on earth. She took another breath and whispered, "So, so beautiful!" and her grip on his hand relaxed even more and then was gone.

Dawson held her hand for a moment longer and then put it gently down on the bed. He got up and went to get Doc Arnie. Doc Arnie checked her pulse both in her wrist and in her neck and then listened for a heartbeat. Then he sighed and straightened up. He looked at Dawson and shook his head. Ashley was gone.

Doc Arnie didn't say anything but noted the time of death on the clock and wrote it down on a pad he carried in his shirt pocket. He sat down in a chair in the corner and stared at Ashley's body for a moment a look of defeat filling is countenance. Then he rose and covered her face with the blanket. He patted her hand affectionately and then walked out of the room. Dawson stayed a few minutes longer then he too got up and went downstairs.

Ashley's funeral was held that evening just before sunset. Ed and the boys had worked feverishly to get the grave dug. Dawson spoke words over the grave drawing heavily from what he remembered his grandfather saying at funerals. Ellen Johnson read Psalm 23 and then Dawson closed the service with a prayer of sorts.

He felt funny praying. He wasn't a religious man. Somehow, however, in this moment it felt like the thing to do. He couldn't walk away from the grave without doing it. It just would not have been right in his mind. When he was done, everyone said 'Amen' and the service, such as it was, was over.

"I could have saved her less than a month ago." Doc Arnie said as he and Dawson and Ed sat on the steps to the front porch. "She'd have gone into intensive care; we'd have pumped her full of antibiotics far more powerful than I had here. There were other treatments we could have done. She'd have made it."

"Don't beat yourself up over it, Doc." Ed said. "You did all you could."

"Doesn't feel that way." Doc Arnie said sadly. "It sure doesn't feel that way."

The door to the kitchen opened and Kelly came out onto the porch.

"Dawson?" she said quietly.

Dawson looked up her to see what she wanted.

"Mom said you promised to take care of me?" she said in more of a question than a statement.

"I did promise her that, yes."

"Can...do I...what I mean is, do I have to come live with you?"

"I guess if you don't want to you don't have to. You are old enough to know where you want to be." Dawson said.

She nodded "For now, I'd like to stay here. I mean...I'm settled here and mom is...here..."

"That is fine with me if it is OK with Ed." Dawson said.

"Sure, honey, you can stay here as long as you like." Ed said.

"Thank you both." She said and then slipped back inside. It was clear she was about to cry.

No one said anything for a long time. They just sat on the porch and listened the sounds of fall around them.

"I guess I will have to be the official record keeper now too." Doc Arnie said. "Someday all this mess will get sorted out, or at least I hope it will, and someone will need to have records of deaths and births."

"Thus begins the new bureaucracy." Dawson said in sly humor.

"Yeah." Doc Arnie said. "It's funny how we are about 'official' records, isn't it? Still, I'll keep them in case the world fixes itself and they suddenly become necessary again."

"I think we need to build another building or two here." Ed said in a musing tone generally gesturing at his huge front yard. "We need a clinic for the Doc here and we need an apartment or cabin or two for the young families. They aren't going to want to live in the same house with Della and me forever."

"Well, we've got about six families in the area and by my count that makes for about sixteen workers. If we have the lumber we could do it pretty quickly." Dawson said. "Kind of like an Amish barn raising, you know?"

"I've probably got enough for the clinic anyway. I've been storing it for ages. Always thought I'd build another barn." Ed said. "It is better spent on a clinic. That will make things better for the Doc here and give him more privacy besides. I mean, professionally speaking, when people beyond our little community discover he is here it will be better for him to have a more private place to see patients rather than using my kitchen where people wander in and out all the time."

Dawson and Doc Arnie nodded in agreement.

    The clinic went up in two days. The men and boys worked hard on their new "community hospital" as they took to calling it. There was a small examining room and a second small room that could be used for surgery. Additionally there was a larger room for two single beds for inpatient care. There was also a small living space/office for the doctor. It was decided he would continue to take his meals in the main house with the family until such time that a kitchen could be added to the building. Furnishings were provided by families who had extras and unwanted serviceable items. Dawson gave him the surgery kit he'd promised and some of the medical supplies he'd set aside at his cabin for his own use. In short order Doc Arnie was set up to actually practice medicine from the 1940's.

    Dawson couldn't help but notice Caroline as she worked with the women to provide meals and warm refreshments for the workers. She knew he was watching her and would occasionally give him a demure little smile. Her husband seemed not to notice.

    "Papa?" Addison asked that evening when they'd gotten back to the cabin.

"Yes, Addie? What is it?"

"Are we going to starve to death this winter?"

"No, honey. We aren't going to starve. Why do you ask?"

"I heard some of the men talking today when they were building the hospital. They said a lot of people were going to starve this winter."

"Well, honey, I suppose a lot of people will. We won't though. We have lots of venison all smoked and set aside and we still have lots and lots of freeze dried food. We will do alright this winter. We will have to work hard next summer though. We will need to grow most of what we need to eat."

Addison nodded her head. She seemed relieved. "OK." She said and gave Dawson a hug.

"I'm going to bed." She said and then went on off to her room.

Annie looked up from her book and smiled.

"Kids!" she said "Where do they come up with this stuff?"

Dawson shrugged and smiled back at her. Just then there was a knock at his front door. Annie jumped up and ran and got her rifle. Dawson drew his handgun and went to the window. He looked out the window at the figure standing in the gathering darkness. Then he opened the door.

"Caroline?" he said as he opened the door. "Is something wrong?" he asked in a worried tone.

"Can I come in?" she asked.

"Absolutely!" Dawson said as he stood aside for her.

She walked into the cabin and he closed the door.

"Can I stay here tonight?" she asked hesitatingly.

Dawson looked at her questioningly.

"Bryan threw me out." She said softly.

"Threw you out?"

"Yes. Threw me out. We had a fight and he threw me out."

Dawson took her into his arms. She seemed to melt into him. Then they kissed.

"I think I should go to bed too." Annie said and closed her book and got up. She then disappeared into her bedroom with Addison.

"What happened?" Dawson asked when they'd finished kissing.

"He figured out I was cheating on him. When he demanded that I choose between him and whomever I was sleeping with, I told him I didn't love him anymore and he threw me out." She then shrugged as if to say, "That's it!"

"How'd you get here? I didn't see your car headlights."

"I walked. Our car ran out of gas. Bryan won't barter for any."

"You walked at this time of night? That was dangerous."

"Not really. It is a nice night – for November, that is."

"Bears. This time of year the bears get very aggressive. They are looking to den up and they are putting on fat for the winter."

Caroline blanched. "I didn't think about them. I just wanted to get to you."

"Well, you are here now and you are safe. That is all that matters, I guess. Come on. Let's go to bed and figure out the world in the morning."

Caroline nodded and then smiled coyly. "I don't think you really want to go to sleep."

Dawson lay awake with Caroline's naked body next to his, her leg draped over his legs and her head on his chest. She was sound asleep. He loved her deeply and wanted Caroline with him. Deep down he was glad she was now going to be living with him. On the other hand, he was concerned with Bryan. Bryan could be hot headed and he did not want to have Bryan show up at his doorstep for a confrontation. If he did, he would likely show up armed and drunk. Dawson knew he would have to deal with it as non-violently as possible for Caroline's children's sake. Killing Bryan would be a bad thing for everyone concerned.

The next morning Bryan did show up.

"I want to talk to Caroline!" he said when he'd been waved to the porch and had gotten to within speaking distance.

"Bryan...Are you going to be able to control your temper?" Dawson asked as Bryan mounted the steps and came to a stop on the porch.

"My temper isn't your concern." Bryan said evenly. "I know she came here last night. I want to talk to her. I figure she's been coming here for a while too. Suddenly things from a couple of years ago are starting to make sense."

"What do you want, Bryan?" Caroline said as she came through the door. She'd apparently overheard him on the porch and came out on her own. Her voice wasn't peevish, it was tired as though she was expecting to have to have the same fight she'd had before over again.

"I'm sorry about last night. I said some things I shouldn't have said. I want you to come home. The boys need their mother." Bryan seemed to be genuinely sorry.

"Bryan, it isn't that easy any more. I can't do 'us' anymore. I haven't been able to for a couple years now, actually. I just went through the motions." Her voice was full of pain.

Bryan nodded his head. Then he looked at Dawson. "Couldn't find a woman of your own so you had to steal mine?"

"Bryan, you don't want to do this." Dawson said softly. "You really don't."

"Yeah? Well, maybe I do. Everything was fine until you showed up. You haven't even been here a month and already you stole my wife."

"Bryan, things weren't fine!" Caroline said desperately. "They haven't been fine for a long time."

"Seemed fine to me until just now!" he said his temper rising. "Then all of a sudden it wasn't fine? That it?"

"Bryan, we've been sleeping together for two years!" Caroline said in a half-lie.

Bryan looked like he'd been hit with a board. "You have not." He said firmly but not loudly.

"We've been together whenever he was here and he's been here more often than you know." Caroline said, driving her point home with another lie. "I only stayed with you because of the boys." That part was true.

Bryan stood silently for a while clearly speechless. Then he nodded his head and said, "I see."

"Bryan, I'm sorry. I really am, but it isn't working for us." She said trying to be as compassionate as she could. "I hate that I've hurt you, but I can't lie about it anymore. It isn't fair to you, or to the boys, or to me. I just don't love you anymore. I am sorry. Really I am."

Bryan didn't say anything right away. When he did speak his pain was obvious. "I'm sorry too, Caroline. "

Then he turned and walked back down the steps and to the driveway. He stopped for a moment like he was going to say something more, but then thought better of it. He took another step and then turned back to the porch.

"Come see the boys when you can. They still need you." He said and then turned and continued on down the driveway to the road.

Caroline fell into Dawson's arms and started to cry. Dawson didn't say anything. He just held her and let her cry.

When winter came, it came with a vengeance. The first snow of the season hit in late November and was a major storm. Wind gusts caused the cabin to groan at times and the occupants could hear trees snapping off and crashing to the ground. When the multiday storm had passed it had dumped fifteen inches of snow on the ground and the wind had drifted it head high in places.

Dawson was glad that he'd lain in enough firewood in the few weeks of good weather he'd had. The winter cold would be held as bay in the cabin as the fireplace got its first major a workout ever. By Christmas the girls had taken to calling Caroline "mom" and the family had settled into a routine of sorts.

Dawson started running a trap line in late December. He was counting on the pelts for barter in the spring and hoping some of what he caught would help vary the diet for the family. Small animals like Raccoon, if done right, were actually quite tasty. He also spent a fair amount of time fishing the river. He had to walk a couple of miles to a calm spot in the river to do this, however. The river behind the house moved too quickly for productive wintertime fishing. So, between hunting, the trap line, and the fishing line he kept fresh meat on the table which stretched out the other food supplies nicely.

In early January, Dawson made his way along the wood line and a now fallow field from a farm long abandoned. The field itself was fruitful for finding pheasants and the aspen growth along the west end of the field provided grouse on occasion. As a result it was a place Dawson hunted on a regular basis. He was moving slowly along the tree line, stopping every other step to look into the woods. He would stay frozen in place for long minutes and then take another couple of steps. Still hunting was only part of the reason he was moving slowly. The winter had dumped another eight inches of snow on top of the fifteen already on the ground. The chill winter wind then moved the snow into sculpted snow drifts that made moving difficult at times.

He was hoping to get a deer, or at least he had when he'd started from the cabin earlier in the day. Now, however, as the afternoon threatened to become evening he'd pretty much decided that the hunt was useless. Still, he could not bring himself to just give up and go home. Fresh venison would be very welcome on the table.

He took another slow step after scanning the woods for movement. Suddenly something did not feel right to him. A feeling that he was being watched stole over him. He'd had the feeling before, but it was usually when he'd been spotted by a deer in its bed in spite of the care he'd taken to move carefully. This time, however, the feeling was more menacing. Something, or someone, was watching him. He knew it.

Dawson carefully peered into the thickness of the undergrowth. He watched for movement or for anything that did not fit with the terrain. Nothing moved. Nothing looked unusual. He checked his back trail but saw nothing. He took another step and again the feeling washed over him.

He did a quick survey of the area around him. If it was raiders he was in a world of trouble given that he was in the open with precious little cover in the event of an ambush. If something else was stalking him it was using natural cover in such a way he could not detect its movements. He needed a place from which to observe and to defend himself. His gaze settled on an old windmill sitting in the middle of the fallow field. It was an old style, open backed-geared windmill that most old farmhouses had on them to pump water for the needs of the farm. This particular one had probably been built to provide water for grazing livestock back in its day. Now it was just a derelict framework with a pump that didn't work. It was about one hundred yards from him. It was overgrown with wild grape vines and other dense foliage. The rooster topped weather vane swung lazily in the dying day's breeze. The wheeled blades, what few that were left of them, spun in the same easy manner as though still pumping water for the farm. He then carefully turned and acted like he'd seen something in that direction that had caught his attention and carefully walked that way. He did not move suddenly or break into a run. The whole way he felt something watching him.

   He finally sprinted the last twenty five or thirty yards to the windmill and forced his way into the grapevine covered structure. The center of the windmill platform was clear; the concrete was oddly only cracked with age but not overgrown. The grapevines had kept most of the snow out of the structure as well. He knew the grapevines were not cover, nor barely even concealment. That had never been his plan. His plan was to either force his pursuer, if there was one, to expose himself while trying to continue the pursuit or to give Dawson something that would obscure his exodus out the other side.

   He found a thicker spot near one of the tower legs in the grapevines and knelt down. He found a hole in the vines large enough for him to see out of clearly and pulled his binoculars from the case on his belt. He scanned the wood line slowly and carefully. It was just as he'd convinced himself that he'd been foolish and that nothing was following him when he saw the movement. Something long and black was slowly moving through the brush just inside the wood line. At first he considered the possibility that someone was clumsily crawling into a better position to observe him. He dismissed this, however, because after a moment or two of observing it, whatever it was, it was clearly moving easily and carefully.

   He stayed perfectly still watching carefully through his binoculars. Finally it stood and moved deliberately forward. He watched it for a second and then took the binoculars down and shook his head to clear his vision and then brought the binoculars back up. He eyes had not deceived him.

   What was moving toward him in a slow but deliberate pace was a large cat, black in color and closely resembling a cougar. He knew it wasn't a cougar. He'd seen cats like this before in the zoo only in much better shape. Black leopards are among the most beautiful of cats. This one however was not the sleek specimen that he'd seen before in the zoos. This one was starving. Its ribs showed clearly and its spine seemed like the scale topped back of a dragon. Dawson felt sorry for the black leopard. Somehow it had managed to escape some zoo somewhere, or had been released by some well-meaning individual. However, it had lost its hunting skills, if it had ever had any, and was now starving to death in a cold and alien place. It had probably only last this long by sheer chance and by scavenging bear kills or on field mice or the occasional rabbit.

He realized in that moment that there had been other probably unintended consequences of the EMP blast he had never considered before. He'd never given zoo animals a thought, but now that he was confronted with it he was sickened at the thought of animals starving in cages, calling for food and finding no relief. Did the cats escape and prey on the zebra or the tame deer? How many dangerous animals were just released by kind-hearted but stupid people? Would the southern American plains become home to the wildebeest someday? Could the same be said of lions and tigers? Would rhinos find a niche to live in? He knew at one time there had been discussions of moving endangered African plains animals to the United States where they might find a safe home in the wild on the American plains. Now perhaps, however unintentionally, it could conceivably have happened.

There were the caged humans he'd never thought of, for example. How many men and women died locked in cells in prisons from lack of food or water? How many escaped? How many cities were now overrun with escaped murderers and rapists who turned them into living scenes from "Escape from New York?"

He wondered about the nuclear plants that by now had created huge dead zones around, and downwind of, the facilities. How many people had died or had become refugees because of radiation? He shuddered to remember that Chernobyl's meltdown had created a 1000 square mile dead zone or exclusion zone around it and would not be safe for habitation for 20,000 years. How many of those zones now existed in the United States?

The black leopard stopped about half way to Dawson and crouched down. Dawson realized that the wind had shifted and the wind was now taking his scent directly across the field to where the cat was crouching. Dawson slowly brought his .308 hunting rifle to bear. He realized that .308 was a little on the light side for taking one of the "Big 5" African animals. However, this animal was dying and dying is a slow agonizing manner. Perhaps in its weakened condition the .308 would be enough.

The cat moved forward, clearly stalking the man it could now smell. Whether the cat could see him or not, Dawson could not tell. About thirty yards out from where Dawson knelt there was a spot of ground with very low grass covering it and oddly very little snow. If the cat crossed that spot, he would have a clear shot with little guess work involved. He wanted to be as merciful as possible. The shot would be head on into the chest cavity or perhaps its head, but Dawson trusted his marksmanship abilities. The difficulty of the shot didn't worry him. The light weight of the bullet did. If he ended up taking a shot into the grass and snow, obstacles he could not see hidden in the grass might deflect the bullet. In that case he could either miss entirely or end up wounding the animal which he desperately wanted to avoid.

Dawson waited. He was hoping the cat would attempt to circle him in search of a way into the vine covered enclosure. He knew it could not come straight at him and gain entry. However, the cat was more desperate for food than Dawson anticipated and it stepped directly forward into the low grass. Dawson settled his sights quickly and just as the cat took its third step into the low grass Dawson squeezed the trigger.

The bullet smashed into the cat at the base of its neck where the neck joined the torso. The cat spun around 180 degrees and then hit the ground. Blood spurted everywhere as it did so indicating an arterial hit. After a second or two of lying on the ground the cat stood on wobbly legs. It turned a little and was clearly going to try to escape even though each heart beat was pumping blood out in a spray onto the snow. Dawson's second bullet caught it just behind the rib cage and angled forward through the heart and lungs before exiting out the other side. The cat took one half step and dropped in a heap.

Dawson did not move immediately. He watched the cat for few moments and then carefully crept out of the enclosure. He approached the cat carefully and then prodded it with his foot, rifle at the ready. The cat was dead. He knelt down and examined the animal, all the while feeling sorry for it. At one time it had been a magnificent beast. It was a male and probably would have weighed nearly seventy pounds in its prime. Now, however, it was a mere ghost of itself and Dawson doubted it weighed fifty. He picked the cat up and draped it over his shoulders and started for home. He could not eat the cat, but neither was he going to waste it. The carcass would serve as bait for his trap line.

When spring finally arrived the little family put in a garden using heritage seeds Dawson had put away long ago. If the season went well it would provide enough to keep them through the winter and provide seed for next year's garden. Dawson had located some wild apple trees in his wanderings and had taken some cuttings from them and was attempting to root them so he could put in an orchard of sorts. Down the road he hoped for dried fruit for the larder. For the next few years, however, the family would have to get what good fruit they could from the wild trees. It would take time for the orchard to produce anything.

In late June a man in a horse drawn solid sided, covered cart came up the road. He stopped at the first barricade and hailed the house rather than approaching directly. This was had become common practice when approaching stranger's houses. The world had changed and practices of the past when the world was safe and generally secure – like walking up and knocking on the front door unannounced – could get you killed. Now the proper thing to do was to call out from the distance and let the occupants get a look at you and wave you in before venturing close.

Dawson bid the man come on up to the house and waited on the front porch, knowing that three rifles were trained on the man in the cart through partially opened windows as he approached.

"Name's Thompson, Harry Thompson." The man said when the cart came to a halt. "I'm a seller of necessary goods and buyer of odds and ends."

"A traveling salesman." Dawson said with a grin.

"My friend, you do me an injustice!" he said in horror. "Back in the day traveling salesmen had a bad name as purveyors of expensive, poor quality merchandise and as being the fathers of illegitimate children. I, on the other hand, sell only the necessary things people need on the frontier. I cannot afford to offer anything but the best merchandise at fair prices."

"Well, Mister Thompson, climb on down and let's see what you got." Dawson said with a smile and slinging his rifle over his shoulder.

Thompson had a wide variety of goods from spices for cooking to clothes to simple tools necessary for simple living. He bartered some of the spices and clothes for the girls and Caroline for some of Dawson's furs and a couple of pounds of venison jerky.

Dawson also was able to get some IMR 4320 gunpowder for a few more furs. The gunpowder wasn't his preferred powder but he didn't know when he would have opportunity to get powder of any kind again. He really wasn't running low on either rifle or pistol powder but having it on hand was, in his mind, a good thing. Gunpowder would become increasingly rare and expensive. Getting it now, before the rarity set in made sense.

"Your doctor bought most of my medical supplies." Thompson said conversationally and somewhat apologetically. "He seemed most grateful to get what I had. Resupplying that will be somewhat difficult, however."

Dawson laughed, "Based on my experience I wouldn't try Carrollton."

"Oh goodness no! Absolutely not. I won't go near that place unless necessary." There seemed to be genuine fear in his voice. Dawson looked at him clearly expecting an explanation.

"I forget you are far removed from the events of the world, my friend." Thompson said. "It has changed in the last few short months. New nations are forming, if you want to call them that. Some of them are beneficial and some of them are...well...a pox on humanity, in my opinion.

"To the east and north of you is the Colburn States. It is an alliance of sorts of what used to be five or six counties in the old days. They've created a constitution of sorts and seem to be fairly civil and fair minded. To the South of you is the Amberton Homestead Association. They cover a large amount of ground as well as being the most populated. The old state capital is their center of government. South of them is the North Copland Alliance. They are nearly as large as the AHA as far as geography and population goes."

"Are we are with whom?" Dawson asked.

"Well, if you haven't been approached by anyone I'd say your little community of sorts if up for grabs. I suppose however that the Holderites would contest that."

"Holderites?"

"Yes...well...they are...how shall I say it? Well, I will be blunt: they are brutal and evil. Their leader is a man named Harlan Holder. He's a delusional little man, short sighted but with visions of greatness. He used to be some minor local politician but he managed to get a couple gangs to do his bidding in exchange for 'favors'. His 'capital' is in Waterford. He started out with just a gang of thugs and a few city blocks and just took over more and more ground until he had his own little kingdom. He took advantage of the chaos and set out to conquer the world by force. He now controls three of the old counties – including, according to his account – this one.

He has a good sized garrison in Carrollton. The garrison there isn't much, but they are dangerous. They are mostly 'good ol' boys' with a very few actual vets in their ranks. They get lots of perks for keeping the peace so they *keep the peace*, if you follow my meaning. Now, Holders 'Storm Troops' are a different story. All combat vets and former cops. When they show up, your goose is cooked. They'd just as soon shoot you and rape your wife and then shoot her as to look at you. Holder uses them to take territory and he uses the militias to keep the peace.

"His main adversary is the Ragarian Union to his north and the Colburn States' west. They are usually at war with one another. So, most of Holder's Storm Troops are up there on the border which is why you aren't likely to see them around here just now. When they aren't at war with each other, they are at war with their neighbors though the Ragarians have learned the hard way not to mess with Colburn, just as the Holderites learned not to mess with the AHA.

"Harlan Holder is a sadistic little man as well. He holds the reins of power by terror and intimidation. It is rumored that his militia members kidnap people from their raids in neighboring territories – farms mostly for food and goods - and either force them to serve in their militia as conscripts, if they are male, or in their pleasure houses as sex slaves if they are female. He feels both are necessary for the wellbeing of his militia's morale and numbers. He does, however, castrate the conscripted males. Only true Holderites can breed in his world, you see. Conviction of minor crimes can land you in the militia or the pleasure house. Conviction for capital crimes will get you publicly tortured and maimed or publicly executed depending on the crime. Harlan Holder does not believe in jail sentences or reformatories.

"The Ragarians are no better, except they do not have pleasure houses. They just have slaves for labor and sex. Rumor has it they even breed their slaves to produce more slaves and have an active slave market. They are just as brutal however in most respects."

"Wow. It didn't take long for that all to happen." Dawson said in amazement.

"It is still happening, actually. No new 'nation' is settled yet. Border disputes are regular occurrences even between friendly states like the Colburn States and the AHA. Nothing is settled yet and probably won't be for another few years. It is all kind of like the big bang that created the universe: right now it is just a big nebulous cloud of hot tempers, fear, and ambition.

"Of course if the Australians and the Brazilians intervene and try to put things back together here in the good old US of A this will all just down in history as a bad nightmare."

"Australians and Brazilians?" Dawson asked.

"That's right!" Thompson said. "Apparently who ever bombed us ignored them and with them being allies to the U.S. they retaliated. As I hear it there are Australian boots on the ground right now on the West Coast and the Brazilians have boots on the ground in what used to be Florida, Mississippi and Alabama. Seems the country was invaded shortly after the bomb went off. The Aussies and the Brazilians stepped up for us. The Mexicans and Canadians have their own troubles and are in pretty much the same state we are."

"You are just a fountain of news." Dawson said with a chuckle.

"Well, it comes naturally. I have to cover a lot of ground to run my business. You just hear things traveling around. Trading information is as valuable as trading goods.

"Anyway, my advice is to avoid Carrollton if you can." Dawson said.

"I shall do that. Indeed I shall." Thompson said as he climbed back into his wagon. "I am working on establishing a regular route. If things work the way I think they will I should be back here once a month or so."

Dawson nodded. "I'll look forward to your next visit then."

Chapter 6

July 6th, 8:30 a.m.

"Hail the cabin!" a voice called from the first barricade.

Dawson gave a quick glance out the window and then signaled to Caroline and the girls to grab their rifles and get into position. What he saw chilled him. It was a group of about twelve uniformed men who were well armed by outward appearances.

"Who calls and what do you want?" Dawson yelled out the window without exposing himself to their eyes.

"I'm Captain Daniel Marsh of the New Order Liberation Militia in Carrollton. We've come to talk."

"Alright. Talk!" Dawson yelled.

"I will approach the cabin unarmed and alone. I'd prefer not to go hoarse by shouting." The captain responded.

"Alright! Come to the porch." Dawson yelled back.

Captain Marsh made a show of handing his rifle off to one of his men and then removing his sidearm as well. Then holding his hands out away from his body to show he was unarmed he approached the house. When he got to the porch Dawson stepped out to talk to him.

"What's on your mind, Captain?" he asked.

"We are just on routine patrol and wanted to make ourselves known. The New Order controls this ground under authority of Chancellor Harlan Holder. It is our charge to defend it and those who live on it."

"That sounds noble." Dawson said flatly.

"We do not intend to cause anyone harm, we only want you to know the terms under which you live in the New Order."

"Terms?" Dawson said just as flatly as before.

"Yes. We notice you have a sizable garden. We will be back in the fall to collect half of your produce. It is the tax that Chancellor Holder demands in exchange for the security our militia brings."

"Half? For security? Near as I can tell we are our own security out here." Dawson repeated flatly but with growing animosity.

"Yes. Half. Be thankful we do not demand more. We are, of course, prepared to collect that tax by force if we have to. If we do, however, you will be deemed an enemy of the state and dealt with accordingly."

"I see." Dawson said.

"Now, our surveillance of your homestead..."

"Surveillance?" Dawson interrupted.

"Yes, we always watch a place before me make first contact. In any event we know you have a wife and two daughters. We will be taking your oldest daughter with us now as tribute. She will be safe and well cared for, I assure you. We will see to her education and medical care while she is with us."

"Hostage is what you really mean." Dawson said.

"Either way, it makes no difference. She will be going with us."

"No. No, I don't think so." Dawson said evenly. "My daughter will stay here with her family."

"Then we shall take her by force as our prisoner. If we must resort to that, however, we will take your wife and youngest as well. Our pleasure houses always are in need of fresh pussy to keep the troops happy."

"That will be pretty hard for you to do when you are dead." Dawson said without emotion.

"I see. You wish to play it that way then. Very well. It is your funeral. I will give you time to reconsider. Talk it over with your family."

With that Captain Marsh turned and strode back down the drive. Dawson went back into the house.

"Everyone stay down and remember what you've been taught. Aim small miss small. Don't just shoot blindly. We have the advantage here."

After about twenty minutes the Captain called again from the barricade. "What is your decision?"

"You already have my decision." Dawson yelled back.

He had barely finished speaking when the first bullet hit the cabin. The reinforced walls did not let the bullet pass through. It had done exactly what Dawson designed it to do. He watched the patrol split into three parties. Six stayed at the main barricade apparently preparing for the frontal assault. Three made their way along the fence to the North side of the house where Addison was watching at her bedroom window. The other three went to the South where Caroline was watching out the bedroom window on that side. Dawson fired his M1A and dropped one of the men moving toward Caroline's side of the house.

He was mostly concerned with the flankers. The only real thing keeping them from coming straight to the house was the multiple strands of barbed wire. While the fence could be cut easily enough, if they were prepared, doing so would expose them to gunfire at least for the moment and he had no idea how Addison or Caroline would react. There was no cover near the fence, so they did hold a marginal advantage – if they shot well.

Suddenly he heard Addison's carbine bark three times.

"THAT WILL TEACH YOU TO MESS WITH A GIRL WITH A GUN YOU SON OF BITCH!!" Addison shouted. Dawson looked toward her bedroom and grinned. He knew he should be upset with her language but he also knew she was on an adrenaline rush that probably bypassed her filters when it came to taunting the bad guys.

The New Order militia responded with gunfire of their own. Dawson managed to get a couple of rounds off and dropped one of the men making the frontal assault as he tried to climb the fence. Annie wounded another as he charged up the driveway at a full run. He lay in the driveway screaming in agony and holding his stomach. Another Holderite tried to run to the fallen man and Dawson dropped him in mid stride. The remaining men dropped back behind the first barricade.

The Holderite fire became more continuous but remained ineffective. The reinforced walls of the cabin did not let anything pass through them so the cabin's occupants could fire out the windows and then duck back out of sight and be safely hidden. The only bullets that entered the cabin were the ones that came through the windows. Dawson was thankful the windows had been opened to ease the heat of the July heat. Otherwise there would have been broken glass everywhere. Caroline and Addison opened fire from their stations indicating that the flankers were attempting to breech the fencing rather than shooting at the house.

Addison opened fire. "YOU WANT MORE?" Addison screamed loudly "KEEP COMING! I GOT MORE FOR YA!!"

Her carbine spat several more times and Dawson could hear someone screaming in pain. Shortly thereafter he saw one man sneaking back along the fence from Addison's side of the house. Apparently the other two of his team were down and he was giving up.

"Odds are even now." Dawson called out to his family. "Five of them and four of us."

Dawson saw the two men from Caroline's side of the house sneak back along the fence on her side of the house but he couldn't get a shot off. The remaining militia members at the fence started shooting at the windows to provide them more protection. The five New Order members ceased fire while they huddled while staying very low to the ground in tall grass. The problem was that the grass was patchy and their concealment wasn't as complete as they thought. Dawson guessed they were rethinking their attack plan. They'd lost seven men. Clearly they were used to just rolling over simple farm families with little firearm experience or individual families who had no defensive plan and wanted largely to just be left alone.

Dawson took careful aim and the figures lying prone on the ground trying to use the grass as concealment and squeezed the trigger on his rifle. The figure flinched visibly and the others scattered. Annie sent several rounds their way but missed. Dawson's target never moved.

"If they try to withdraw we can't let them escape." Dawson said to Annie. "Anyone getting away will likely come back with a larger force."

Annie nodded. "OK. I'll do my best."

Suddenly the Holderites opened fire again. Dawson stayed low and could see one of the men was running up the drive as fast as he could. He noted the man had shed his pack and his weapon. He was holding something small in both hands. Getting a good aim was difficult because the Holderites were targeting the window openings and firing as rapidly as they could. He still managed to get a shot off and missed. Then he waited. The flaw in the New Order plan was that unless they wanted to risk shooting their own guy once he got near the cabin they'd have to stop shooting.

"Wait till they stop shooting. He's got some kind of grenade: either tear gas or frag. We won't get much time to aim so be quick and be accurate." He said to Annie.

"I will." She said, "Nobody is raping me again."

Dawson was right. The militia stopped shooting. Dawson and Annie popped up and quickly aimed at the man who was still running at them but preparing to throw whatever was in his hand. Both rifles went off and the New Order militia member spun around screaming as he fell to the ground. Shortly thereafter the grenade went off. The shrapnel from the grenade finished him.

The remaining member of the militia unit gave up. They started to carefully pull back using a version of a Parthian retreat as they did so: moving away from Dawson and the cabin while firing backwards at it. Once they were at about 200 yards they gave up being careful and trying to stay concealed, thinking they were safely out of effective range of most 'farm folk'. Dawson dropped one almost as soon as he stood up. He dropped a second as the men started running directly away from the cabin on a bee line for safety. The third he dropped at about 300 yards when the man stopped for a moment to look back instead of continuing on. Had he continued on, Dawson likely wouldn't have been able to take him.

"Everyone gather in the dining room!" Dawson called out.

Addison and Caroline came into the dining room. Neither seemed injured other than a couple of scratches caused by flying pieces of wood from the window frames. The walls had done their job. Dawson was satisfied.

"I dropped two of them!" Addison said excitedly. "I did what you taught me and I hit them. I wasn't even scared. It was great!"

It was obvious Addison was on an adrenaline high. Dawson chuckled.

"You did good." He said to Addison and ruffled her hair a bit. "Everyone stay here. I'll go outside and clean up. You don't want to see what's out there, so stay in here and wait for me to come back." Dawson said as he drew his sidearm. He carefully opened the cabin door and stepped out. He cautiously went around to Addison's side of the cabin. One man was hung up in the fencing. Addison had hit him with one round to the forehead and another to the chest. He suspected he chest hit was intentional while the headshot was just luck. The second man had obviously bled out with a bullet wound to the leg that must have hit an artery. He then checked the bodies in the drive and in the front barricade. One of those men was still alive so Dawson finished him with one round from his Sig.

Once he was sure the cabin area was safe he checked the men who had been retreating when he'd shot them. They were all dead. Two of them were young - real young. He guessed they couldn't have been older than nineteen and likely were younger than that. They'd probably been attracted to the promise of free food and warm housing and all the women they wanted in the pleasure houses. He regretted the waste of their lives, but they'd made their choices and had now paid the piper. He dragged them up to the front barricade one at a time. Once that was done he went through their gear and set aside anything he thought the family might need. Shirts, underwear, ammo, toiletries, food, and so on would go into the larder in the basement for use later. Their weapons were also kept for use or for barter depending on the need or opportunity.

About an hour later Ed and two of his sons arrived.

"Looks like you had a dust up too." Ed said as he surveyed the bodies piled by the front barricade.

"Yeah. We did."

"So did we. They messed up the house pretty well but no one was seriously hurt. Nothing we can't fix though as far as the house is concerned. They all ended up like these ones did."

"Well, I don't suppose these will be the last ones Holder sends. Sooner or later someone else will come calling to enforce Holder's claim." Dawson said stoically as if the fates had already decreed it.

"Yeah, probably. We'll have to be more watchful from now on. I'll probably rotate the boys though the barn steeple to keep watch at our place. From up there they can see most of the countryside. Maybe I'll build a platform in the silo for observation purposes. We can see even more from up there."

Dawson nodded. "Yeah. Probably a good idea. Too bad we don't have one of those old hand crank air raid sirens. If we had a platform in the silo and one of those we could alert the whole community at once."

Ed nodded but didn't say anything. There wasn't any need. Wishing for something no one had any means of obtaining was useless.

"I'll go get the backhoe and bring our bunch down here." He said. "We'll bury them all out there in the open somewhere and cover it over with that fallen tree and rocks. No one will know what happened to them."

Dawson nodded. "Yeah. Let's do that."

Chapter 7

August 11th

Dawson had left the house early to go fishing. His plan was to catch some nice sized trout and smoke them for the coming winter. In better days he'd fished the river with a fly rod. He'd enjoyed the challenge and skill required in placing the fly exactly where it needed to float to a given place where fish might be hiding. Now, however, it was strictly survival and he used the classic hook and bait. Fly rods and fun were no longer part of the equation.

The plan had been moderately successful. He had not caught as many fish as he'd planned but he did catch a few. The way he looked at it, a few was better than none. They would do.

"Where's Caroline?" he asked as he walked into the cabin with his catch.

"She went back to her old house. It's her son's birthday and she wanted to wish him a Happy Birthday." Annie said without looking up from the stew she was cooking.

Dawson nodded in acknowledgment. He wasn't worried too much about Bryan anymore. He had long since cooled off and had actually stopped by once or twice to ask Dawson for tips on smoking meat and fish and had wanted to know what traps to get off Thompson if he had any the next time he came by. Bryan had never been much of an outdoorsman, in spite of having set himself up for being completely off grid. Pretty much everything was new to him when it came to survival living and survival skills. Dawson was pretty sure nothing was going to go wrong if Caroline showed up to celebrate her son's birthday.

He set about cleaning the trout he'd caught and never gave Caroline's absence another thought. All in all she'd be home shortly after lunchtime. He couldn't imagine her staying overly long. Besides, he knew she had gardening she'd wanted to get done. The woman loved her garden. She always had as long as he'd known her. The fact that the apple tree cuttings had taken root so well was more because of her skill than his. She was a master at it. He smiled when he thought about that.

He had just finished the last fish when he heard Annie yell, "Where's all that smoke coming from?!" He looked up and saw her pointing off in the general direction of the Harrison farm. Dawson turned to look in that direction but his view was obstructed by several large shade trees in his yard. He then rushed to where Annie was standing, still pointing off into the distance. A large black column of smoke was rising thick and fast above the tree line.

About that time Ed's pickup careened into his driveway. Ed's two oldest boys were in the back carrying their rifles.

"Looks like a fire at the Harrison place!" Ed yelled. "Come on!"

Dawson paused long enough to grab Annie's AK-47 and jumped into the bed of the truck with the boys. Ed then quickly turned around and sped off toward the smoke. It didn't take long to get there, although the ride had been anything but smooth. Ed ignored potholes, ruts and obstructions in his haste to get to the fire. A house fire was the single worst thing that could happen to a family given the times.

The pickup slid to a halt as Ed slammed on the brakes once they'd hit the Harrison farm yard. The house was fully engulfed in flame. There was no hope of saving it. No one was around. Whoever had set the fire had gone.

"What the hell?" Caleb said more in a statement than a question as he pointed off toward the garden.

Dawson turned to see what had caught Caleb's attention. Caroline's sons stood along the garden fence with their arms outstretched on the top rail of the garden fence. At first glance they seemed to be resting casually against the fence in an identical pose. A second glance was all that was needed to see it wasn't the case. They'd been shot: tied to the fence and executed. The youngest, the birthday boy, who was only eight years old, was actually suspended off the ground.

Dawson looked at the dead boys and then back at the house. Ed grabbed him knowing what he was about to do.

"If she is in there, there's nothing you can do for her." He said firmly.

Dawson started to struggle out of Ed's grip.

"Dawson! If she's in there, she's already dead. You can't save her. It is too late. Think of Addie and Annie. They need you alive!" Ed said more firmly and loudly through gritted teeth to emphasize the point while tightening his grip on Dawson's jacket and giving it a shake against Dawson's chest.

Dawson stared at the burning house in panic and then came to himself and looked at Ed. He nodded his head and quit resisting.

"Let's get her kids down off that fence." Ed said quietly. "We can do that much for her."

They went to the fence to cut the children down from it. As they approached they could see that the poor boys had pretty much been used for target practice. It wasn't just an execution. It had been an exercise in perversion and hate. The youngest, especially, seemed to have been a favorite target for whatever reason. Perhaps he'd screamed the loudest when shot? Dawson wondered. He'd seen things like that in the Middle East. Insurgents would torture suspected spies by shooting them in the extremities until they got what they wanted. It looked like something similar had gone on here.

The thing that bothered him was that he hadn't heard any shooting. The Harrison farm wasn't that far from his place. He should have heard shooting long before they saw the smoke from the house fire. It was something he'd have to take into consideration from now on. It appeared that whoever did this was using suppressed weapons. On the other hand, over history weather had sometimes kept whole battles from being heard even though people were within range of the sounds. He was concerned either way. If they were making suppressed weapons standard practice, coming to someone's aid in the community would be more difficult. The only reliable mutual defense would depend on Ed building that platform in his silos.

Caleb and Mike went and found some tarps in the barn. They carried them out to the garden and spread them on the ground while Ed and Dawson cut the boys down from the fence. Then Ed and Dawson wrapped them up while the two boys started digging graves. When they'd finished burying Caroline's boys the crew could only stand back and watched the fire burn itself out.

By sundown, the fire had pretty much burned itself out and was a smoldering pile of hot rubble. Ed and Dawson approached the house to see if they could find any bodies near the door way they could just grab easily. There wasn't any.

"We can't really get in there tonight." Ed said. "We might as well go home and come back tomorrow. It should be cool enough by then for us to be able to get in and see if Bryan and Caroline are actually in there."

Dawson nodded. "Yeah. You are probably right."

Reluctantly he got into the pickup and Ed drove him home.

"I'll be back first thing tomorrow morning." Ed said. "I'm real sorry Dawson. I really am."

Dawson nodded his head, "Yeah. Thanks, Ed. I'll see you in the morning." He then went into the house.

"Where's mom?" Annie asked when he came through the door.

"She...won't be coming home." Dawson said, his voice catching.

Addie let out a loud wail of despair. "She's dead!!" and ran off into her bedroom. Annie looked at Dawson for confirmation.

He nodded his head, "Yeah. Likely so. We couldn't get into the house to know for sure. We'll know tomorrow."

"Her boys?"

"Dead. That is all we do know for sure. They were...dead in the yard. Smoke likely got them." Dawson lied.

Annie nodded and her eyes teared up. "I'll go comfort Addie." She said her voice catching and quickly left the room.

That night Dawson's dreams were filled with images of burning houses and the sounds of terrified screams. He woke up twice in a cold sweat absolutely certain the screams he heard were real. After the second time he gave up. He went into the kitchen and made himself a pot of coffee. Morning was a long way off. He poured himself a cup when the coffee was done. He took a sip and then put the mug down. Dawson then burst into tears.

The sun was just beginning to color the sky when Ed's truck pulled up the driveway. Dawson doubled checked his sleeping teenagers and then went out to the truck. Ed was somber and it was clear the he, like Dawson, hadn't slept well.

"You know who did this, right?" he said as the truck slowly made its way down the rutted service road.

"Yeah. I do." Dawson said quietly but determinedly.

"You know that there isn't much we can do about it, right?"

"Yeah. I do." Dawson said without emotion.

"You know we may not find her in there, right?"

"Yeah. I do."

"And you know if she isn't in that house there isn't much we can do about that either, right?"

"Yeah. I do." Dawson's voice never changed.

The sight that greeted them when they pulled into the drive made Dawson's stomach churn. The remains of the house that still stood looked like a cold blackened skeleton watching over the heaps of burned furniture, charred rubble, and piles of ash. Here and there smoke rose from spots that were still hot and still smoldering.

Neither Ed nor Dawson made any move to get out of the truck. Neither wanted to find what they thought they would find lying somewhere in the rubble and ash. Finally Dawson drew a long deep breath as though steeling his nerves.

"Well, I guess we won't learn anything sitting here." He opened the truck door and got out. Ed followed his lead and they walked together to the burned out remains of the house.

It was clear the search was going to be slow. Bookcases had over turned as walls had collapsed, the ceiling had fallen in dropping burning furniture from the second story and it would have been easy for a body to be hidden under rubble or a piece of large furniture that fell when the wall gave way or dropped from the rooms above. After about half an hour of searching they found the first body. It was burned beyond recognition; its extremities were mostly burned away so that only the upper legs and arms remained along with a charred grotesque head and torso. The heat had burst the abdomen open.

"I'm guessing that is Bryan." Ed said. "Caroline's shoulders weren't that broad."

They managed to get the body into a body bag that Doc Arnie had sent with Ed and carried it out to the lawn. Then they went back inside. After another half hour of looking Ed found the second body under an old iron framework bed that had fallen from the second floor when the ceiling collapsed. This body was in no better shape than the first and Dawson could barely bring himself to look at it.

"It's Caroline." He said. "That is her rifle." He said pointing at the soot and ash covered AR-15 lying on the floor next to the body.

"How do you know?" Ed said, "An AR is and AR."

"I gave her that rifle to carry. I etched all my rifles with that mark on the receiver in case they were ever stolen. You know; something extra to positively identify it by for the police if it got stolen." He said as he pointed at the firearm.

Ed nodded. "Damn."

They got Caroline's body into the other body bag and carried her out to the lawn and laid her down next to Bryan. They then set about digging graves. They finished the first grave and buried Bryan.

"Should we bury Caroline here with her kids or back at the cabin with you?" Ed asked carefully.

Dawson was silent for a very long time and Ed patiently waited for him to decide. "She loved her kids as much as she loved me but I think she would want to be with them."

Once they'd buried Caroline's body they stood in silent mourning over the family that was no more. Then they got into the truck and drove away.

"You suppose she was dead before they burned the place down?" Dawson asked quietly as the truck made its way slowly back down the service road.

"Dawson, we have no way of knowing that. Don't torture yourself thinking about it. If she wasn't you don't want to know that. If she was, it doesn't matter."

"Yeah, I guess." Dawson said. He suspected they'd burned the house down over her, though. Bryan and she were not in the same place in the house indicating maybe they were trying to defend it from different places. To Dawson it looked like they set fire to the house to drive them out or kill them. Knowing Bryan the militia had probably come to collect their 'tax' and Bryan had gotten hot headed and belligerent. After that it all went downhill.

'Enemies of the State' Captain Marsh had said. That was how they would have viewed him and her and reacted accordingly. Dawson decided from that moment on, he was at war. Holderite, or New Order Liberation Militia (as they officially called themselves), patrols were something he'd avoided since the encounter with Captain Marsh's patrol. Now, he would hunt them. He could not bring Caroline back, but he could avenge her.

Chapter 8

Dawson made his way down the main street of Carrollton two weeks after Caroline's death. 'Carrollton: the circle of Hell Dante never found.' Dawson thought to himself as he walked along the street. He had one thing on his mind. Deep inside something told him to go home. No matter what he did here, he wasn't bringing Caroline back. Still, here he was. Walking the streets of Carrollton looking for he didn't know what but knowing he was going to do something.

Bloodlust: that was what his old C.O. had called it. That desire to kill something or someone without regard to innocence or guilt. He was focused however. He wasn't going to go about killing innocent civilians in the streets just because they lived in Carrollton, despicable town that it was. He hunted the guilty. Of course, in his mind being guilty meant only that his prey was wearing a New Order uniform. The higher the rank, the more he was interested in them.

The streets of Carrollton were moderately busy at this time of day so Dawson fit into the crowd without drawing notice. Yet he was busy noting how the streets were laid out and how the guards moved on their street patrols as he pretended to be going about other business. It didn't take any expertise to note that they were at best poorly trained and equipped. He disregarded them in an offhanded manner. They weren't his target in particular but they would be easy prey if he chose to take them.

When evening fell he debated on finding an inn or a motel but decided against it. He decided that would it would be best to see Carrollton at night if possible. Sleeping in doorways or alleys did not appeal to him but lurking in them did. The problem was he didn't know where anything was in Carrollton so there was a certain amount of risk.

"Y'all look lost." A woman's voice said from behind him in a soft southern drawl.

He turned to look to see who'd spoken to him. The woman was blonde, dressed as a hooker, and had more makeup on than any woman should wear at any one moment.

"I've been watching you." She continued. "You're just wandering aimlessly all around this shithole of a town." She took his hand and when Dawson tried to pull it back she tightened her grip. "Come on, sugar, I'll take care of you tonight."

"I'm really not in the mood. My wife just died a couple of weeks ago. I'm really not thinking of companionship."

She chuckled. "Neither am I. I just need a good poke."

"I said I'm not interested."

"Ya' sure?" she said as she pulled her jacket open exposing her breast. "These poor girls could use some tender attention." She looked at him temptingly, her eyes dancing in a challenge and her tongue licking her lips sensuously.

"No, sorry." Dawson said and tried to pull his hand back again. She tightened her grip still more.

"Mystie! Put those away!" a passing guard ordered. "You're in public and on the main street for Christ's sake!"

"I'm working he'ya!" she spat back at him as he passed on by them. "You didn't mind seein' 'em last week!" Then she turned her attention back to Dawson. "Come on!" she urged. "I'll be real good to you. You remind me of one of my brother's friends. I always treat my brother's friends real nice." Her voice became a purr.

"I'm not in the mood." Dawson said struggling to remain both civil and calm.

"I know, sugar, but I am. I need what you got." She purred.

"Sorry." Dawson said as he jerked his hand out of hers suddenly so she couldn't react. Then he started on down the street. She grabbed his jacket and pulled him back facing her.

"Y'all's really are thick, ain't ya?" she said through gritted teeth. "Ya' DON'T want to go that way. Trust me!"

"Why? I'm looking for the hotel."

"Because you'll more fun with little ol' me!" she said as she shot a look over his shoulder and he turned his head to follow her glance. A group of militia members were coming up the street.

They seemed unlike the rest of the guards and militia members Dawson had seen on the streets – and much better equipped and wearing Viet Nam tiger stripe camouflage uniforms and not old Army MultiCam or the woodland camo that preceded it.

'Storm Troops!' Dawson thought to himself.

"Alright." He said taking her hint. "Let's go."

"I knew y'all wanted a little." She said rather loudly and took his hand and started to walk away, almost a little too hurriedly in Dawson's estimation, but he kept up. She led the way back up Main Street until they got to Elm Street and then hung a left. Dawson allowed her to keep on leading him but all the while preparing for whatever violence she might be leading him into. To him, it smelled like a setup.

They continued on down the street for a couple of blocks still moving at the same hurried pace. Eventually they came to a house with women sitting on the porch in the lantern light showing off their bodies for perspective customers. They politely ignored Mystie and Dawson as they came up the steps and went into the house.

A grizzled man sat behind a desk that looked like an old fashioned hotel front desk. He looked up at Mystie and Dawson when they walked in and he started to say something but Mystie cut him off.

"Not now, Alfie. I'm working. He ain't my cousin visitin' from Mobile an' I got bills to pay." She charged on ahead and made a turn to the climb the stairs to the next floor where most of the bedrooms likely were. Dawson pulled back.

"Now, sugar," she purred, "My bed is in my room up they'ah. We all have our own workspace and I know you really want to see mine." She winked at him sexily and pulled her jacket open a bit, giving Dawson another look at her chest. There was a look in her eyes, however, that told Dawson not everything he was seeing was for real. She gave his hand another tug and he followed her on up the stairs. At the top of the stairs there was a hallway with two doors on either side. The hall ended in another door. She led the way to the last door and took a key out of her bra and unlocked it.

Mystie winked at Dawson and went on in. Dawson could see the room was just a bedroom so he followed her in.

She lit the oil lamp on the table near the door and then closed it behind them and then heaved a heavy sigh.

"Thank God that's over." She said dropping the southern accent. Dawson stood in shock. Her accent had been nearly perfect. He never suspected it was fake.

"I'm sorry for the way I handled that." She said in a genuine tone of voice. "You have to play the part around here if you want to be the 'gray man.'"

"I'm not following you." Dawson said.

Mystie sat down in a chair at a small table and lit the oil lamp in the middle of it. Then she turned to face Dawson. She sat silently as if taking his measure. Dawson could sense something dangerous about her. She seemed like a coiled snake.

"My name is Melania." She said finally. "You are...?"

"Dawson VanOrder." Dawson said not wanting to volunteer any information yet kicking himself for giving her his real name.

"You don't remember me, do you?"

"Should I?" Dawson asked answering her question with one.

She nodded her head. "Angel Logistics."

Dawson said nothing but tried not to react to the name.

"Your team trained some of my people for some special security work a few years ago. I remember you."

"Sorry. Wrong guy." Dawson said. "I never worked with Angel Logistics.

"Who were those militia guys in the street?" Dawson asked hoping to change the subject.

"Holder's special forces."

"They looking for something special?" he asked.

"Yeah...me. They just don't know it. They are looking for some guy called 'the Wolf' which is me." She sighed. "We can drop the cat-and-mouse routine. We are on the same side unless I'm completely mistaken. If I am mistaken, one of us isn't leaving this room alive."

"Same side? There are sides?" Dawson asked trying to sound innocent.

She reached into her belt and produced a pistol and put it on the table beside her. "Damn thing digs my side something fierce when I sit down." She complained. "I need a new holster or something, I guess." Then she looked at Dawson and smiled.

"Yes, there are sides. All wars have sides. A war is two packs of wolves fighting over territory and sheep. If you aren't sheep you're a wolf. I can tell you aren't a sheep so the question is which pack of wolves do you belong to? Something tells me you belong to mine not theirs."

"Maybe I am a sheep." Dawson said.

"Really? A sheep?" her voice reflected deep skepticism. "You are carrying a hunting rifle, but you carry yourself like you are more used to carrying a combat weapon than a sporting one. Your pistol could just be any old pistol but I'll bet it was your A.L. service pistol and it is a Sig P220 in 40 S&W. Your knife isn't a hunting knife either. Oh, it will pass as one, but it isn't. Now, which pack?"

"My own." Dawson said evenly.

"Well, my dear Mister VanOrder, she said as she stood up and started to remove her clothes. "I'm afraid that may work for whatever private little war you've got going on, but in the larger picture the question is where your private little war fits into the real war." She walked shamelessly across the room in just her panties and took a t-shirt and a pair of black cargo pants out of her dresser.

"Real war?" Dawson asked as she started to get dressed.

"Yeah. You might have noticed there is a war going on. It is kind of hard to miss. People get killed, people get taken hostage, buildings get burned, and towns get occupied. Just a small insignificant war on the cosmic scale; certainly not on par with World War Two, but it is still a war and where there is a war sometimes the really dangerous wolves don't attack in the open. We don't. You and me. We make it personal and quiet and we scare the shit out of the other wolves.

"I don't know about your private little war, but mine is about vengeance." She said. "I let those bastards grope me, ogle me, and fuck me and all the while I play like I'm the easiest whore in town. But it is all a cover and I do it for only one reason. I will have my vengeance Mr. VanOrder. They will pay." There was steel in her voice and deep anger. "So can we stop with the game playing and be level with one another?"

Dawson nodded. "Alright." He said.

"Good. Now, what's your little war about?"

"Same as yours. Vengeance."

"Wife, lover, child?" she asked.

"Wife." He said simply. "They burned down the house over her and executed her children."

"I'm sorry." She said softly. "I know it is a hard burden to bear; the being left behind, I mean.

"I made my way here from Denver after the blast. My family lives north of Myerstown, or at least they did. I came home to a burned out hulk of a house, my parent's bodies rotting on the front lawn with crows feasting on them, and my little sister missing. She died down here in Carrollton's pleasure house. I couldn't save her. I can, however, avenge her and my parents."

Dawson nodded. "I'm sorry for your loss. It hurts."

"Yeah...it hurts," She agreed "which is why we have the underground."

"Underground?"

She opened another dresser drawer and pulled out a black sweatshirt and ski mask. She put the sweatshirt on before answering.

"Yeah, underground. No one else is around to hurt them so we do. We burn shit down, make shit blow up, kill people when we can get the right targets. Vive la rébellion!" she smiled in a way that clearly meant she wasn't smiling.

"I see." Dawson said.

"Look, Mister VanOrder, you can run your private little war if you want. I'd rather you ran yours along with ours. Together we can make them pay for what they'd done to our families and our homes and our communities."

"What is your plan?" Dawson asked in a semi-professionally curious manner.

"Long term? Kill Harlan Holder. Short term? Kill Mason Conway the new commander of the New Order Militia here in Carrollton County. The pleasure houses were his invention when he was just one of Holder's advisors for a long time and he personally ran the pleasure house here until his promotion. In Holder's order of things, he is the new number three man in the command structure. My sister died in his custody, and he will die in mine." She said it all matter-of-factly as though Mason Conway had already been handed over to her.

She looked up at him. "My team is meeting to take care of business with Commandant Conway. I'd like you to come along. We could use you. If you can't or won't, I'll trust you to stay here until I get back and that you won't roll over on me afterwards. You know; professional courtesy and all."

Dawson looked her for a moment. He knew he should not trust her. He did not remember her from the training exercise she'd mentioned but she seemed to know about his former employer which was a surprise. Maybe she had been part of the exercise. He hadn't paid much attention to the attendees at that event. It was his last assignment before he 'retired' to make Janie happy. He never thought he'd see any of them ever again. To him they'd just been faces.

On the other hand, his gut told him she was on the up and up. Seven years of relying on his instincts taught him to trust his gut. It was always more accurate than his brain.

He nodded. "Alright. I'll go along. Why not?"

She smiled. "Good. Leave your rifle here and you'll find another sweatshirt in the bottom drawer over there. It should fit you. It is usually way too big for me. I only wear it when I have to wear body armor – even then it is big on me."

Melania opened her closet and pulled out two rifles with folded stocks. She unfolded one and checked the action. Then she got several magazines off the closet shelf.

"M1 carbines?" Dawson asked in skepticism. "How did you get those? No one has those anymore."

"Sources." She said simply. "Perfect little gun for what we do. We aren't refighting the Battle of Bulge. We don't need anything that can shoot 600 yards."

Dawson looked at her skeptically.

"Look, not a lot gun-show gun dealers lived much past week two of the collapse. Most of them were old, out of shape, medicine dependent geezers. My source was smart enough to know not to raid gun stores and compete with drug crazed looters. He waited, listened, let others do the hard work, and then took advantage. We got all he had of these. Cost us dearly I'll admit, but they work like a charm."

She handed Dawson one of the carbines and three magazines.

"We shouldn't need these, but then we shouldn't be here in the first place." With that she pulled a spiked combat tomahawk out of the closet and slipped into a loop on her belt while Dawson checked his weapon's action for functionality.

"Now, let's go kill someone." She said. The she opened her bedroom window and slipped out.

They went out to a small roof outside her window and then dropped down to the ground below. Staying low and in the shadows they made their way into the alley and toward the center of town. They'd traveled several blocks when Melania slipped into a deep doorway and crouched down. They were at a junction where five alleys came together. Dawson followed her lead. After about five minutes a cricket sounded, only it wasn't a cricket. It was a clicker like children use to annoy their parents.

Melania responded with a clicker of her own and three figures materialized out of the shadows.

"Your friend needs his face blackened." One of them said when they got up close enough to whisper and be heard. "He shines like the bloody moon."

Melania nodded. "I know. I knew you had face black. I don't."

"Here." The man said after fumbling in his pockets for a moment. "Complements of Arties Army Surplus store in beautiful downtown Worthington."

Dawson took the offered paint and quickly applied it to his face.

"Now, you look like a right proper commando." The man said.

"The Commandant moved his bedroom." One of the others said. "He decided he didn't like the upstairs room so he moved downstairs to the room next to his office. Even had a carpenter put a door between the two rooms. Too bad he chose one of our guys to put it in otherwise you'd be in the wrong room tonight killing some lowly private." There was a certain gloat in the man's voice.

"War does seem to sometimes hinge on such rolls of fortune." Melania whispered. "I'll accept it when it rolls my way."

The others nodded and tried to suppress a laugh which told Dawson there was an inside joke involved with that comment.

"Let's move out." Melania said after they'd had their private laugh.

The team made their way quickly and quietly down the alley ways. The closer they got to the barracks the slower they had to go. Guards were patrolling pretty much everywhere and getting past them was tense and nerve-wracking. They were almost discovered twice on the way in and once they almost stumbled into a pair of guards that came from out of nowhere.

They made their way to the window of the Commandant's bedroom. Melania tried to open it but it was locked shut. She looked at the team and shrugged. They moved down and tried the office window. It slid open but the wooden frame made a loud cracking noise in protest as it went up. They all quickly looked around to see if the noise had alerted anyone. When no one appeared the team quickly and as quietly as possible made their way through the window and into the room.

One team member cracked open the door to the bedroom and then nodded. He carefully and slowly opened the door and Melania and Dawson slipped into the room. Two the team members stayed by the bedroom door while the third followed Melania to the Commandant's bed.

The commandant's aide was sitting in a chair next to a desk along the far wall where a single oil lamp was burning on low barely lighting the room at all. He was awakened by the cold of the steel muzzle of Dawson's pistol against his forehead pinning his head against the wall. His eyes flew open and before he could speak Dawson put his hand on the man's mouth to silence him. Once he was certain the man wasn't going to call out he pulled his hand away and put his finger to his lips. The aide nodded his understanding.

Melania jumped bodily on the sleeping commandant, pinning his arms under her legs and stuffing a sock into his mouth in mid snore. The other team mate jumped on his legs pinning them under his bedding as well. The Commandant's eyes flew open in surprise and shock and he struggled to get up but it was useless. They had him pinned. She gave the sock an extra push into his mouth to make sure he couldn't spit it out. He protested but the sock muffled him.

"Now, Mason." Melania said quietly and threateningly yet somehow still conversationally. "You don't know me and you probably don't remember my sister. She was in your pleasure house. She died there. You had her raped and tortured there. I get it: things happen in war, etc. I get it. I really do. But something else happens in war, Mason. People get try to get even. I'm getting even, Mason. I'm the one blowing up your buildings, killing your men, and setting fires around town. Why? To get even. But it isn't enough Mason. I need to clear the board between us. Level the playing field. I'm the Wolf and I've come for you."

The Commandant had quit struggling by now and was watching wide eyed as Melania spoke to him. Terror was written on his face.

"You've heard of me, no?" Melania asked feigning vanity.

He nodded his head, his eyes still wide with terror.

"Now, Mason, I've always wondered what I could do to make us even. I thought about killing your wife and children. Getting into Waterford isn't that big a deal and they are such soft targets....you look surprised, Mason. You shouldn't be. By the way, does your wife always have guests at 1:00 in the morning? Seems a strange time to be entertaining in her bedroom, don't you think? I've always wondered about that. Well that, and why your roses haven't been dusted properly....What? You are surprised? Of course I know Mason. I was there. I saw them – well them and her.

"But you know, Mason, that wouldn't have been enough nor would it have been fair. Your sweet innocent family is probably completely unaware of what you are doing out here in Carrollton. No, Mason, to be even we have to get more personal.

"Then I thought I should just take your manhood: cock and balls. All of it. Leave you useless to your wife, who probably is cheating on you tonight in your own bed at home." Melania reached behind her and grabbed the Commandant's genitals and gave them a not so gentle squeeze. He groaned in pain and protest.

"Then I realized that wouldn't be enough either. She probably wouldn't miss them and I still wouldn't know why you did the things you did. I still wouldn't know what makes you tick. So I thought I'd see what was on your mind. Have this little chat with you, like this: face to face. Just two grown adults getting to know one another better. That is more civil don't you think?"

He nodded his head but was still clearly terrified.

"So, Mason, what **is** on your mind? Anything you want me to know? Any insights into why you think doing what you do is a good thing? I'm curious and I am really willing to listen."

The Commandant tried to say something but the sock kept him muffled and unintelligible. Melania leaned down and made a face indicating she couldn't understand him. He kept trying. Finally she sighed in mock frustration and straightened up.

"I'm sorry, Mason, I can't understand a word you're saying. I guess I'll just have to see what is on your mind another way. Now, how will I do that?" she looked thoughtful. "I know! I'll just look!" she said as though having a bright idea. She reached down and pulled the tomahawk from its loop.

"This will work!" she said. The Commandant began to struggle for all he was worth but he really didn't have time to struggle much.

Melania planted the spike deep into his forehead. His eyes crossed and he groaned and then lay still.

His aide let out a yell for help, but Dawson's pistol, still planted firmly against his forehead went off. The lack of distance between the muzzle and the target muffled the shot some but it was clear the barracks was now alert.

"Just as I thought." Melania said to his now lifeless body. "No excuse at all." Melania pulled a note she'd written from her pocket and pulled the sock out of his mouth and replaced it with the note.

"Come on!" Dawson said "We gotta get out of here!"

Melania nodded and jumped off the dead body. They made their way out the window just as guards came into the room. One of Melania's team members fired a few rounds at them and then the team took off down the alley. Going quietly or in the shadows wasn't an option. The team had to fight both a running battle both from the front and the rear.

One of the team was hit and went down. Melania quickly looked at him, obviously thinking of not leaving him behind. He never moved once he was on the ground so the team made their way away from the barracks fighting all the way.

"Everyone go different directions!" Melania said once they'd gotten back to the alley junction they'd met in. "Take to the roofs if you can." With that the team scattered. Dawson, not being familiar with the area felt abandoned. Bullets ricocheted off the buildings around him so he had to do something quick.

He took off running down the alley toward Elm Street looking for any means to get to the roof. He found none. However his pursuers seemed to have fallen behind or had given up not knowing which way to go at the junction. Once he reached Elm he quickly darted across the street and then climbed up on to the small porch and into Melania's room. She was changing out of her black outfit into her 'working clothes' which meant she removed everything.

"Quick! Get out of your clothes! All of them!" she ordered him in a quiet yet harsh voice.

"Huh?" Dawson asked in surprise.

"Get out of your clothes and put that rifle in the closet. Get that paint off your face! You're in a whore house. If they search the place, naked people are what they expect to find! Do it!"

Dawson did as he was told all the while feeling completely ill at ease. He glanced out the window and saw guards swarming the streets in search of the commandos. Then checked the mirror to make sure the paint was completely off his face.

"They'll be in here any minute!" she said urgently. "Fuck me!"

"What!?" Dawson said in disbelief.

"I said 'fuck me!' You're in a damned whore house. That is what happens here. Fuck me or at least make it look like you are!"

There was a sound of angry voices downstairs and women were screaming in fear.

"Now!" Melania said. "Do it and make it look good!"

Dawson quickly got into bed with her and got between her legs. He'd barely gotten on top of her when the door burst open and two militia members stepped into the room.

"OH GOD!! OH GOD!!!" Melania screamed in her perfect Southern accent. "FUCK ME HARDAH!! HARDAH!! OH GOD I'M CUMMING!!!" faking an orgasm and then as though suddenly realizing their 'private moment' had been intruded on she pushed Dawson off of her in wide eyed fear and started to scream in fear and surprise. It sounded genuine. She looked genuine.

The guards looked around without venturing further into the room and then turned and left.

Melania and Dawson sat for a long while where they were listening to the sounds of the search both inside and outside the house. The house quieted down pretty quickly. Dawson got up and started to get dressed.

"No!" Melania said quickly. "Not yet! Get back into bed."

"Huh?"

"Trust me! Do it!"

Dawson got into bed and Melania took his penis into her mouth. She started to suck on it and had only just begun when the grizzled man from downstairs burst into the room. It was clear he was angry and looking for someone to explain what was going on.

Melania looked up at him and in her southern accent said in exasperation, "Alfie! This man paid me for all night! He's had his pleasure interrupted twice now. Now git outta here and let the man enjoy what he bought!"

Alfie grunted and then strode from the room, closing the door behind him when he left. Melania then let out a short laugh and laid back on the bed next to Dawson.

"I'm sorry." She said after a moment. "It was the only thing I could think of at the moment."

"That's alright." Dawson said. "It was weird but it's alright."

"I remembered something someone told me once in a training seminar I went to: 'Do whatever you have to do to go home. No trick is too dirty. No tactic too uncivilized. No action is taboo.'"

Dawson was quiet for a moment. "I said that."

"Yes. You did." Then she paused for a moment and seemed worried when she spoke. "I hope the others got away."

"Me too. They seemed pretty competent. They probably did alright."

"They are competent. Two are ex-seals. The one that got killed was a ranger."

"What did the note you left behind say?" Dawson asked.

She grinned. "It was my calling card. It simply said, 'the Wolf has come.'" I leave it behind to taunt them and make them afraid." Then she rolled over on top of him.

"You know you'll have to stay the night here, right? You can't go out into the streets tonight. The militia will be on extra alert. You won't make it home. They will arrest you just for being on the streets."

"I thought of that." Dawson said nodding his head slightly.

She looked at him for a moment and then her expression changed.

"I'd really like to finish what you started." She said with a sexy grin. "I really would. Raids make me horny."

The next morning Dawson made his way out into the streets of Carrollton. The raid had been successful. He made his way to the eastern gate and saw that the guards had been tripled. Steeling his nerve he kept approaching.

The guard captain stopped him. "No one leaves the city!" he said sharply.

"I have children at home. Their mother is dead. I can't leave them alone too long." Dawson protested.

"Sorry. City is locked down. No one leaves. Period."

"I don't understand. Why can't I leave? I've got kids to think of." Dawson said feigning a parent's frustration.

"Look, I know you got kids. We had a murder last night and until the word is given no one leaves! Now go back into town and find a place to stay. That is all I can tell you." The captain was clearly tired of dealing with people who insisted on leaving. He'd probably heard every line in the book of reasons and excuses and wasn't in the mood to listen.

Dawson nodded and turned and retraced his steps. He made his way downtown to a pub and ordered a light lunch and paid for it with three .308 rounds in barter. Once he'd eaten he went back out onto the street. He really didn't know what to do. Going back to Melania's was not an option, unless they could convince Alfie that he enjoyed her so much he was back for another night of fun. He finally decided to bide his time and cut his way out through the fence after dark. By then the guards should be a little less vigilant and more like their old selves.

He happened to be walking down the street when he saw Melania, dressed as a hooker making her way down the street on the other side. She saw him and smiled coyly but they did not greet one another. Suddenly she was surrounded by militia guards. They threw her hard against the wall and, in spite of her struggles, quickly bound her hands behind her back and led her away. She quickly looked back at Dawson, a look of fear filling her face. Dawson fought the urge to find a way to rescue her, but realized that at the moment there was none. She must have known what he was thinking and shook her head to keep him from doing something to help.

All afternoon Dawson tried to find out where she was being held, but no avail. The only upside to her arrest was that the guards had gone back to their normal lazy routines and the guards at the gates had been reduced in number. Now, however, Dawson was not leaving town now that he could. He could not leave a team member behind.

About 5:00 in the afternoon he noticed a printed handbill nailed to a telephone pole. He pulled it down and read it aloud as though someone was listening to him.

"Public Execution to be held at 5:30 p.m. on the Field of Judgment by order of Acting Commandant Lyle Ashford for crimes against the State."

Dawson asked a passerby where the Field of Judgment was and was told it was at the far end of Elm Street out near the city's defensive fence. Dawson made his way there and arrived there early. Melania and her three team mates were already on the field in in cages. He could tell they'd been tortured. He guessed Melania had probably also be violated. If he could somehow get them free and eliminate the few guards standing around in a lackadaisical manner he could easily cut the fence behind them and escape.

He was making his way toward the cage as innocently and invisibly as he could when a number of new militia arrived. It was the crew he'd nearly encountered the night before. They took up positions near the cages and around a raised dais nearby. Dawson no longer had any hope of accomplishing what he'd planned. All he could to was wait – and improvise if possible.

At 5:30 p.m. three men in long black robes walked onto the field and took seats on the dais. A microphone was set up on the dais near the judge's chairs and another in front of it and facing it. Dawson realized they were being powered by batteries charged with a solar charger. A sound check was conducted and then the judges stood.

"Let the Court of Punishment come to order!" one of them said into the microphone. Then they sat down as did the crowd gathered to see the proceedings. Very few of them had brought lawn chairs with them so most sat on the ground.

"Bring out the first prisoner." The same judge intoned.

The guards opened a cage and dragged, literally, one of the prisoners out. They then had to hold him up so he could stand before the second microphone.

"Thomas Gardner. You have been found guilty of murder and crimes against the State. You have also, however, also provided the State with information without which we could not have brought your accomplices to justice. This court therefore for sentences you to confinement in the New Order Militia hospital until such time that your wounds are properly healed. Thereafter you are to be castrated and pressed into service with the militia as a conscript for the rest of your natural life. It is so ordered. Take him away.

"Next prisoner!"

The cage was opened another man was dragged from the cage as Gardner was dragged to a waiting cart and hauled away. The second man was able to largely walk with only a small amount of assistance. He stood before the microphone as erect as possible. His shackles were removed, but a militia member stood behind him with a bayoneted rifle pointed at his back.

"Have you anything to say before sentence is passed?" the judge asked.

"Fuck you and fuck this court!" he said defiantly.

"Edward Givens you have been found guilty of murder and crimes against the State. Having no extenuating circumstances you are hereby sentenced to death by firing squad; the sentence to be carried out forthwith. Take him away!" the judge intoned. It occurred to Dawson that the judge had said this same thing so many times he no longer gave it any thought or even put any emotion into it. His voice was nearly a monotone.

Givens was roughly dragged across the small field and placed in front of a single hole in the ground. A detachment of five of Storm Troopers stepped forward in formation and turned toward the prisoner. Four were armed. The other was clearly the squad leader.

"Aim!" their squad leader ordered. There was a clatter as the rifles were brought to bear with practiced precision.

"Fire!" the command came and the rifles fired immediately. Givens just disappeared into the hole. He'd barely hit the bottom when a regular militia member stepped forward, threw a bucket of lime into the hole and then stepped back.

"Bring out the next!" the judge said.

He, like Givens, was pretty much able to walk. He then stood before the microphone and was unshackled.

"Have you anything to say before sentence is passed?" the judge asked in a voice that showed he was growing bored.

"Have you heard the one about the priest, the nun and the donkey?" he asked and was promptly hit with a baton so hard across the shoulders it caused him to drop to his knees. He groaned in pain as he went down.

"Robert Mitchell, you have been found guilty of crimes against the State and of murder. Having no extenuating circumstances to mitigate your punishment you are hereby sentenced to death by firing squad. The sentence is to be carried out immediately. Take him away." The judge intoned in the same monotone.

He was dragged to the hole and forced to stand. His execution was as precise as Givens' had been.

"Bring out the last prisoner!" the judge ordered.

Melania was pulled from her cage and dragged to the microphone. She stood on shaking legs and appeared about to faint. Her shackles were removed as the other's had been.

"Have you anything to say to the court before your sentence is passed?" the judge asked.

She said nothing.

"Your accomplices have gone to their deaths having divulged all the information they knew related to your crimes. You however, have yet to divulge the name of the fifth conspirator. Divulge his name and the court is prepared to be merciful, and spare your life, in spite of your heinous crimes. Divulge his name or where he can be found and the court will sentence you to five years in the Waterford pleasure house." The judge said; his voice not in a monotone for the first time.

"He is the Wolf." She said in a shaky voice. A nervous gasp rose from the small crowd.

"The Wolf?" the judge asked. "You know no more. His name or where he is?"

"He is the Wolf." She said flatly and matter-of-factly. "He will come for you just as he came for the Commandant. He is the Wolf."

"I see. So even now you refuse to cooperate and save your life?"

"He is the Wolf." was all she said.

"I implore you one last time: give us his name!" the judge sounded almost panicked that she wasn't cooperating nor apparently fearing for her life.

"He is the Wolf." she said more confidently. "He will avenge my death."

"I see. Very well. We do not know your real name so you shall therefore die as a nameless person forgotten by history before your bones are dust. Because you have refused to cooperate with the court and because there are no extenuating circumstances to mitigate your sentence, you are hereby sentenced to death by firing squad. The sentence is to be carried out immediately. Take her away." The judge's voice was not a monotone. He sounded genuinely angry.

Melania was then dragged over to the hole. On the way she looked around desperately as though looking for help. She spotted Dawson in the crowd and their eyes locked. "Fight on!" she mouthed to him.

The guards placed her in front of the hole and then stood aside. The firing squad took position.

"Aim!" ordered the squad leader.

Melania jutted her chin out defiantly and pulled her shirt open, flashing the firing squad in one last act of defiance.

"Fire!" Came the order and the rifles went off immediately, pushing Melania backwards a step to the very edge of the hole. She dropped to her knees and looked at Dawson for a moment and locked eyes with him. In spite of the distance between them,

Dawson saw the light in her eyes flicker and then go out, and then she fell over backwards into the hole.

The next morning Dawson made his way home. He'd cut his way out of Carrollton through the city fence in the middle of the night after he'd retrieved Melania's M1 carbines and ammunition. He'd also cleansed her room of any other items that might expose the remaining underground members. In time he would make contact with them but at the moment there were things to do. Far behind him the alarm sounded again and Carrollton was locked down while the militia searched house to house again. Three more bodies had been found that morning: the underground turncoat who had informed on Melania was found dead in his hospital bed in the militia hospital. The judge was found at home in bed by his wife when she woke up next to him in their bed. The third was the new acting commander of the Carrollton Militia. He was found lying dead in the same bed his predecessor had been found in. All three men had a knife in their chest pinning a note to their bodies. The note read simply: "The Wolf has come."

September gave way to October in a gentle warm way. Dawson started to put away small game and all the fish he could get in preparation for winter. He also laid in the winter wood supply. Addison had taken charge of the garden and Della had come down to teach her to can vegetables and dry the jerky.

Annie had turned eighteen in September and Dawson knew it would not be long before she, like her sister, would want to move out and start her own family. He did not approve of the way things were being done in terms of sixteen and eighteen year olds marrying, but then the world now was much like the late 1800's and such things weren't uncommon on the frontier. Like it or not, he was on the frontier.

In late October Annie went missing. She'd told Dawson she was going to check the apple trees and never came back. Dawson was beside himself with worry. He thought at first she'd changed her mind and gone to the Johnson's to see her sister. She was not there. Addison had no idea where she'd gone either. The next stop was at the Myers house and again, she was not there. She was, however, discovered in Lucas Fry's bed at the Fry farm about two miles east of the Johnson's farm. Dawson was angry with her for three reasons: first she just disappeared without a trace and had worried him to death. Second, she was in bed with Lucas Fry, a boy two years older than herself. Third, she'd walked all the way to the Fry house without anyone accompanying her which was an incredibly dangerous thing to do, considering the time of year with the bears foraging food in preparation for denning up for the winter and with the constant worry of Holderite patrols.

When he blew up at her, she'd protested that she was old enough to run her own life and that she loved Lucas. In any event she and Lucas stepped over the oak branch and Annie moved in with the Fry family a few days later.

Dawson watched the line of armed men walking single file down a ravine floor about a mile from the cabin. He'd been out hunting deer when he stumbled across them. They weren't being particularly quiet as they moved along which told Dawson they either felt superior to anyone who might challenge them, or that they were certain they weren't going to run into anyone. They made an enormous amount of noise walking through the fallen leaves on woodland floor, almost as if they were school children playing in them. He stalked them for another mile and waited for them to stop to rest. When they did he took up a position on the ridge behind a big log.

"Scum of the earth" he mumbled to himself. He guessed from appearances it looked like patrol was en route to the Johnson farm or perhaps to the Myers farm. They were probably out to rekindle the debate on territorial jurisdiction for the territory around the farms. On the other hand, they were packing light so it was possibly just a raiding party out looking for outlaw raiders or easily obtained supplies to take back to Carrollton.

Dawson brought his hunting rifle to his shoulder. He was lying behind a log, looking down on the patrol. They had no idea he was there. He set his sights on one of the Holderites in the middle of the line and squeezed the trigger. The .308 bullet slammed into its target and sent the man sprawling. Before the line could react a second bullet sent another one into the next life, though not instantly. He laid on the ground screaming and writhing for a few minutes then went still. The four remaining members of the patrol had dived for cover as the second bullet had whizzed past them and were now trying to determine where the sniper was.

Dawson waited them out. He wasn't interested in a prolonged firefight given that ammunition was something he did not care to waste. As a result he wasn't going to give away his position by just firing bullets into the logs, stumps and rocks they were hiding behind. He could see occasional movements of arms and hands and knew they were signaling each other commands. Obviously the leader of the patrol was still among the living. He waited knowing that one of them would try to slide out and flank his position or at least the position they thought he was in. After a few minutes of waiting he caught movement to his right in the ravine and knew at least one of them was moving to do just that. He estimated where the movement was heading, waited a few more moments and when he saw a slight change in terrain caused by the crawling man's body, he fired.

It wasn't a kill shot like he had hoped for but it did connect. He instantly heard the man screaming in agony and calling for help. Bullets kicked up dirt in front of him in response to his shot. They had figured out where he was. He did not return fire. He waited as he ducked a little lower behind the ridgeline but stayed where he could keep an eye on the men below. The agonized screaming continued.

Suddenly two of the figures below him jumped up and started to run away. He pushed himself up a bit and set his sights on one of the men but didn't have time to fire before gunfire from the patrol below him dropped them in their tracks. Apparently the running figures were conscripts trying to escape with their lives, Dawson figured. Their own people wouldn't have shot them otherwise.

That left one member of the patrol below him hiding behind a large log.

"You got a wounded man over there!" Dawson called out loudly. "See to him!"

"Yeah. I get up and you shoot me. No way!" Came the response.

"See to your man! I'll hold fire while you do as long as you get up without your rifle."

There was long pause. "Alright! I'm moving to help him. I've dropped my rifle!"

Dawson watched as a man warily stood up and then quickly went to the fallen man's side. He couldn't see exactly what the man was doing, but it appeared that he was checking the wound and talking seriously to the wounded man. He gave him a drink from his canteen.

"You gut shot him!" the man shouted up at Dawson. "I got nothing for it. Have you got anything?"

"At home, but not here and home is a long way away. Looks like his luck has run out!" Dawson yelled back.

The Holderite bent as though saying something to the fallen man then he pulled his knife from its sheath. In a quick motion he thrust it into the fallen man's throat. The man twitched a couple of times and then laid still. The Holderite cleaned off his blade and put it back into its sheath.

His blade was barely back in the sheath when Dawson's bullet hit him square in the chest. He looked surprised and then dropped to the ground face first.

"I told you I wouldn't shoot you while you tended him. I never said anything about what would happen once you were done and I didn't say anything about taking prisoners." Dawson muttered.

He got up and made his way down to the fallen men. He checked their packs and took anything he thought he could use, especially ammunition, clothing, MREs, and first aid supplies. A couple of them wore new boots, or at least boots not yet truly broken in, so he tied the laces together and took those. He noticed the two who had been shot in the back trying to run away had what looked to be new BDU pants on so he took those as well. They weren't bloody or torn and he hated to leave them. He grimaced when he saw the sloppy castration job that had been done on them. This confirmed to him his suspicion that the fleeing men were conscripts.

"I coulda done better with my pocket knife, friend" he said to the last one. "Sorry you got caught up in this."

He then started for home. He knew the bears would likely find them soon enough. If they didn't the coyotes would. Either way he didn't want to be there when they did. Leaving the dead men unburied probably would have seemed uncivilized in a day gone by, and he was certain someone somewhere would mourn their loss, but it just was the fortunes of war as far as he was concerned.

The last thing Dawson did before he left the scene was to take one of the militia member's field knife and pinned a note to the man's chest. "The Wolf has come" it read.

When Dawson walked through the front door of the cabin that evening he was greeted by the delicious smell of stew cooking. He was also greeted by Kelly, Ashley's younger daughter.

"Hi daddy!" she said cheerily and with a smile.

"Well, hello, Kelly."

"I'm moving in here with you and Addie if that is OK with you." Kelly said.

"OK. Why the change? I mean I'm glad to have you but I thought you were happy at the Johnsons'."

"Well, I felt guilty with Addison being here alone."

"I'm thirteen!" Addison said adamantly. "I don't need a babysitter!"

"I never said I was here to babysit." Kelly said to her patiently. "I just thought with dad being away so much this time of season trying to put food away for winter it might be safer if you didn't have to defend the house alone if something went wrong."

"She has point, Addie." Dawson said, "You are a great shot with that carbine of yours but a second rifle at a time like that would be very helpful."

"OK." Addie said in frustration knowing she wasn't going to get anywhere even if she did think she could hold off the entire New Order militia alone.

"Now here is something for you both to think about. Neither of you are trained in any kind of tactical area. All you know is how to shoot. You have to plan ahead and you have to plan well. 'If he does this, what will I do?' 'If he does that, what will I do?' 'How will I make him do what I want him to do?' You have to think ahead. Reacting to what he does in a haphazard manner won't do anything but get you killed. I tired of burying people I care about."

That evening he was surprised to see Kelly and Addie sitting at the table studying a map that Kelly had drawn of their yard, house, and fences. They were talking quietly with one another and tracing routes on the map. He smiled to himself. He was sure they would not think of everything but at least they were planning something.

Chapter 8

Christmas Day, Noon

"This is our second Christmas together." Ed said from the head of the table. "Before the bomb went off none of us really knew one another. Now however, we depend on one another in ways we never imagined."

Dawson looked around the huge dining room. The whole community had managed to get into the room for Christmas dinner together. Prior to the bomb he'd never met the Fry's, but now his daughter was married to one. He'd barely met the Myers family but now he knew them pretty well. He'd known the Johnsons very well and the Harrisons pretty well before the disaster hit.

"We've had a rough couple of years." Ed admitted to the crowd. "We've lost Ashley Jensen and the entire Harrison family." Dawson noted that the Fry family all crossed themselves at the mention of the deceased community members. Somehow he liked that they did that.

"On the other hand, we've gained a lot too. Doc Arnie has come to live with us and we'd be in dire straits without him. We've had weddings and we have a couple of grandchildren on the way both for us and the Fry's. This afternoon Ellen is stepping over the oak limb with Johnny Myers. We've built our own hospital and we've started new families. We've beat back the New Order militia on several occasions and they don't generally bother us much anymore and we haven't had any casualties that Doc Arnie couldn't fix. For that we are all grateful. Now, I'm going to stop talking so we can eat!" With that he sat down and what had been a quiet room was now filled with laughter and conversation.

Dawson joined in the conversation and looked around the room. It had been an interesting couple of years for him too. Somehow he'd ended up with five daughters. Soon he would have grandchildren of sorts with Cassie, Tanya and Annie all pregnant. The joy, however, was overshadowed by the loss. He missed Caroline terribly. He'd long ago accepted her death, but he could not ease the pain. Nothing he could do, no deals he could make would bring her back. His soul was empty.

After dinner the whole community crowded tightly into the living room to celebrate Ellen and Johnny's wedding. Ed performed the ceremony that Dawson had created. Dawson realized that this was the first time he'd not been the father of the bride and didn't have to officiate. It seemed odd to not be on the other side of the limb on the floor. Once they had stepped over the limb and kissed the crowd let out a cheer.

"Well, son, getting married on Christmas means you have no excuse to forget your anniversary!" Ed laughed as he clapped Johnny on the shoulder.

"Excuse me!" Doc Arnie called out above the crowd. "Excuse me!"

The crowd got quiet as Doc Arnie made his way to the front of the room.

"I have something I'd like to say and something to ask." He said as Ed stepped aside to give him speaking space.

"I came here because of an emergency – an emergency I could, unfortunately, not set right. I was welcomed by you all in the kindest of ways in spite of that failure. I've done the best I could for you when you were sick or wounded and now it looks like I'll be delivering your babies." The room chuckled at his tone of voice which reflected a certain anxiety over the prospect. "Della has been a godsend to me. She is an excellent nurse and sometimes I think you all really would do fine without me as long as she was here. However, there is one person I've come to care about very deeply: so deeply in fact that I cannot think about life without thinking about sharing it with her." He paused for a moment as though gathering his courage.

"Well, the thing I want ask is this: Kelly, will you be my wife?"

Dawson was shocked. He didn't know Kelly was even interested in Doc Arnie. There was almost a twelve year age difference between them. He should have been outraged, he supposed. But he wasn't. They were a long way from anyone and people with spouse potential were rare. People just adjusted and made allowances. He like the rest of the crowd turned to look at Kelly who was blushing beet red.

"Yes!" she said as she burst into tears. "Yes!" The crowd parted so she could go to Doc Arnie and the two held one another and kissed. A cheer when up as they did.

"Well, they are standing in front of the oak limb." Cal Myers called out. "Get up there Dawson! You are the father of the bride. Do your thing!"

Dawson got up and stood before the couple. He went through the service and they stepped over the oak limb. Everyone cheered again. For now, in that moment, the community was happy.

"Daddy?" Addison said that night as they sat in front of the fire in the fireplace at home. Snow had started falling in heavy wet flakes as they had walked home from the Christmas celebration. Addie had fallen very quiet as the snow fell around them during the walk. Dawson was sure that she was remembering Christmases past, which were far happier than the last two had been.

"Yes, Addie?"

"Will I forget my real mom and dad?" there was a worried tone in her voice.

"No, sweetie. You won't forget them. Some things may become a bit hazy as the years pass but you won't forget them.

"Will they forget me?" she asked. There was a real fear in her voice.

"Well, Addie, I don't know exactly how things work in heaven. I'm pretty sure, though, that they will never forget you. Jesus didn't forget the disciples after he died did he?" Dawson was amazed to hear his grandfather speaking through him. What he'd just said sounded just like something his grandfather would have said.

"No." Addie said softly.

He gave her a wink, "I think that means we don't forget the people we love when we die. Your mom and dad still remember you and still love you."

Addison sat quietly for a few moments and then said softly, "I wish I could talk to them."

"I know. I feel the same way about a lot of people – especially Caroline. I think we will all get that chance later though. We just have to be patient."

"Do you think Millie will remember me?" she asked as tears began to form in her eyes.

"Yes, honey, I'm sure Millie will remember you too." He said as he stood up. He walked over to where Addison was sitting on the floor and sat down next to her. He took her into his arms and just held her. She cried hard for several minutes and then pushed herself away from Dawson, still sniffling and breathing in a stutter breath that children get when they cry too hard.

"I think I'm going to go to bed." She said softly.

Dawson watched her go into her bedroom. It had been well over a year since her parents had been killed and her friend had died. In all that time Addie hadn't really cried all that much. To see her cry hard now was comforting to Dawson. She was finally allowing herself to grieve.

In mid-January Dawson stopped the remains of the Harrison farm. He'd made stopping there a routine thing to do when he was traveling in that direction. Somehow stopping by Caroline's grave and talking for a few minutes made him feel better inside. He missed her more than ever and wished beyond all imaginings that she was still alive somewhere. He knew deep down that if she was still alive, she probably would have been better off where she actually really was. Thinking about her in a pleasure house in Carrollton or Waterford sickened him.

He sat down in the snow and started to talk to Caroline, filling her in on the girls and the community. Somehow telling her about everyday things made her feel less dead to him. It was irrational but sometimes grief expresses itself in a healing way via the irrational. He wasn't too worried as long as he didn't lose touch with reality and start thinking she was actually alive or imagined her talking back to him.

When he stood to leave he noticed what appeared to be fresh tracks leading into the barn. Upon investigation he was perplexed.

It was a single set of tracks that came and went fairly frequently. Had the tracks been made by a group of people he would have assumed it was a passing patrol and shrugged it off. This, however, would seem to indicate that someone was using the barn for shelter.

He opened the door carefully and stepped inside. At first he saw nothing out of the ordinary. Bryan's tractor sat exactly where Bryan had left it, now covered in a thick layer of dust. The cow's stall, long empty since the cow had been taken to the Johnson farm, had cobwebs growing across the opening while the gate stood open just as Ed and Dawson had left it when they'd move her. Dust drifted lazily in the sunlight filtering through holes in the old barns sides. He cast a casual gaze at the loft expecting to see the carefully stacked bales of hay that Bryan had put away – far more hay than his cow would ever need – in the loft. He was about to turn and go when he realized the loft was not all neatly stacked anymore. A large quantity of hay bales were now displaced and piled helter-skelter in a mound off to the side along the barn wall.

Dawson slung his rifle and climbed the ladder to the loft to investigate. Once he was in the loft he pulled is pistol and inched forward carefully. From this angle he could see an opening about two feet square going back into the hay like he used to make when he was a kid on his uncle's farm when he built hay forts in the loft. He could also see that the loft had been disturbed and then bales put back into place. Someone had built a shelter by hollowing out a living space in the main loft and discarding the extra bales in a pile by the wall.

He knelt down to look into the door. The doorway ran back about the length of two bales of hay. A red, blue and green plaid blanket hung down over the opening at the far end of the 'hallway' the bales created. He was about to stand back up to look around the loft more closely when someone turned the lights out. He felt something smash into the back of his head and then knew nothing more.

The world was a blur. Nothing was in focus. Dawson could see a light or rather he could see multiple lights but he knew it was only a single light. His head pounded and he squinted in pain. He tried to bring his hand to his head to rub it but found his hands were tied behind his back. It was then he noticed his ankles were bound together as well.

In the kaleidoscope of light before him he could make out a figure squatting in the shadows. The figure, like the light, was multifaceted and indistinct. It appeared to pay him no attention at all, but rather was intently working on something in front of it that Dawson could not make out. He groaned in pain and passed out again.

The next time Dawson awoke he could see more clearly. The Kaleidoscope effect was largely gone and the pain in his head was diminished greatly. As his eyes finally came into complete focus, he could see more clearly that he was inside some kind of structure lined with hay bales or made of hay bales. The ceiling above him was partially made of wooden planks that held the hay above them up and kept them from falling inward. There was no heat source, yet the small room was warm enough to be comfortable. He realized it was probably warmed by trapped body heat, or heat from a recently lit lantern. Paper wrappers were strewn around the soft hay covered floor. His backpack was thrown against the wall near the door. It had been opened and ransacked. His rifle was nowhere to be seen, nor was his pistol and knife. Judging from the very low light in the small room, Dawson judged the time of day to be either just before sunrise or just after sunset.

He tested the ropes on his wrists and found they were, for the most part, unyielding. He knew that given enough time he could work his hands free, but the nearly instantaneous release he was hoping for from sloppily tied knots wasn't in the cards. He didn't bother testing the knots on his ankles. Once his hands were free they would be no problem and until his hands were free having his feet free was pretty much useless. He settled in to wait.

The gloom of the small room grew deeper as time passed telling Dawson that the day had ended and night was falling. As he waited he worked at the bindings at his wrists, and seemed to make some headway however slight. Still he was encouraged. He heard noises outside the shelter and stopped working the ropes. The blanket parted and a short wild looking man crawled into the room with a lantern. He clicked the electric lighter for the propane lantern and once it was burning he set it down on the floor and turned to the backpack by the door.

In the lantern light he could see the man more clearly. His black hair flew wildly in all directions and had hay embedded in it. His thick black beard also had hay embedded in it. His clothes were the remains of what had been expensive late fall outdoor wear and were clearly not warm enough to be worn in winter. The little man was lucky to have not frozen to death so far. His eyes were ice blue and had a piercing look to them - or perhaps a wild look brought on by deprivation. Dawson judged him to stand about 5' 3" tall.

"Food." He mumbled to himself. "Have I eaten it all?"

He opened the backpack and began to rummage through it turning his back on Dawson. He reminded Dawson of something he'd seen in movies where the mentally deranged imp or dwarf threw things out of backpacks searching for something important. This man didn't exactly throw things but he wasn't exactly ordered in his search either.

"No more food." He said in disappointment. "Now I am hungry again. No more food." His voice took on a singsong as he spoke.

"Cow! I have a cow!" he said as though remembering something. "Strong cow too. Good cow." He giggled to himself. "I can eat the cow!" He paused for a moment and then seemed to be perplexed. "How can I cook the cow? Fire will burn down the house. Can't have a fire. Lantern isn't hot enough. Oh dear…oh dear… can't eat the cow raw. No. Can't do that. No."

"Water." Dawson said weakly. "I need water."

The man spun around in surprise and shock as though he'd not known Dawson was in the hay room with him.

"He speaks!" the man said in both wonder and fear. "He speaks!"

"Please, I need a drink of water." Dawson repeated weakly.

"No! No water!" the man said "I must have time to think...to solve...No! No water!" then he spun back around and returned to his dilemma. "Heat...must have heat to cook with."

"Build a fire outside the barn. You can cook outside without burning down your house." Dawson said trying to be helpful.

The little man spun around and appeared shocked and surprised again as though he'd forgotten Dawson was there.

"No! No water!" he said emphatically and then spun back around with his back to Dawson. He continued to mumble to himself in a kind of singsong voice. "Need a fire...small fire...hot fire...cook the cow...need a fire."

Dawson sighed, "If you build the fire outside the barn you can cook your cow outside where it is safe."

The little man spun around clearly angry at having this thoughts disturbed. "I SAID NO WATER!!" he screamed in rage, "NO WATER!!" Then he spun back around and huffed indignantly. In moments the singsong returned but this time he began to rock back and forth a little as he mumbled to himself. "Need a fire...hot fire...small fire...cook the cow...eats it hot...need a fire....cook the steak...cook the rump...need a fire...hot fire..." Suddenly he whirled around again and screamed "NO WATER!!" then he dove out the door way.

Moments later he stuck his head back through the blanket a look of panic on his face. "Matches!! Matches!!" He grabbed the backpack and started to dig through it, tossing items over his should in a frantic search for matches.

"I have some matches in my pocket." Dawson said hoping to find a way to calm the deranged man down and perhaps get himself untied.

The little man whirled around and glared at Dawson, his nostrils flaring in rage. "I SAID, NO WATER!!!" He screamed, rage dripping off every word. Then he quickly returned to his rummaging in backpack.

"NO MATCHES!!!" he let out in a loud cry of despair. "No matches for the fire...no way to cook the cow..." he broke down into broken hearted sobs and curled up in a fetal position on the hay covering the floor.

"Hungry again...always hungry...no cow...no fire...hungry again." He whimpered. Then he appeared to fall asleep. Dawson started to work on the ropes and knots again taking advantage of the little man's slumber. He was making some small progress when the little man awoke.

He looked around the room as though taking inventory and seemed surprised to see Dawson but didn't say anything. He got up and crawled into the corner opposite Dawson and pulled out a small backpack of his own that he had hidden under the hay on the floor.

"Letter...read the letter..."he mumbled as he almost reverently pulled an envelope from the backpack. Keeping it up off the floor so it wouldn't get wrinkled or soiled he then crawled back over to the lantern. He slowly opened the envelope and carefully pulled out the letter and opened it as if it was ancient and fragile. He held it lovingly so he could read it in the lamp light.

"Loves me..."he sighed. "Coming home soon...loves me..." His face lit up in rapture and he closed his eyes as if dreaming of a joy filled reunion. His smile was large and seemed to erase the desperation that Dawson had seen etched on his face before.

Dawson watched him without speaking. It seemed best to let the little man enjoy whatever escape he found in that moment. He knew the little man had probably been driven mad by the death of whoever wrote that letter and her final words were his only remaining lifeline to any happiness. There was nothing to be gained by intruding on his dream.

The little man sat like that for nearly fifteen minutes and then reverently refolded the paper and slid it carefully back into its envelop. Once it was safely back inside he once again carefully crawled across the floor and returned the envelope to the backpack ever so carefully. He then reburied the backpack under the hay. Once that was done he curled up in the hay and fell asleep.

Dawson returned to working the ropes and knots. It was an arduous task. The little man clearly knew his knots and trying to figure them out with his hands behind his back proved challenging. However, around 4:00 a.m. Dawson managed to free his hands. It did not take long to free his feet. Once he was free he began to carefully and quietly repack his pack while keeping his eye on the sleeping little man.

Once the pack was repacked Dawson carefully and quietly picked it up. He paused momentarily eyeing his pistol tucked securely under the little man's belt. The pistol was expendable. Dawson liked it, but it wasn't his favorite. He debated leaving it with the little man. With it he could defend himself in a small way, or perhaps shoot small game. He took the three spare magazines from his belt and put them, and his zippo lighter, on the hay next to the lantern. The little man would easily find them there.

Carefully and quietly he crawled out of the hay room. Outside the opening Dawson found his rifle leaning against a horizontal beam for the barn. Dawson toyed with leaving it behind as well. He had another hunting rifle. Besides, the little man had likely put it there for quick access in the event he needed to defend himself. He picked it up and checked the action as quietly as possible. It was loaded and ready to go. He looked momentarily at the little doorway and decided leaving one firearm in the hands of a crazy man was dangerous enough. He slung the rifle over his shoulder and then made his way down the ladder. Once on the ground he quietly exited the barn and made his way home.

"Where have you been?" Addison said in a tone of voice that told Dawson she'd been worried sick. "You've been gone three days! You were only supposed to be gone for the afternoon!" Then she ran across the room to Dawson and hugged him desperately. "I thought you were dead!" she said as she started to cry.

"I'm sorry, sweetie. I really am. I was careless and got kidnapped, but I'm home now."

"Kidnapped! Who?" her voice was now filled with both surprised wonder and fear.

"I don't know. A strange little man living in the Harrison's barn. He's completely mad. So, stay away from there."

Addison nodded. "I will. I promise."

"Good. Now let me get these things off. I'm starving." Dawson told Addison all about the little man while he shed his winter clothes and got some stew out of the pot by the fire. As he sat there eating it, he could not help but think of that desperate starving little mad man. When he was done eating he knew what he had to do. He took a nylon bag and put a quantity of dried fruit and jerky into it along with some smoked fish. Then he went to the basement and put a new pistol on his belt and grabbed three magazines for it and went back upstairs.

Addison looked up at him in concern when he started to put his winter clothes back on.

"Don't worry, sweetie. I won't get caught this time. He is starving, however, so we need to take care of him for now. It isn't his fault his mind is broken. Actually, I'm surprised there aren't more people like him. We will be kind to him and help him with what we can."

Dawson opened the door and trudged through the snow back to the Harrison farm. Once there, he carefully edged his way back into the barn and hung the bag on a nail driven into the doorframe. Then he slipped away and went back home.

Two days later Dawson made a second trip to the Harrison farm with another bag of food. He was gratified to see that there were the remains of a cooking fire in front of the barn. At least the little man had figured out how to cook his cow. Dawson smiled as he hung the bag of food he'd brought with him on the same nail the he'd hung the first from. He wondered if the cow was completely imaginary or if the little man had found a dead deer which in his damaged mind was a good as a cow. In the cold of the winter it would have been frozen solid and still be perfectly edible.

He noticed a set of tracks leading around behind the barn so he followed them. They led to what had been Bryan's smoke house. He opened the door and stood in shock. Lying on the floor was a man's body. Dawson couldn't tell if the man was militia or not because his clothes had been removed, as had part of his left leg. A hack saw lying on the floor next to the body told Dawson all he needed to know. The little man's problems were larger than Dawson could handle alone.

He debated what to do. He could just kill the little man. Cannibalism was taboo – even if you are crazy or desperate. On the other hand, if the little man was completely out of his mind, which Dawson suspected, perhaps getting him to Doc Arnie was the wisest thing. Dawson really didn't think Doc Arnie could help his mind, but once Doc Arnie had examined him they could find a way to confine him and keep him from harming others or himself. He decided to do that.

He suspected the little man had not resorted to cannibalism except out of desperation. After all he'd rummaged through Dawson's pack looking for food and he'd not offered to harm Dawson in any way. Besides, Dawson had no way of knowing how long ago the leg had been taken or even if it had actually been consumed. The first bag of food Dawson had left behind had been taken was now discarded on the floor next to the door. The food had been removed, not dumped out.

He made his way back to his cabin and settled in for the night. The next morning he and Addison made their way to the Johnson farm where Dawson told Ed and Doc Arnie about the whole ordeal.

"Oh my goodness." Doc Arnie said in stunned disbelief after Dawson had finished. "You are certain he removed the leg?"

"No, I'm not certain but circumstantially it would appear that way. He talked about eating his cow and there is no cow anywhere around either live or dead."

Doc Arnie nodded. "Well, he is clearly in need of help regardless of the issue with the leg. Let's have a look at him and make a decision as to what we can do, if anything." He paused, "And we do need to acknowledge at the outset there may be nothing we can do for him at all."

"And then what?" Ed asked.

"We do what we must, I guess." Doc Arnie sighed.

"You mean…." Ed gasped.

"No…nothing that drastic. However he may need to be permanently confined. If he requires that, we will be using food and building space for someone who makes no contribution to the welfare of anyone and may be a danger to everyone. These are things we must consider."

"Alright…we'll cross that bridge when we get to it." Dawson said. "Ed and I will head out and see if we can't bring him in."

"Be as gentle as you can, OK? He may be a handful or he may not depending on what has happened to him and what drove him where he is."

Dawson nodded. "Sure thing, Doc." With that he and Ed headed out to the Harrison farm.

Dawson and Ed carefully approached the Harrison farm keeping watch for movement or for any signs of life. They really had no way of knowing where the little man might be and they didn't want to scare him off. Because Dawson had been there recently he noticed right away that the snow around the burned hulk of the house had been disturbed. Fresh tracks were everywhere. He signaled Ed to go slow and watch carefully. They could be walking into an ambush.

They hadn't gone too far when a rifle went off and a bullet whizzed past Dawson's ear.

Ed and Dawson scrambled for cover as another rifle opened up on them. Dawson ended up behind Bryan's four bottom plow. Ed dove behind a medium sized boulder.

"See 'em?" Ed yelled.

"No. Still looking." Dawson yelled back. "Wait! Got 'em!"

Dawson raised his rifle and fired two shots into the burned out house. He failed to connect, but he hadn't expected to because he couldn't see his target clearly. To him it was a black target mixed with black surroundings. Before he could get situated one of the attackers broke cover and ran for the barn. He dove through the door before either Ed or Dawson could fire a shot.

Suddenly guns could be heard going off inside the barn. One was a rifle and the other a pistol. The pistol fired first. Their distinctive sounds made that very clear. Dawson fired another round into the burned out house and got no reply. The shooting in the barn stopped. A man staggered out of the door and then fell into the snow. He never moved once he'd hit the ground.

"Cover me!" Dawson said loudly to Ed as he jumped up and ran toward the barn. He dove through the door and rolled to his feet. No one had fired at him as he ran across the open ground. He hoped the crazy little man wouldn't fire at him now. He didn't want to kill him.

He quickly climbed the ladder and found the little man lying in the hay outside his hay room door. He looked at Dawson wildly and tried to reach the pistol which had fallen from his grip and laid a couple feet from him. Dawson was faster and kicked the pistol away to the barn floor below. A heavy flow of blood was coming from the little man's upper arm and thigh.

"Damn!" Dawson said and looked around quickly to assess the wounds and the condition of the little man. The leg wound was the most dangerous. He quickly shed his backpack and pulled a tourniquet from a pouch and put it in place near the man's groin. He pulled it tight and then looked at the little man who was motionless with fright.

"This is going to hurt and you are going to hate me." He said as he started tightening the windlass. The tighter the tourniquet got the more the little man screamed. It didn't take long for Dawson to shut off the flow of blood to the leg however. Once that was done he turned his attention to the arm. He pulled an Israeli bandage from his pack and put it on hoping the constant pressure of the bandage would stop the bleeding. It did.

"Now we have to get you to Doc Arnie." He said. "I've got no idea how to get you down from here."

"Backpack. Backpack." The little man said in near panic.

"Don't worry; I'll make sure to bring it."

"Thank you." The little man said.

At that point Ed came into the barn and when he realized where Dawson was he climbed up to join him.

"Shit!" was the first words out of his mouth.

Dawson nodded. "We gotta get him to Doc Arnie fast."

"Is that a tourniquet?" Ed asked as though he'd never seen one. Then it occurred to Dawson he probably hadn't. Dawson, on the other hand, had seen too many of them.

"Yeah. Don't touch it! Help me get him down."

It was a clumsy climb down but no rope was available to lower the little man to the main floor so they had to carry him. Once he was on the ground they took a piece of sheet metal Bryan had set aside for emergency, bent the front of it upwards to keep snow off and attached a makeshift rope made of baling twine. Then the carefully put the little man on the improvised sled.

"Backpack...backpack." The little man said urgently.

Dawson nodded. "Yep. Be back in a second." He quickly climbed the ladder and retrieved the little man's backpack. He handed it to the little man once he'd gotten back onto the barn floor. The little man clutched it with his good arm as though his life depended on it.

"Are we going to get shot at getting out of here?" Dawson asked Ed.

"I doubt it. The tracks in the house head on off west and whoever made them was moving pretty fast too. I think the gunfire here in the barn unnerved him, like they didn't know anyone was in here."

"Good. Now all we got to do is get him to Doc Arnie before he freezes, or I do." Dawson said as he took off his heavy coat and covered the little man with it. Then he picked up the rope. "Come on. Let's move!"

The rope broke three times during the hurried three quarter of a mile trip to Doc Arnie's clinic. Once there they had lots of help to get the little man carried inside to the surgery so Doc Arnie could treat him. Doc Arnie immediately set to work on the leg and closed off the wound and packed it all the while cursing his lack of anything resembling an IV or blood to transfuse. Fortunately the bullet, in passing through only nicked the artery rather than severing it. Once Doc Arnie was satisfied it likely wasn't going to burst open and it had been well sutured he'd packed the rest of the wound and slowly released the tourniquet.

"You always carry one of these?" he asked Dawson as he released it while directing his entire attention on the wound. His voice was completely a detached professional near monotone.

"I do. Habit, I guess."

"Not a bad habit. A bit unusual but not bad. Most people don't carry such things."

"Army training. I just never quit carrying one when I got out. Always carry one especially when I'm in the woods. Never know when accidents will happen." Dawson shrugged.

"Or firefights." Doc Arnie continued without changing his professional tone of voice. He then turned to the arm and began to unbandage it. Della was prepared with more pressure bandages in case the wound hadn't settled yet. It did bleed quite a bit once the bandage was off but Doc Arnie set to work immediately with sutures and closed off the bleeders. He then set on closing the wound. Then he released more of the tourniquet so as to not over stress the sutures he'd put into the artery or damage the tissue in the leg below the tourniquet and wound.

When they were done Dawson, Doc Arnie and Ed collapsed into chairs in the examining room, leaving Della in the surgery with the little man. Doc Arnie heaved a sigh of relief.

"He was very lucky you knew what to do when you found him." Doc Arnie said. "Most people would have panicked and he'd have bled out."

"We had to learn some field medical stuff in case …. Well, we were going to Iraq."

Doc Arnie nodded in understanding. "Well, you did good. He's not out of the woods by any means but we've done our best with what we have. He's lost a lot of blood. His blood pressure is dangerously low."

"Doc!" Della said urgently as she poked her head into the room.

Doc Arnie looked up and jumped to his feet and went into the surgery. Dawson followed him. The little man lay on the table as he had been but now his color was gone and his breathing was extraordinarily shallow and it seemed to be more like a gasp than a breath. Then it stopped altogether. Doc Arnie checked his heart and then stood up and looked dejected.

"Lost him. I needed blood and haven't any. I was afraid he'd lost too much."

"I got to him pretty fast!" Dawson protested.

"I know you did. The problem is that there is a point past which even if you get the bleeding stopped entirely there is no recovery. The body just doesn't have enough to work with. Our friend here had two terrible wounds. While you were stopping the one, the other kept bleeding. Add to that his poor physical condition, malnutrition, and so on it was just more than he could handle. It wasn't your fault."

Dawson reached out and picked up the backpack which had been placed on a table behind him in the room. He opened it and carefully took out the letter and opened it up.

"He treated this like a religious icon." Dawson said as he opened the letter in response to the unasked question hanging in the air as Doc Arnie and Della looked at him.

"What does it say?" Della asked.

"It is dated October 14th – a week before the blast that gave us all this." Dawson said gesturing around him. "He probably got it the day the shit hit the fan." He then turned back to the letter.

"Dearest Edwin,

I thought in this day and age of electronic messaging I would sent you one of those quaint old love letters like we used to send each other back in the old days of the 1980's when we were younger and far more innocent. The world has changed much and not all of it for the good.

By the time you receive this I will already be on my home to you. My work here in Britain is complete and I shall be homeward bound by the middle of next week at the latest. I cannot wait to see you again, my love. I hate that our work often separates us like this. However, as we both know, it is for a greater good and hopefully the world will be a better place and more peaceful for what we do.

Please give my best to our colleagues at the university. They are all such dears and I miss them – though not nearly as much as I miss you.

I love you with all my heart and forever,
Miranda"

They stood silently for a moment and looked at the little man's body.

"So, your name was Edwin." Doc Arnie said. "I'm sorry, Edwin, that I could not do more for you. You must have missed your wife terribly. Just know you were among friends at the last. You were not alone."

"I'm going to guess losing his wife is what drove him crazy." Della said as she took his hand gently in sympathy.

"Well, perhaps she is still alive in England or perhaps the East Coast." Doc Arnie said. "I'd hate to think her flight went down over the ocean somewhere."

"I think he sensed she was dead and could not deal with it." Dawson said. "I think knew it the moment I saw the smoke from Caroline's house. When you love someone you just know."

"Maybe." Doc Arnie said. "Maybe. But whether he did or didn't and she was or wasn't, he was lost without her."

Dawson carefully put the letter back into the envelope and then put the envelope inside Edwin's shirt. "He should have this with him." He said in more of a mumble than anything else. "It's kind of a way of burying them together."

"Hail the cabin!" a now familiar voice called from outside at the barricade.

Dawson looked out the window and saw a familiar wagon and driver. Thompson was making his sales visit in spite of the mid-February cold snap. Dawson opened the door and waved him on up to the cabin.

"Top 'o the morning' to ya" Thompson said in a fake Irish accent when they were within speaking distance. Clearly he was in good spirits.

"Gone Irish have you?" Dawson asked with a laugh.

"Well, I guess that would be nice if I could." He replied. "You know luck of the Irish and all. With all this damned snow and cold, my business is much less profitable and I need all the luck I can get."

"What have you got this time around?" Dawson asked with a laugh.

"Oh, pretty much everything." Thompson said as he climbed down from the driver's seat. "I try to carry some of everything, you know. Fine goods for the discriminating buyer, as I always say." He dropped the sides of the wagon down, revealing various goods and items he'd taken in barter.

"Any powder?" Dawson asked.

"Well, Dawson, my friend, you are in luck. Just day before yesterday I took in three one pound jars of IMR 4895 which, as you know, was originally a military powder used in the 30-06. It will do anything you need it to do for your "hobby.""

Dawson thought for a moment. "I got two AR-15s"

Thompson thought for a moment. "Just two, 'eh? Hmm....five would be more like it I would think. After all, powder of any kind is getting scarce."

"Three." Dawson replied.

"I can't go less than four." Thompson said. "I'll have trouble getting rid of them as it is."

"Well...I guess I'll have to pass then. Too rich for my blood."

"Now, now...don't be so hasty. How about three AR-15s and that bear skin you've got drying on the wall over there?"

"It isn't tanned yet. It is still drying."

"That is fine. I won't have it long. That, I know I can get rid of at a profit."

"Alright. Done deal, then."

They shook hands on the deal. As they shook on the deal it occurred to Dawson how the world had come back full circle to a time where deals were sealed with a handshake and not necessarily with a signature on the dotted line. In the current circumstances a man's word had to be his bond. Otherwise, he was in deep trouble if he ever needed help from his neighbors.

"Heading into Carrollton?" Dawson asked as they took the bear skin down.

"Oh goodness no!" Thompson said. "My last trip there was a disaster. Against all common sense I ventured into that town to see if I could get some supplies I'd grown short on. I almost ended up a conscript in their infernal army. No, no...I only get my commercial wares now in Alton, well inside Colburn. The good people of Carrollton will have to suffer with their less than state of the art goods.

"Speaking of Carrollton, you might want to be more watchful from now on. Rumor has it that the Ragarians and the Holderites are on the verge of a truce, if not an outright treaty of peace. If they are, that means that the Holderites will have far more men to commit to pacifying your little community's rebellion out here."

"Rebellion?" Dawson asked incredulously. "How can we be in rebellion?"

"Well, from what I gathered during my rather tense and thankfully short visit to Carrollton, they are claiming all territory to the Colburn border. Some of the more radical ones are claiming more than that. In any event they will most likely seek to 'persuade' you to bend the knee to Mr. Holder's malevolence."

"Yeah...well, they tried that once. It didn't work out too well for them."

"I am sure it did not. However, I also am sure they did not send a full expeditionary force of Storm Troops. If they had done that, your daughters would be in the pleasure house in Carrollton or Waterford and you would either be dead or castrated and serving as a conscript."

"I'll keep an eye out." Dawson said acknowledging the truth of what Thompson had said.

"Good." Thompson said. "I'd hate to lose my source of 'discovered' rifles."

"I do seem to have a knack for finding them lying around." Dawson said with a grim grin.

"Yes. I've noticed that. A gift, I am sure." Thompson said as he threw the bear skin into the back of his wagon. "Now did you need anything for the ladies in the family?"

"I'll go get Addie. She can tell you herself if she needs or wants anything. Hang on, I'll be right back."

He returned a few moments later with Addie. Addie looked over Thompson's wares as though looking for a lost engagement ring and finally settled on only asking for a couple of books. Barter was easy on those and she went back into the house happy with her find.

"Well, Dawson, my friend. Be well until we meet again." Thompson said as he packed up his wagon. "I shall return as soon as I am able."

"Take care of yourself, you old swindler." Dawson said with a laugh. "And stay away from patrols."

"I shall do my best!" Thompson said, "I shall do my best."

Chapter 9

Spring finally came. The winter had been hard and cold and the warmth of spring was a welcome relief. Ellen Myers had decided that children needed schooling so she had started a small school at the Johnson farm. There had also been a community meeting when the first thaw hit and it was decided that the Johnson farm, being fairly centrally located would become the community hub. A couple of new families were added to the community as well; holdouts that prior to the last winter hadn't felt the need to do anything but be independent. The winter and rumors of increased New Order interest in the area convinced them to join.

As a result trees were cut and a stockade of sorts was being built around the family compound, enclosing the hospital, all of the Johnson buildings, in addition to open ground for an eventual school house and a couple other small cabins. This gave people a fortified place to flee to if they needed to. No one was calling it "Johnsonville" yet, but Dawson figured that was only a matter of time. That was how towns came to be.

Ellen's husband was starting a saw mill so usable lumber would not be too far off in the future and then building would begin in earnest. Thompson agreed to find nails and other necessary items as part of his service to the community and his customers. He also reasoned it gave him a safe place to rest and recoup so it was in his best interest to help out.

With the school starting, Addison had moved temporarily to the Johnson place as did the other school age children. Dawson had to laugh to himself though because Addison, being almost fourteen, had considered herself too old for school now. She finally agreed to go when Ellen asked her to also serve as a tutor for the younger children. When the school started there were eight children enrolled.

Dawson had agreed at the meeting to be the main hunter for the community and provide extra meat that could be jerked or smoked and put away for emergency and to support the growing community population of the Johnson homestead. He also knew that this job would mean he would not be able to put in a garden as he usually did, but he was assured he would be provided for in recognition of the fact that his job would keep him busy. He also knew that his job also meant he was the first line of defense in intercepting New Order patrols and for alerting the community should a larger body of troops move into the area. As a result he started hunting with his M1A rather than his normal hunting rifle. It was a heavier rifle to carry than he would have preferred, but it was good for game and necessary should he need additional firepower against threats to the community.

In late April he was moving carefully along a ridgeline when he heard a number of shots in the not so far off distance. He knew no one from the community was likely going to be out hunting right now given that everyone was working to put in gardens and crops. They also knew that hunting in the spring or summer was counter-productive. The game animals they needed were raising their young and killing an adult meant killing babies. As a result he changed into "scout" mode and patrolled the area for New Order incursions. He now crept along as stealthily as possible and made his way toward the sound. Eventually he could hear men talking and laughing.

He shook his head. Only Holderites would be so brazen as to make that much noise. They were used to rolling over farmers and were likely certain they would not meet a challenge they could not master. He slowed his pace, homing in on the talking and watching carefully for sentries or stragglers.

He made his way slowly up a gully face fairly certain his quarry was on the other side. From the number of voices he guessed it was a foraging patrol not a body of troops. He crawled carefully up the incline toward a log lying on the crest of the gully. It was his hope that from there he could remain concealed and observe what was going on, on the other side.

Once he was in position he could see very clearly what the situation was. The gully dropped of steeply below him. It was unlikely anyone could come at him from that angle. However, the steep incline gave him an unobstructed view below. Below him were about twelve New Order militia members all standing around a downed deer that was lying behind a fallen tree trunk. He also saw that the gully bottom they were in angled away from him to his right. Near where the group stood it curved sharply and angled away from him to his left as well; so sharply in fact that anyone going that way would have to expose themselves entirely to his rifle. He noted any cover and/or concealment they might try to use in either direction. While they could not attack him frontally if he was discovered, they could still try to flank him. He would have to make sure that did not happed should it come to a firefight.

"Hell, Carlson," a voice said, "Anyone could have shot that damn deer from there. What the hell you bragging about?"

"I ain't bragging!" came the protest from below.

"Oh no? Then what is all this 'one shot one kill' shit you been spouting."

"Well, I did! It ain't bragging if you done it! You guys all missed and it was running. I dropped it with one shot!"

"Ya' coulda stabbed it with your knife you idiot! It was that close."

"It was not that close. It was a good shot!"

"Shut the hell up, all of you!" another voice said. The speaker was clearly agitated and in charge. "Just gut the damned thing out and get it butchered. We ain't got time to fuss over who did what. Our job is to scout the area, report back, and bring what we can find in the way of food back to Carrollton when we do." Dawson figured out the speaker was a guy wearing full combat gear including a set of body armor. Dawson watched him for a moment. He didn't know where the guy came from but it was clear he was the only real dangerous one in the group. From his demeanor and stance, Dawson could tell he was a combat vet. Overall, the rest of the patrol seemed poorly equipped. All were wearing some semblance of a uniform but beyond that they were pretty rag-tag. None of them wore helmets except the last speaker, nor did they wear body armor. The weapon of choice seemed to be on the AR platform, most likely in .223 or .556 although two were carrying hunting rifles.

He toyed with withdrawing and alerting the rest of the community. However, he dismissed that just as he had with the Diablos a couple of years ago. He pulled his suppressor from the pouch he carried it in and screwed it on to the barrel. At this range, it wouldn't help all that much, but it might make them think he was further away than he actually was. In any event he hoped it would cause enough confusion to allow him the opportunity to gain an advantage and hold it.

Mentally he did an inventory of what he was carrying: Three extra magazines of twenty round each, his sidearm with two extra magazines of thirteen rounds each. He grinned to himself. If he needed more than eighty rounds for the M1A he was in more trouble than he'd counted on. 'After that I'll call in artillery support' he said softly to himself as he double checked to make sure the magazine in the rifle was seated.

He eased the rifle up to his shoulder as he lay in the leaves behind the log, exposing only enough of himself to get the rifle aimed properly. His plan was to get the armored guy to turn fully toward him so he could get a shot into his face if possible. If not, he'd take him out by any means he could.

Dawson carefully took aim at the man kneeling down to begin to field dress the deer. He knew this would be his only perfectly aimed shot. He slipped the safety off and squeezed the trigger. The bullet hit his target square in the chest and stirred up a figurative hornet's nest.

The armored guy spun around in surprise to see where the shot had come from. Dawson, who had already shifted his aim to the man's head, got one quick shot at his face and hit him square in the bridge of the nose. He dropped like a rock off a cliff. By now the rest of the patrol was diving for cover. Dawson waited and did not fire at the moving targets. He would pick them off one by one as best he could when opportunities presented themselves. Three of the men dove behind the log in front of the deer, including one that was literally dragged to the ground as though attached to his teammate.

Bullets impacted all along the gully crest making it clear they knew where he was in general, but not in specific. He smiled and did not move or fire. He knew anything he did would help them locate him. Now the waiting game began.

Suddenly a single group of five men jumped up from the deadfall they'd hidden behind and started running as fast as they could down the gully. Dawson drew a bead on them and squeezed off a round. One of the men dropped, hit squarely in the back. Before he could fire another round however, the squad below him opened fire on the fleeing men. The remaining four died within moments of the first.

Now began a long war of silence, nerves and patience. Dawson hoped they were short on both of the last two. Dawson knew all he had to do was keep an eye on the remaining seven men and keep them from flanking him. They, on the other hand, only vaguely knew where he was and any attempt to locate him or change positions would expose them to his field of fire. Suddenly one of the men behind the log in front of the deer jumped up and seemed to be pulling at something attached to his wrist. Why he suddenly jumped up wasn't clear. Perhaps his nerves had failed him and he was trying to flee, but the anchor attached to his wrist was unyielding. Dawson dropped him and in return the squad in the gully below sent dirt and wood flying everywhere. His shot had given him away to them. Dawson ducked down and started screaming as though in pain.

"We got 'im!" one of the men yelled and jubilantly jumped to his feet.

Dawson's bullet took him in the shoulder, exactly where Dawson had intended it to hit. The man fell to the ground and starting yelling for a medic. The medic tried to move toward the fallen man but Dawson's bullets kept him in place.

The squad once again peppered his position. A flying piece of wood nicked Dawson's cheek but, other than that the bullets were harmlessly thrown. The medic tried to take advantage of the suppressing fire but Dawson put a round into the man's leg and sent him spinning. Blood spurted everywhere. It hadn't been the hit Dawson wanted, but it would do the job. The medic fumbled for a tourniquet in his bag and once he found it he fumbled around getting it removed from its packaging. He almost got it applied before he began to lose consciousness. In the end, he never made it, however.

"We give up!" one of the men called from below. "Cease firing! We give up!!"

"Stand up and throw your rifles at least fifteen feet in front of you!" Dawson called.

Four men stood up and tossed their rifles away.

"Where's the fifth guy?" Dawson yelled. "I can count!"

"Can't stand up!" one of them yelled.

"Can't or won't?" Dawson yelled back.

"Can't!"

"Says you."

"Look! We got no quarrel with you." He yelled back up at Dawson

"Yeah? Well, I got one with you." Dawson yelled back. "You remember the Harrison place? You people burned it down over them. They were nice folks. Had three small boys. You killed them all."

"We didn't kill them all." The man yelled back. "I wasn't there but I know we didn't kill them all."

"Oh yeah?"

"Yeah! I fucked her myself in the pleasure house in Carrollton last month. She was still alive then." Apparently the Holderite thought using raping a woman as proof of life would somehow appease Dawson.

"How do you know it was her?" Dawson yelled back doubting his story.

"My buddy was the one of the ones that took her off the farm. He said they shot her kids up and burned the house down. We took turns on her."

Dawson didn't respond verbally. His rifle went off and the bullet slammed into the man's shoulder. The man looked shocked.

"We surrendered!" He protested as he dropped to his knees grabbing his shoulder.

"That was for raping Caroline Harrison last month." Dawson yelled in anger.

A second bullet slammed into the man's chest almost as soon as Dawson was sure his words had been heard and had registered. The man pitched backwards and never moved.

"Now, any of you got anything you want to confess?" Dawson yelled as he changed his point of aim.

One of the men panicked and tried to pull his sidearm. Dawson dropped him within moments of the pistol clearing the holster. The others took off running. Dawson had no trouble dispatching them either.

He then turned his attention to the last member of the patrol who still remained behind the log.

"You got anything you want to confess before I kill you?" Dawson shouted angrily down at the log he knew the man was behind.

There was no answer, nor was there any movement. After about ten minutes Dawson began to wonder if perhaps the other person actually was incapacitated or unconscious though he couldn't figure out how that could have happened. The spokesman for the remaining squad members had used the word "can't" when describing why he would not stand and show himself. Slowly and carefully he made his way down the steep side of the ravine, making sure to keep some kind of cover between him and the log. Once on the ravine floor he rushed the log and jumped over it, prepared to fire point blank into the person on the other side of it.

He laid there on the ground with his face buried in the leaves. He did not move and appeared to be unconscious. Dawson shoved the person's leg with his foot and only then did the person move. They rolled over slowly and stared up at him with terror filled eyes. The militia member wasn't a man. It was a woman.

"Slave?" he asked harshly, keeping his rifle trained on her.

There was a long pause and she said nothing. Dawson did a quick visual survey. She had no weapons. Her uniform, if you wanted to call it that was comprised of ill-fitting pants and a jacket that looked like some kind of light military field jacket from an overseas military and at was least three sizes too large for her. The sleeves were long enough that her hands were completely covered. It didn't even look like she had sheath knife on her belt.

"Slave, I'd wager." He said finally.

She nodded with the same terror filled eyes.

"I am not going to hurt you." He said trying to allay her fears some. "They are all dead, so they aren't going to hurt you anymore either. Come on, sit up." He handed her his canteen as a gesture of hospitality. She slowly sat up and desperately reached up for canteen, dragging the other dead man's arm up with hers as she reached for it. Only then did he notice her hands were bound together with nylon handcuffs and then to the other man's wrist. Apparently it was to keep her from falling behind or running away.

"Here, let me cut those things off you." He said gently. "You won't need them anymore." He said as he watched her drink from the canteen eagerly. When she'd finished she held out her hands to be cut free. He cut her bindings and then cut her free from the dead man who'd been attached to her. He stood for a moment giving her an appraising look once she was free of the nylon bindings. She had short red hair that had been haphazardly cut short just below her ears, had blue eyes, and he guessed her to be in her mid-twenties which would make her six or eight years younger than himself.

"Look, "he said as she rubbed her wrists in relief. "You're going to have to come with me. It will be nightfall soon and you can't stay here. This place is in the middle of nowhere and there are bears about. They are pretty cranky this time of year."

She nodded blankly and got up. Dawson checked the bodies and packs of the fallen Holderites to see if they had anything that could be of use to him. He took their ammunition even though it wasn't the right caliber for his current rifle. He could use it for barter with the traveling merchant or just keep it for his own ever growing arsenal. He took some of their clothing items – underwear and t-shirts from their packs – and some personal care items like toothpaste, soap, medical items, and so on. He picked up their rifles and slung them over his shoulder. He would use them as barter as well. Then he headed off toward home.

The whole way home she didn't say anything in response to his questions or comments. So after a while Dawson trudged on in silence. They arrived back at his cabin just after darkness had fallen. He made his way through the spiked barricades and choke points he'd built to prevent a full on assault on his cabin, crossed his large front yard and finally arrived at the front door. Once inside he dropped his burdens on the floor in a corner and looked at his companion.

"Sit! Get comfortable. I'll stoke the fire and take the chill off the place." He said warmly, trying to be hospitable.

She nodded fearfully and took a seat on the floor near the fireplace. Dawson put some small pieces of wood on the embers in the fireplace and then nursed the fire back to life. She sat staring blankly into the flames.

"Take your jacket off." Dawson said lightly trying to get her to smile. "Stay a while."

Her back stiffened as though receiving an electric shock when he told her take her jacket off. She then reached up and unbuttoned the jacket and slowly took it off. She was naked underneath it. She turned toward him expectantly, fearfully, and making no effort to cover herself.

Dawson couldn't help but take in her body with his eyes. He saw she was more petite than he'd thought and that her breasts were probably among the finest he'd ever seen; full, perfectly shaped, and screaming for fondling. He got up and got a t-shirt that he'd taken from the dead militia members out of his pack.

"Here." He said as he handed it to her. "Put this on."

She looked at him with a confused expression on her face, but she slipped the t-shirt on. Dawson began to realize how abused the poor woman had been.

"What's your name?" Dawson asked for the twentieth time since he'd rescued her. This time she answered softly and timidly,
"I don't know."
"You don't know?" Dawson asked in a surprised tone.
"You have not named me yet."
"I haven't named you? What do you mean?"
"When I was born my parents named me...Brandy, I think. It was a long time ago, I think. When the Ragarians kidnapped me they named me 'Elsa.' When the Holderites stole me from my master with the Ragarians they put me in their pleasure house in Carrollton and named me 'Slut.' So I am 'Slut' unless you name me something else." Her voice sounded distant and disconnected from reality.

"What do you mean unless I name you something else?"
"The Ragarians killed my husband and my baby and raped me until I quit fighting them. If I did not serve them properly they raped me some more. They took away my name; at least I think they did. When I had been trained properly, they named me Elsa and they sold me to my master who kept my name Elsa. He raped me a lot too if I was not obedient and sometimes just for his pleasure. It was his right, he was my master. The Holderites raided my master's farm and stole me from him and they named me "Slut" and made me let them fuck me in their pleasure house. They had a veterinarian sterilize me so they could fuck me without consequences because my name was what I am: a slut to be fucked not to have children. They sterilize all the women slaves that way because we are just livestock. Sometimes they would torture us too just for laughs. It was their right, they owned us. They kill us for fun sometimes too. It is their right. Slaves usually do not live very long.

"Now you have stolen me from the Holderites. I am your slave now. I am who you say I am and I will do what you tell me to do and you can do to me whatever you want. It is your right as my master. I know my place. I will not burden you by being disobedient." She said softly, matter-of-factly, and yet still oddly distant and almost monotone. Dawson was shocked. The mental damage done to the woman was devastating to the point where she could excuse evil out of hand and call it a 'right.'

"Brandy you are not a slave anymore. You are free to do whatever you want to do."

Brandy stood and took off the t-shirt and pulled off her pants. She sat back down next to the fire. "I am your slave now." She said blankly as though that was her comfort zone. Dawson shrugged.

"Did you know Caroline Harrison?" he asked hoping to find a spark of life in her.

She screwed up her face as though thinking hard and then answered softly, "I think so. I think her name was Caroline. The Holderites took away her name too and named her Skippy because after they got done raping her and training her she would spread her legs for anyone without fighting. I think she is gone now."

"Gone? What do you mean gone? Did they move her?"

Brandy slowly shook her head, "Her mind is gone, I think. She has gone away. When they come to fuck her she just lies down and spreads her legs and lets them have her. She just lies there until they are done. She does not move or make any noise; she just lies there. She does not talk to anyone very much anymore. She just waits by herself for the next group of men to come and use her."

Dawson sat silently. Caroline was his love: a beautiful woman both physically and in personality. Dawson could see her standing in the doorway of the house when he'd left to go fishing that morning; her brown hair blowing slightly in the breeze, brown eyes dancing with contentedness, her lithe body only slightly filling the doorway. If what Brandy said was true, she was a broken woman now, probably beyond repair. He shook his head to clear the tears forming in his eyes both from sorrow for Caroline and from frustrated rage. There was nothing he could do for Caroline even if she was still alive, which seemed a dim hope given what Brandy had just told him.

Dawson sat silently for a long time staring at the naked woman sitting on his floor. It was obvious that two or maybe three years of being raped, and otherwise abused had messed with the woman's mind to the point where she could not remember a time when she hadn't been abused. He was at a loss as to what to do.

"Why were you with that patrol? You clearly weren't there for combat purposes. Did you run off and get caught or something?"

"No. Sometimes they take a slave with them when they go out. The slave is to pleasure them and make them happy. It is their right to do that. They own the girl."

Dawson sat quietly for a long time. He felt a growing rage deep inside. Somehow he would have to fix this. He just didn't know how.

"Hungry?" Dawson asked changing the subject "Let me get some supper on."

He put together a simple dinner and then put it on the table. Brandy watched him the whole time as though expecting to be beaten or ordered to do something.

"Soup's on!" Dawson finally declared, "Isn't much. Just some venison and wheat berry stew but it is hot and it isn't too bad either."

Brandy got up from beside the fire and came over to the table and looked confused. Dawson looked at her for a moment and then gestured toward the chair on the other side of the table where he had put her place setting. She hesitantly pulled out the chair and sat down.

"I am allowed to sit at the table with you?" she asked in surprise.

Dawson looked at her as though wondering if she was serious, "Yes. Of course you are. Where else would you sit?" He wasn't being sarcastic when he asked; he was just surprised.

"My master on the farm made me sit on the floor next to him and he would feed me from his plate on the table. My owners at the pleasure house fed us all from a big bowl on the floor."

"From...a bowl......" Dawson said and sat thunderstruck. 'My God.' He thought to himself 'What kind of monsters are they?"

She dug into her stew like it was the first meal she had, had in a long time. Dawson let her eat in peace, curiously watching her as he ate is own supper. He got up and served her a second helping when she had finished the first. She ate it a greedily as she had the first helping. He had a huge number of questions but wasn't sure he wanted to hear the answers. As she ate, his mind kept wandering to Caroline. She didn't deserve what happened to her. None of those women did.

When they had finished he put a kettle near the fire to heat water for dishes. Brandy returned to her spot by the fire. Dawson got out his guitar and quietly played a few songs while waiting for the water to heat up.

"My master plays nicely" Brandy said softly as he put the guitar away.

"Thank you." Dawson said politely "that was kind of you to say."

Brandy blushed a little at his kind words. Obviously she was not used to that.

He took the hot water to the sink and poured some of it in. Then he set about doing dishes. Brandy stayed where she was, staring blankly into the fire. When he was done he sat back down by the fireplace in his chair.

"Do you want to fuck me now?" Brandy asked softly in a tone that indicated she knew what was next.

Dawson's heart went out to the woman. Truthfully, yes he wanted to have sex with her, but only because she was a beautiful woman sitting naked in his living room. However, there was no way he was going to do it. She was expecting to be raped again just like all her other supposed masters had done and he wasn't going to play that game with her.

"No, Brandy."

She looked at him despairingly, "Have I displeased you? Are you going to punish me?" there was a tinge of panic in her voice.

"No, Brandy. I am not displeased with you. Not at all. And, no, I am not going to punish you. You aren't a slave."

"I am your slave." She said softly but emphatically. "You took me from the Holderites. I belong to you now." Then real panic filled her face and her voice as though something had just occurred to her. "You are going to sell me to someone else!"

"No, Brandy, I am not going to sell you to anyone. I cannot sell you."

Relief flooded her face, "I am your slave." She said again. "You took me. I am yours."

Dawson sighed. This was clearly an argument he was not going to win tonight.

"Well," he said, "Let's get you settled in for the night. I'll pull out the hide-a-bed for you to sleep on."

"I won't sleep with you?" she looked panicked again.

"Brandy, it is alright. You deserve your own bed. You deserve your own space."

He got up and pulled out the hide-a-bed and then got some sheets and blankets out of the closet and made up her bed.

"There!" he said when he was done. "I'm heading on off to bed. You can stay up as long as you like, just don't wander out the door. We have a couple of bears in the area and they've been pretty active lately. They could be prowling outside looking for food. They do that on occasion and this time of year they start to get really aggressive. If you need extra blankets they are in the closet over there."

Brandy did not move and after a moment's pause, Dawson went off to bed.

The next morning Dawson woke up to the feel of a naked body in bed next to him. Whether she was awake or not, he could not tell, but his normal morning erection was solidly against her back. He did not move. Brandy seemed to be breathing in a sleeping type rhythm so he guessed she had slipped into bed with him during the night and the current closeness of their bodies was coincidence not design on her part. The question was how to pull away, get out of bed, and not wake her.

He failed. As he started to move she woke up and she did not attempt to move away from his erection. In fact she moved just a little so that it even tighter against her body. Dawson had not expected to suddenly tight against her like that and pulled back out in almost a panic. Everything in him was screaming to take her. His sense of right and wrong, however, would not let him.

Brandy rolled over and looked at him with a lost look in her eyes, like she had failed him in some way or he did not like her.

"Brandy, I will be honest. I do want to have sex with you. You are a beautiful woman. Any man would be crazy to not want you. Well, either that or gay. But right now you are vulnerable and I don't want to take advantage of you. I don't want you to think I am treating you like the others have treated you for the last few years. When and if, we have sex it will be because you and I agree you want it. Not because you think I am making you have it."

She looked at him like she didn't understand him.

"Brandy, do you remember when you first got married?" he said in frustration at her lack of comprehension.

She slowly nodded her head.

"Do you remember how you felt on your wedding night? How you wanted to be with your husband, how you wanted to make love with him?"

"Kind of." She said softly "Sometimes I think it was not real because I don't remember him taking me."

"Brandy, he did not take you. You went with him on your own. You were married. You loved him. Don't you remember?"

Brandy did not respond for a long time and then she slowly nodded her head and her eyes started to fill up with tears. "I remember they killed him. I remember they killed my little Jessica....my precious little Jessica." Suddenly her eyes filled with tears and she let out a loud anguished wail as though years of pent up grief suddenly found release. "They made me watch as they killed her!!" she wailed loudly between sobs, "They made me kneel over a bench and tied me to it so I could not move and I had to see her. Then they tied my baby to a post in front of me and used her for target practice!! She was so tiny, just a baby, and they shot her to pieces!! They raped me and laughed at her and at me the whole time they did it!! They dragged me away with them and left the pieces of her little body scattered on the ground for the crows!" Suddenly she broke into even harder sobbing and tears gushed from her eyes in near fountain of grief. The long pent up grief flooded out of her uncontrollably.

Dawson instinctively pulled her to him and held her while she cried. She cried hard and heavy for nearly twenty minutes and then drifted off to sleep, spent from exhaustion. Dawson slid out of the bed and covered her up. Then he went to make breakfast.

He could not imagine what Brandy had endured. Visions of what she'd told him played out in his mind. He could not imagine the grief Brandy had carried all this time; grief that had found no release for fear of punishment, grief that was compounded with each assault on her body and her mind. The men that took her were evil; as pure an evil as ever existed. He found himself growing angry at the men who took her and abused her just as they had done to Caroline.

He was just about to sit down to eat when Brandy slipped into the room. He got up and fixed her a plate and put it in front of her chair, then gestured for her to be seated and eat. She ate in silence, occasionally wiping her eyes as though still crying.

After breakfast Brandy went back to her place by the fire and Dawson did the dishes. He had just finished the dishes and was about to join Brandy by the fire when someone called from the barricade.

"Hail the cabin!"

Brandy gave him a panicked look and Dawson grabbed up his rifle as he sidled up next to the window. As he looked out he saw Ed Johnson and his son-in-law Mike standing at the first barricade; a curtesy to give Dawson clear view of them and to identify them as friends not foes.

He opened the door. "Ed! Mike! Come on in. I was about to put a fresh pot of coffee on. Take a load off!" Dawson called to them.

Ed and Mike entered the cabin and then stopped short when they saw Brandy, still naked, cowering on the floor along the wall next to the fireplace trying to huddle into the smallest space she could occupy.

"Sorry." Ed said in embarrassment, "Didn't mean to intrude." Both he and Mike turned toward the door.

"No! It's alright. Sit! I got a lot to tell you." Then he turned to Brandy, his voice was soft and gentle when he spoke; "Brandy, honey, I really need you to go into the bedroom and put on that t-shirt and shorts I set out last night for you to wear. Would you do that for me, hon?"

"You aren't going to give me to them or sell me to them?" she asked fearfully.

"No, honey. No. They are not going to take you anywhere and they aren't going to harm you. Ed and Mike are friends. They are here to help me protect you. No one is taking you anywhere." Dawson tried to sound as reassuring as possible. Brandy was clearly on the edge of panic.

Brandy quickly got up and ran for the bedroom as though escaping.

Ed looked at Dawson inquiringly.

"It's a long story. It's going to take more than one cup of coffee to tell, too, I am sure. Have a seat." Over coffee Dawson laid out the events of the previous day starting with the firefight to prevent the Holderites from getting to the Johnson farm to the events there at the cabin the night before. He then told them all that Brandy told him about her experience. When he told them about Caroline Ed's face clouded with anger. Mike's response was instant;

"We gotta get her out of there!"

"Now, Mike, we don't know it is her or even if she is still alive, which I sincerely doubt." Ed said, "We found two bodies in the ashes of their place, remember?" His voice was filled with anger however.

Yeah, and I remember you couldn't tell who was who. One of them could have been a Holderite and you'd never have known the difference. We got to at least try to get her out if it is her." Mike responded.

"How?" Dawson asked sympathetically but pragmatically. "Look, I want Caroline out of there more than either of you; probably more than both of you combined. But here is the truth: the New Order militia is about two hundred strong. If you count conscripts their numbers are probably around three hundred fifty.

That isn't counting any of the Storm Troop numbers. There is probably a hundred or a hundred and fifty militia garrisoned in Carrollton. There's only six of us if we all go, but that would leave your farm unprotected, which you don't want to do, so I would think that leaves maybe four of us to do it. We have no chance."

"We could sneak in. You know; kind of a guerilla operation." Mike said insistently.

"Yes, we could sneak in. As I remember Carrollton the town borders are pretty porous unless you are on the roads. Getting in would not be a problem. Getting out would be. Given how popular the pleasure house is supposed to be, I doubt we could get in and out with having to shoot someone. Gunfire will attract attention and attention like that means a running firefight while trying to protect a woman who may or may not be all that mobile or willing.

"You have a wife and a baby on the way. Ed has a whole family to worry about. Either of you getting killed or captured is a disaster for the family and, frankly, for the community."

"Too bad we can't scout the place out to find out if she is in there and what the lay of the land is." Ed said.

The three sat quietly sipping on their coffee.

"We can." Dawson said quietly.

"Can what?" Ed asked.

"Scout it out."

"How? You just laid out how dangerous it would be."

"I laid out how dangerous it would be to do an extraction. Scouting is something different entirely. I haven't been in Carrollton since we rescued Doc Arnie. They don't know who I am and they won't likely remember me from before. I'll take some pelts to trade – which I will do and then I can poke around a bit and see what I can find out."

"Too dangerous." Ed said. "I know you love Caroline and you want to rescue her if she is still alive, but the odds of her being alive are very long. Very long indeed. You may end up getting captured and killed, if they are feeling charitable. Castrated if they aren't."

"For Caroline, I'll risk it."

"What about your friend there?" Mike asked gesturing toward the bedroom where Brandy had disappeared.

Dawson sighed. "Yeah…she'll be a problem."

"Tell you what. I'll have Tanya come down and stay with her. Actually I'll send Tanya and Addison both now that I think about it. Addison has wanted to visit home lately anyway so that would work out pretty well. Just let me know when you want to go and I'll bring them down here." Mike said.

"Alright. Give me a couple of days to get some things around." Dawson said, "Then I'll be off to Carrollton."

"Master?" Brandy said that evening as they sat by the fire.

Dawson looked up from his reading. Brandy had been very quiet ever since Ed and Mike had gone home. Something was obviously on her mind. Dawson was certain that she was about to tell him what it was.

"Brandy, honey, I'm not your master. I am your friend. You can call me Dawson."

She nodded and then looked perplexed.

"Sir?" she said as though somehow 'Sir' was a happy medium between calling Dawson by his first name and calling him her master.

"Yes, Brandy?" Dawson said in resignation.

"They will kill you."

"Who, honey?"

"The militia in Carrollton. They will kill you if you go after Skippy. They will catch you and they will kill you." There was genuine fear in her voice.

"Brandy," Dawson said gently, "Her name is Caroline. She isn't who they say she is. Don't worry about them killing me. I have to come back to take care of you. I won't let anything happen I can't get out of."

Brandy sat for a long time staring into the fire.

"The pleasure house is on Evergreen." She said. "Only militia men can go in and use us. Someone is there all the time. They come to use us any time of day or night and there are always guards around." Her voice sounded distant as though speaking through a dream or a recollection of what had been. Her eyes had a faraway look to them as she stared into the fire.

"You love her don't you, Master?" she then said in suddenly clear voice.

"Brandy, I'm not your master." Dawson repeated patiently. "Yes, I do love Caroline."

Brandy nodded. "I am glad someone loves her. Everyone should have someone who loves them – even slaves. Slaves...can't love anyone." Her voice trailed off as though in pain. Then she sat silently for another long time, staring mindlessly into the fire. Then she looked up at Dawson.

"Are you going to fuck me tonight?" she asked. Her voice lacked the fear that had been in it before. She sounded more curious than anxious.

"No, Brandy. I'm not going to have sex with you."

She looked troubled. "I'm not pretty enough, am I?" her voice trembled. "They always told us that the pretty girls got fucked, ugly girls got tortured."

Dawson sighed. "Brandy you are a very pretty woman. Very pretty. But right now, it would not be right for us to have sex. You need to heal and sort through the last couple of years and grieve over your baby and husband. You've never been allowed to do that."

"I miss her." Brandy said her voice growing distant again. "I miss my little baby. I loved her so much." Tears started to run down her cheeks.

"Come here, Brandy." Dawson said without thinking and then put his book aside.

Brandy obediently got up and stood before him, trying to control her crying as though willing herself to stop.

"No, come here." Dawson repeated indicating his lap.

Brandy sat down on his lap clearly expecting to be fondled or groped. Dawson put his arms around her and cradled her against his chest and held her gently as a father would a small child.

"Now, tell me all about her and if you want to cry you can cry all you want." He said softly.

Two days later Dawson stood outside the cabin with Tanya and Addison.

"Now, Brandy is pretty fragile." He told them. "Just go with the flow with her. She will most likely just sit by the fire and do nothing. I think she is sorting out her life right now. If she wants to talk like she is a slave, don't correct her. In her mind she still is one and it is too confusing right now to explain otherwise. Like I said, she's pretty broken mentally. I haven't seen much in the way of PTSD, but there could be an episode so play it by ear.

She may want to talk about life with the Ragarians or the Holderites. If she, does be prepared to hear some pretty awful and shocking things. Don't offer an opinion or express disgust. It is a way of making sense of the life she'd been forced into. If you say anything it may keep her from getting it all out of her. She needs to do that."

"Got, Dad." Tanya said. "You can count on us."

"Addison, you know where the rifles are and how to defend this place if you need to, right?"

"Yeah, Dad. I know. Don't worry. Tanya and I have this." Addison said in her I'm-nearly-fourteen-years-old-and-not-baby-anymore tone of peevishness.

"Good. I knew I could count on you. Now it is going to take me a couple of days to walk to Carrollton and a couple of days to get back. I don't plan on spending more than a day or so in Carrollton so I should be back inside of a week. Ed and Mike will check on you a couple times a day just to help with things that may need doing." His tone of voice was that of someone running down a checklist before leaving the house in the care of the children for the first time.

"Dad, we will be fine." Tanya said with a chuckle. "Just go and find Caroline."

Dawson nodded. He picked up his back pack and put it on. He slung his hunting rifle over his shoulder and picked up the large bundle of furs he was using as cover to get into town.

"Just remember..." he said after he'd taken a couple of steps.

"Dad!" Tanya interrupted. "We got this. Don't worry."

Dawson nodded and headed off toward Carrollton.

Chapter 10

Dawson approached the guard post at the city limits of Carrollton about sundown. It had taken him two days to get there.

"State your business!" the guard ordered when he'd gotten up to the gate.

"Just came to trade off some of last season's furs I've got left. Damn traveling peddler wouldn't take off my hands." Dawson said gruffly.

"Let's see 'em!" the guard demanded.

Dawson swung them down from off his shoulder and let the guard look though them.

"Some of 'em ain't bad." The guard said knowingly. "Probably best place to go would be to see if Carney down at the tannery wants 'em. Other than that, I'd try Gibby at the General Store."

"Thanks. I appreciate the help. I need to pick up a few supplies and this is about all I got left."

"If you need a place to stay, I'd try the Major's Manor down off Main. It ain't much but it is better than the street."

"Thanks again. I was wondering about finding a place to stay."

The guard turned to his partner. "Go ahead and open her up. He ain't no military unit." He said as though explaining to his partner the perfectly obvious.

Dawson walked through the gate and heard it swing closed behind him. He made his way to the Major's Manor and rented a bed for the night. The Major's Manor was more like an old fashioned army barracks rather than a hotel. Rows of bunk beds lined the large open upstairs room that ran the length of the Manor. He stowed his gear in his assigned locker and went downstairs to get something to eat. Dinner was served buffet style on the dining room. From the looks of the buffet, food wasn't all that plentiful in Carrollton. Either that or the Major's Manor was cutting costs.

He sat down and started to eat. The décor was pleasant enough although the lighting was being done with the old fashioned oil lamps. They gave the room an oily smell but not terribly repugnant. A few other diners were eating there as well.

"I tell you I heard they were culling the livestock tomorrow!" A nearby diner said loudly and excitedly to another.

"They ain't going to do that in broad daylight." The other said calmly. "Besides what purpose would it serve if they did?"

"Hell, I don't know. Public entertainment? I'm just telling you what I heard." The other said sullenly. "If they are, though, it would give us a chance to see what the militia gets for themselves. I heard they were culling the ones that don't produce much anymore or are sick, but they still should be worth a look."

"Look," the other diner said, "John, I got no interest in what they do with their livestock. All I want to do is finish my business here in this shithole of a town and get the hell out of Dodge. I hate this place."

"I know. I just think it would be cool to watch them do the culling. I hear they got a whole system for putting them down all humane like. I think it would be fun to see."

"Yeah, well I don't. Not interested at all."

Dawson listened intently but tried to appear completely oblivious to their conversation. He guessed that the 'livestock' wasn't cattle or sheep. Most likely they were talking about women from the pleasure house. Brandy had said they called the women their livestock. If what they were saying was true, the militia was every bit as evil as he imagined. The fact that non-militia members used the same term to describe the women told him how pervasive the mentality had become in Carrollton.

He finished his meal and made his way outside. Once on the street he attempted to appear to be just on an evening stroll. Militia members patrolled the streets in a both a clear attempt at intimidating anyone who might contemplate breaking the law and to reassure the good citizens of Carrollton that all was safe and secure. Eventually he came to Evergreen St. and turned to walk down it.

Evergreen was obviously the "Red Light District." He hadn't gone far before he came across the first brothel. The girls sat on the porch displaying their bodies with no regard for modesty. One of them called to Dawson and offered him "today's special" if he was interested. Dawson smiled and waved and kept on walking. About midway through the second block he came to what he assumed was the pleasure house. It was a rundown old home that had no signage on it all. The windows were boarded over, giving the building an abandoned appearance. Only the presence of guards on the front porch gave a clue that it wasn't just another home in a rundown neighborhood.

He stood momentarily and took the measure of the place. Trying to quickly memorize the lay of the yard and the manner in which the guards did their jobs. A sudden woman's scream from inside the building brought a round of knowing laughter from the guards. Dawson went on down the block and then sneaked down a back alley. Eventually he got a look at the back of the house. The back door had been boarded over as had the back windows on both floors. He noted they'd used scrap boards to board the windows rather than plywood. He guessed that was to let at least some light into the building. Entry or exit out the back would be nearly impossible without attracting attention, however. As he continued on down the alley he could see that the windows on the side of the house had also been boarded over. The only way in or out was the front door.

He returned to the Manor and made his way to his bed. He had felt a little apprehensive about potentially sharing the room with a large number of strangers. To his relief, it appeared that the only other overnight guests numbered about half a dozen. He got into bed and fell asleep.

The next morning Dawson got up and made his way to the tannery. He asked for Carney when the clerk turned to wait on him. The clerk nodded and mumbled something that sounded like, "jusaminute" and walked off.

Shortly thereafter a big burly man, with coal black hair and a large coal black beard and sideburns came into the room.

"Name's Carney." He said in a booming voice that was a large as he was. "How can I help you?"

"Well, I got a few furs left I was hoping to get rid of. They are the last of last season's catch. I caught more that the peddler wanted to take off my hands." Dawson said.

"Well, maybe I'll take 'em and maybe I won't." Carney boomed. "Let's take a look at 'em."

Dawson swung the large string of furs off his back and dropped them on the table next to him. Carney started to go through them with an expert's eye. Dawson could tell the man knew his fur.

"Some of it is pretty nice." He said finally. "What you want for 'em?"

"Well, actually, if I could get a couple of cowhides I'd consider that even. I'm needing to make some harness."

"Just two?" Carney asked

"Yeah, I know I'm underselling but…"

"Look, Mister…"

"Billings." Dawson said. "Cal Billings."

"Look, Mister Billings, I run an honest business here. I don't gyp anyone and I don't want it out that someone got out of here with less than their furs were worth. It's just bad for business. I'm probably the last of the honest businessmen in this godforsaken town. So here's my offer: You got a lot of real prime mink and weasel here and some really fine fox and coon. So I'll give you two cowhides, half a dozen steel snares, and a gallon of oil for working that leather. That should come in handy for making that harness you mentioned. I'd give you more if those coyote skins had been in better shape."

"Oil for the leather? Wow that is hard to come by. You sure you want to do that?" Dawson asked in surprise.

"I wouldn't have offered it I wasn't sure."

"I'll take it." Dawson said.

"Good. Wait here and I'll have one of the guys bring your stuff out to you. By the way, if you get any good bear hides I'll give you top trade for those. Got a big demand for 'em. Keep that in mind. Anyway, it's been a pleasure doing business with you, Mister Billings."

They shook hands on the deal and Carney went back through the door into the tannery. Shortly thereafter a man came out with two cowhides all rolled up tightly and a gallon plastic jug.

"Snares are inside the hides." He said as he dropped the bundle down on the table.

"Thanks. I appreciate that." Dawson said.

"Hanging around town or heading home?" the man asked genially.

"Oh, probably heading on home."

"Not stayin' for the culling?" the man asked in surprise.

"The culling?" Dawson asked in mock surprised interest.

"Yeah. Militia is culling out some of their livestock. You know; the useless ones in the herd. First time ever that they are doing it in public. They usually do that in the basement of the pleasure house. I heard they hang 'em upside down and slit their throats and let 'em bleed out down there. This should be quite a show today. There's been lots of activity down at the field. I heard they were doing it around 3:00 this afternoon." The man seemed quite enthused about the coming murders.

"Thanks. I may just hang around." Dawson said, "Nothing at home needs immediate attention anyway. This sounds kind of exciting."

Dawson spent the rest of the day wandering around town getting the lay of the streets, doorways, and alleys. He paid particular attention to the alleys. If they actually did raid the place the alleys would like be their best routes. He had to commit it all to memory. Not knowing how things were run, he didn't want to risk being searched on the way out of town and having the guards find notes and maps on his person. His memory would have to do.

He also noted the armaments the militia guards carried. While they were supposed to be a military unit they had a surprisingly wide array of weapons. Some carried AK-47s while others carried AR-15s. He even saw a couple carrying old CETME rifles. Those that carried pistols as well as their rifles had more variety yet. Dawson laughed to himself. 'Looks like every man for himself if they run out of ammo. No way could they share magazines reliably.' He thought.

At 2:30 he was at the pleasure house to see if there was any activity. It was obvious something was in the works because there was a much larger group of New Order militia men present that one would expect for just recreational activities. He found a hiding spot down the block where he could see the front of the building fairly clearly with only a few obstructions to his view.

About 2:45 a guard came out leading a string of six women. None of them were clothed at all. The first one was a slender woman with long brown hair. Dawson couldn't get a clear view of the woman but she looked like Caroline. Before he could move to get a better view the line of women had turned and was slowly making their way down the street away from him, heading toward the main street. Dawson realized that while the women were connected to each other by ropes around the neck none of them resisted at all. They didn't cry out or beg for mercy or anything. They docilely and quietly followed the guard who led them. The rest of the guards had fallen in alongside them probably to both protect them from gawkers and to keep them from bolting.

Dawson followed them to the main street where the little procession turned right. Dawson sprinted down and alley, trying to guess where they were headed so he could get a look at the first woman. When he came out of the alley, he realized he'd over shot the parade and that they had turned down an alley he didn't know anything about, heading away from him. He quickly tried to catch up but when he got caught up seeing clearly was not likely. The procession had entered a large open area that was already filled with spectators. The women were led through the crowd to the front of the field where they were contained in a narrow livestock chute and locked in.

A couple of militia members with rifles stood waiting casually in front of a large hole dug in the ground. A step or so from them but between them and the chute stood a third man who looked like a militia officer. He was carrying a clipboard and his sidearm. Dawson tried to push his way through the crowd but found the going difficult. Everyone wanted a view and no one wanted to give way.

"Bring out the first one!" the man with the clipboard shouted brusquely. The front of the chute was opened and a woman was pulled rather roughly out of the chute. She didn't resist at all, but followed along behind the guard in a completely docile, mindless manner.

Dawson could see that this woman looked a lot like Caroline but just when he would have gotten a clear look at her face a man with his small kid on his shoulders stepped in front of him blocking his view completely. By the time he got where he could see again she was standing with her back to the crowd in front of the hole. Two guards stood about a step away on each side of her, apparently in case she bolted at the last second. They had attached ropes to her wrists which they held pulling her arms out slightly from her sides.

The man with the clipboard walked up to her and looked her over. She stood motionless the whole time as though completely unaware of what was going on or what was happening around her. The officer checked his clipboard as though comparing notes, nodded his head and carefully pulled her long brown hair over her shoulder and down her chest, exposing her back clearly to the men with rifles.

He then stepped well aside and one of the men leveled his rifle. The man with the clipboard nodded his head again and the guard fired once, striking her square between the shoulder blades. She pitched forward into the hole ripping the rope from the two guard's hands. She went forward so violently that she first struck the far side of the hole before dropping down into it. A loud cheer went up from the crowd as she fell forward and then down.

"Bring out the second one!" the clipboard man barked without checking to see if the woman was dead. Apparently it did not matter.

Dawson was filled with rage. The woman had certainly looked like Caroline. If so, he was too late. She was dead or soon would be. He pushed his way back through the crowd and then went back down the alley. He paused for a moment to decide what to do. Staying in Carrollton was not high on his list of things he wanted to do. Still he had to know if Caroline was dead. He decided to wait around.

When the last of the women had been executed Dawson made his way back toward the field against the flow of the crowd who laughed and joked as they exited the execution area. He then approached the men at the hole who were getting ready to fill it in.

"Can I help you, citizen?" the man with the clipboard asked crispy while moving his hand to his sidearm.

"Well, maybe. Hell of a show you put on." Dawson said feigning enthusiasm. "I was wondering though about that first woman. I think I did her a couple years ago in the pleasure house and I haven't been back since. I was wondering was that woman named Skippy?"

"How'd you get into the pleasure house?" The man asked suspiciously.

"Well, truth be told I wasn't supposed to be in there. However, I'd done a huge favor for a militia captain who got his patrol into some trouble up near the border. He gave me a pass to get in on his authority as a thank you for the help." Dawson said.

The man nodded in understanding. "Well, I can't help you with names on the livestock that gets brought out for culling. They just put down a number on my paperwork and a brief description of what she looks like. In her case she was cow number one. I don't know anything beyond that. I'm sure someone somewhere has a record, but it ain't me."

Dawson sighed in disappointment. "Can I take a look into the hole?"

"Why you got such an interest in a worn out cow like her?" he asked.

"Well, back then she wasn't worn out and well...we had fun and I remember it like it was yesterday." He grinned at the man in a lascivious manner.

The man shrugged. "Knock yourself out. Just don't get in my men's way. They need to fill that hole in and move on."

"No problem. Just a quick peak and I'm gone."

Dawson stepped up to the hole and peered down into it. He could not see anything of the first woman except her hair and the back side of her head. Her face was buried under another woman's body. It was then that he saw the head move slightly.

"That one is still alive in there." He said pointing down into the hole.

"That a fact?" the man with the clipboard asked, seemingly unconcerned. He walked up to the hole and looked in for himself. "Humpf. That cow as a will to live, I'll give her that. Well, she's probably not the only one down there like that." Then he looked at the men with shovels. "Fill it in boys. We got other work to do!"

The men threw in several buckets full of lime and then started filling in the hole. Dawson stood in shock and then turned and walked away. He knew he would be back. Sooner or later he would be back. If Caroline was lying at the bottom of that hole, he would personally kill the men that put her there.

Dawson turned away from the hole and walked on out through the alley to the street. He was going home.

When he got to the guard post at the gate the same guard that had admitted him to Carrollton was on duty.

"So, how'd the trading go?" he asked in a friendly tone.

"Not bad. I got two cowhides that I really needed, some oil to work the leather with, and a few snares."

"Told ya Carney was an honest man." The guard said with a smile.

"Yeah, he told me to come back if I got any bear hides. Says he needs them bad."

"Probably does. Seems like everyone in town wants one for their bed covers lately. Nice and warm, you see? Saves on having to buy as much firewood."

"Makes sense." Dawson said with a nod of his head.

"Well, guess I need to get down to business." The guard said changing the subject. "I need to check your pack. I have to make sure you don't have anything in there you shouldn't."

"Seems like you'd have done that on my way in too." Dawson said with a laugh as he took the pack off his back.

"Yeah. I've thought that myself many times. But I only do what they tell me to do. Anything else will get you into trouble."

He quickly looked through Dawson's pack and then nodded his head.

"Well, friend, have a safe walk home. See you when you've got some of those bear skins for Carney." He then turned to the guard running the gate. "Well, open it up! He ain't no deserter or anything. Let him through." He said impatiently.

Dawson picked up his backpack and quickly shouldered it. He nodded his head in farewell to the guard and went on through the gate smiling. Carrollton had not seen the last of him. The Wolf would come again to visit.

Three days later Dawson, Ed and Mike sat at his table in the cabin. Brandy sat on the floor, like a spaniel that hadn't seen her master in weeks. She put her head on Dawson's thigh and held onto his leg tightly. Dawson laid out what he'd seen of the town, drew a few rough maps of things, and told them about the execution of some of the women from the pleasure house.

"I imagine that if they are killing some of the women from the pleasure house like that, they must have fresh ones coming from somewhere." Ed said.

"Either that or they can't afford to feed them." Mike said drearily.

"Either way," Dawson said "we don't know much more than we did before as to whether Caroline is alive or not. However, I am pretty sure – not one hundred percent mind you but pretty sure - the woman I saw die was Caroline. I'd know her backside anywhere."

"They do it for fun." Brandy said from the floor. "That is all it is."

The men sat for a moment looking at one another. This was the first time Brandy had offered to join a conversation much less make an observation about the motives of the Holderite militia.

They realized that while Brandy may be silent and out of sight, she was still listening.

Ed sighed. "Well...I'm at a loss here. I don't think we can get in and out without getting caught or killed ourselves. We'd need about a hundred more guys to do it. We don't have near that many. Hell, we don't have near half that many."

"No, we don't. From what I saw of the pleasure house a frontal assault is the only option. A frontal assault will be loud, messy and fruitless without more numbers on our side. We've pretty much run out of options. We need help."

"Has that peddler been through lately?" Mike asked.

"No not lately." Dawson said. "He's about due any time though."

"Maybe he has contacts that would help us out?"

"We can ask." Dawson said.

"Alright," Ed said in a determined tone, "whoever sees him first asks him. I want to clear out that damn town. Whether Caroline is alive or not, I want to clear it out." The others nodded their heads in agreement.

The men talked for a while longer and then Ed and Mike left to go home. Dawson stood in the doorway and watched them disappear around the bend in the road. He sighed. In some ways he was mourning Caroline all over again.

"Master?" a small voice from behind him said.

"Brandy, I am not your master. I am your friend." He said patiently as he turned to face her. "Anyway, what is on your mind?"

"Why didn't you give me to your friends?"

"Brandy, I cannot give you to anyone. That isn't something I can do nor is it something I would do."

"Do you want to ...?" There was a worried tone that hadn't been there before when she had asked. At first her voice was more fearful. Now she seemed very worried. It wasn't the same worry that had been in her voice before though. This time she seemed different.

"No, Brandy, no. I do not want to have sex with you right now."

"I am not pretty enough, am I?" she asked in a slightly grieved tone.

"Brandy you are very pretty." He said gently.

"Have I displeased you, then?" She said fearfully.

"No, you have not. Never in a million years." He said gently and reassuringly.

She stood silently questioning him. It was painfully obvious she was used to her masters making sexual demands all the time even to the point of sharing her with others. She was confused as to why he did not do the same. It also seemed like she was confused about something else he couldn't put his finger on.

Dawson sighed both in frustration and in pain for Brandy.

"Brandy, did your husband give you to his friends for sex?" he asked gently.

"I don't think so. I don't really remember. I've forgotten most of that life."

"Did he rape you at every tick of the clock?"

"No. I don't think so."

"Of course he didn't. You were his wife. He loved you. He only had sex with you when you both wanted it because you were his wife."

She was quiet for a long time as though thinking.

"Master, if I were your wife would I still be your slave?" Her voice was curious in tone as though pondering something new that had just occurred to her.

"Well, Brandy, you are not my slave now so if you were my wife you would not be my slave. If you were a slave, you would be my wife, not my slave."

She nodded her head in understanding. Dawson suddenly had an idea and he sensed something was starting to click in Brandy's mind.

"What is your name?" he asked her as though changing the subject.

"That is about all I worry about. If a Holderite patrol wants an old shriveled up, droopy tits woman like me they are harder up than anyone imagined.

"Well, you aren't shriveled up and your....." Dawson voice trailed off in embarrassment, having caught himself about to say something she might have found offensive.

"Well? And my what?" Della asked in a playful demand her eyes lighting up as though challenging him.

Dawson just grinned, and blushed deeper red.

"Well?" Della demanded.

"And your tits don't droop." Dawson finished in embarrassment.

"Thank you!" Della said genuinely. "A woman needs to hear that occasionally from someone other than her husband. However, my dear, things are moving south. They always do. Damn gravity anyway." Then she laughed.

"So, I assume you didn't travel all the way over here just to embarrass me." Dawson said.

"No, actually I didn't. Embarrassing you was just a side benefit." She said with a sly smile. "We've been so busy at the clinic lately that Doc Arnie hasn't been able to check your guest over. He sends his apologies on that. He wants me to give her a quick preliminary physical and make sure there aren't any obvious diseases or injuries that he needs to attend to. He plans on stopping by himself this afternoon but wants to make sure he brings what he needs if there is something unusual involved.

Your Brandy has been through a lot of trauma both physically and mentally. From what Tanya says it sounds like you are giving her a safe space for her to heal mentally as much as possible. Now we need to make sure she is mending physically as well if she needs it."

"I'm pretty sure she is as OK as she can be." Dawson said.

"Tanya was too, but we really should know for certain. She deserves what health care we can provide. She is part of the community now. Which reminds me; we added two more families to the community while you were gone to Carrollton. The Harding's and the Smithson's decided that they'd had enough of self-reliance."

"I'm afraid I don't know them." Dawson said. "I'm not from around here."

"They live further east, out past the Fry place. The Smithson's own a farm and have a small beef operation still going. The Harding's live in a mobile home across the road from the Smithson's. They don't have much except for enough space for a garden. He's an amateur blacksmith though. Seems they used to do those Renaissance reenactments. He made simple iron odds and ends to sell. He's gotten pretty good at making horseshoes and plow bottoms. They will earn their keep pretty well. They will probably move into the compound by winter. Ed convinced them that the mobile home wasn't the place to be in winter and his blacksmithing would be more beneficial if more centrally located. We do need their garden though, so we'll have to see what actually happens. Maybe we'll just build them a better home with safer heating and call it good."

They made their way to the cabin as they continued to talk about happenings in the community. Mildred Fry had had a baby boy they'd named John. Cal Myers fell out of his hay loft and nearly broke his leg but was on the mend. The new school was scheduled to be finished within the month as lumber came available. Then the interior would be started and a fireplace installed.

When they got to the door Dawson opened it and gestured for Della to go on in. He followed her through the door. Brandy stood in the bedroom doorway, naked as usual, with a concerned look on her face.

"Brandy, this is Della. She is a nurse and...." Dawson started but never finished what he was going to say. Brandy let out a scream of terror and ran back into the bedroom.

Dawson looked at Della in confusion and then followed Brandy into the bedroom. He found her curled up in a corner between the dresser and the walls as though trying to find and even smaller space to hide in. He sat down on the floor in front of her and said nothing. She stared at him, her eyes wide in terror.

"Can you tell me what is wrong? Why are you scared?" Dawson said gently and quietly.

Brandy just stared at him wide eyed and terrorized as though unable to speak.

"Were nurses evil at the house?" he asked after a long period of silence.

Brandy nodded her head slowly, but never taking her eyes off Dawson and never becoming less fearful.

"Did they hurt the women at the house?"

Brandy nodded her head, "They made slaves die." She said quietly, her terror very plain in her voice. "There is a room they used. They only came at culling time. You are going to cull me!" the panic and terror filled her voice and tears began to well up in her eyes.

"No, Brandy no. You are safe here and you always will be. No one will hurt you in any way as long as I am here." He reached out to touch her to reassure her but she pulled away in fear so he pulled his hand back.

"Brandy, did you ever watch the movie "The Wizard of Oz?" Dawson asked.

Brandy nodded her head but confusion replaced part of the fear in her eyes.

"Do you remember Glinda the Good, the Witch of the North? She was the woman in white that gave Dorothy the ruby slippers. Remember her?"

Brandy nodded her head slowly but her look did not change.

"Now, she was a witch, right? Dorothy dropped her house on a wicked witch, the witch of the east, which made the wicked witch of the west very angry. They were both evil witches, but the witches of the north and south were very good witches. Right?"

Brandy did not move nor did her expression change.

"Now, we know from this that some witches are evil and some witches are good. Just because they are a witch doesn't mean they are always evil. The same is true with nurses, Brandy. Some nurses are like the evil witches. However, some nurses are like Glinda – very, very good. They never hurt anyone and only want to help make them live longer and better. Della is a good nurse. She has treated my daughters and she has treated me. She never hurt any of us. She helped Mildred Fry deliver her baby which is a very good thing.

"Now Della is here to make sure you are healthy. She wants you to live a very long time and be very happy. If you are hurt or sick she wants to fix it so you can do that. Not only is she a nurse, she is my friend and I trust her very much. I promise she won't hurt you. If she even tries I will kill her on the spot. I promise. OK?"

Brandy nodded her head slowly and let Dawson take her hand. She reluctantly let Dawson pull her to her feet and she held his hand tightly as they walk about into the kitchen-dining area.

"Della, this is Brandy. Brandy is very scared. The nurses at the pleasure house were evil and she thinks you are here to hurt her or kill her.'

Della looked shocked. "Oh, sweetie, no. No, no, no. Absolutely not. All I want to do is take your blood pressure, listen to your heart, and check your temperature. Then I want to check your body for infections or sickness. Dawson can stay right here if you want."

Brandy nodded her head slowly but it was clear she was still very afraid.

"Now, come on over here and sit down." Della said "This won't take long, I promise."

Dawson took Brandy to one of the dining chairs and she sat down. Della took out an oral thermometer and told Brandy to open her mouth. "Now put this under your tongue and don't bite it. Don't talk either." She said as she took Brandy's wrist and began to check her pulse. After a couple of minutes she pulled the thermometer out of Brandy's mouth and checked it.

"Well, perfectly normal – exactly normal actually. That is a good sign." She smiled at Brandy warmly. "And your pulse is good too considering you are scared to death right now. I'm not going to take your blood pressure right now because I'm pretty sure your BP is way high at the moment. Just promise me that if you have any headaches or dizziness or chest pains you'll come to the clinic right away, OK?"

Brandy nodded her head slowly never taking her eyes off Della. It was clear she did not trust her.

"Now stand up and let me have a look at you." Della said. "Dawson do you have a bathroom scale?"

"Yeah. Somewhere."

"Could you please fetch it?"

"Sure. Hang on."

Dawson had to let go of Brandy's hand and she looked at him pleadingly.

"Brandy, I'll still be in the room. I just need to get the scale from the bathroom.

As he picked up the scale he found it humorous suddenly that the room he was in was the 'bathroom.' That was the only function it served now. The tub was all that remained usable, although he had jury rigged the toilet so that Brandy could use it until she was comfortable using the outhouse.

He brought the scale back into the room where Della and Brandy stood. Della was just finishing checking out Brandy's body. She then had Brandy step on the scale.

"Very good! You are perfectly healthy or seem to be." She said once both she and Brandy had sat back down. "Now, sweetie, do you have any pain or itching or discomfort in your vagina?"

Brandy looked at her blankly and then nodded her head a little.

"Which?" Della said gently.

"It itches sometimes." She said softly.

"Can I see?" Della asked

Brandy looked at Dawson for reassurance.

"Do you want Dawson to leave the room?" Della asked.

Brandy shook her head. "No!" she said emphatically, and very much afraid.

"OK." Della got down on the floor in front of Brandy. "Now can you spread your legs for me, sweetie?"

Brandy looked at Dawson who nodded his head encouragingly. Brandy spread her legs widely as though expecting to be mounted. Della gently examined her and then sat back on the floor.

"Well, sweetie, you have what looks to be a standard run of the mill yeast infection. We can fix that up pretty quickly. I'll tell Doctor Arnie and he will come by this afternoon with the medicine. He may want to double check me, maybe not. Either way we'll get you fixed up right away. Then you will be completely healthy."

Della then stood up and stretched her back a bit.

"Not as young as I used to be." She laughed looking at Brandy first and then Dawson. "Not at all. Well, I've done everything I need to do here. Dawson, can I speak to you outside for a moment. Ed wanted me to pass on some news."

"Sure." Dawson said.

Once outside and the door was closed behind them Della turned to Dawson.

"Have you had sex with her?" Della asked bluntly.

"No." Dawson said honestly.

"Good. She probably only has a yeast infection or maybe a bacterial infection but I can't rule out an STD. Given where she's been it could be. On the other hand, Ed tells me that she sits on the floor a lot so she could just have picked up some bacteria of some sort and she just has a standard infection. Doc Arnie will know for sure. In the meantime stay out of her pussy."

"No problem, Della. She keeps asking about sex but I'd feel too much like I was treating her no different than the bastards in Carrollton."

Della nodded. "Good. She needs the safety. Doc Arnie will be around this afternoon. You might want to prepare her for that. My guess is that doctors in the pleasure house weren't any nicer than the nurses."

"She says the only doctor they got to see was a vet. The militia considers them livestock so they only get veterinarian visits. She said she was sterilized by one."

Della nodded her head. "I suspected as much from what Ed told me you'd told him. That bunch needs to go away as violently as possible." She said, clearly meaning it.

"Yeah. I intend to make that happen." Dawson said.

Chapter 11

Dawson made his way through the streets and alleys of Carrollton carefully avoiding contact with any of the guards that patrolled the streets. The darkness of the moonless night made it easier to do, but he still needed to be careful and quiet. He was dressed in black from head to toe and carried his AR on his chest with a two point tactical sling. He wished he had a suppressor on the AR, but one was not available so he hoped he'd not have to use the rifle.

He paused momentarily as the alley he was in crossed Evergreen not far from the pleasure house. There was a real temptation to raid it instead of his intended target but quickly dismissed it as far more risky and less productive. Still the single guard on duty at 2:30 a.m. made going in very tempting, especially if Caroline was still alive – which he had grown to doubt. The more he reflected on what he saw at the public executions the more convinced he was that he'd seen Caroline being murdered.

Sticking as close to the shadows as possible he darted across the poorly lit street and down the alley on the other side. He stayed in the alleyways as much as possible and when he could not, he stayed in the shadows. He finally reached the last alley he needed to traverse. It ran past the back of the warehouse being used as an armory for the militia.

He actually did have a plan for what he was about to do, but admittedly its success would depend on the continued amateurishness of the militia he'd seen in his firefights with them in the field and had been observed in the streets when he was in Carrollton before. There had only been a couple of militia members who behaved like combat vets before he'd killed them in the field. The rest were gung-ho soldier wannabees, scared kids who joined up for food and shelter, and draftees and conscripts who were all completely clueless.

He approached the warehouse as silently as possible expecting the rear door to be well guarded. His assessment of the professionalism of the militia was borne out by what confronted him as he watched from the shadows. Instead of at least half dozen guards protecting the vulnerable rear door to the storehouse of munitions, only one guard sat in a chair leaned back against the wall on two legs, clearly fast asleep.

Dawson shook his head in amazement. In former days he would have suspected a trap. The visible guard would only have been bait to get an attacker to expose himself to the real defenses. The New Order militia however wasn't that smart and they weren't that organized. Their only claim to power was fear and brutality. Brains never entered into the picture except as an occasional surprising highlight.

Dispatching the guard proved to be no problem. He'd drawn his knife and cut the man's throat in mid-snore. The guard had struggled some before dying and even attempted to call out an alarm, but Dawson had no trouble silencing the voice and controlling the struggling until the man bled out. He picked the dead man's pockets and discovered a couple of keys that may or may not have gone to the warehouse in some way so he took them. He left the man's newly minted New Order cash he found in his pocket. Dawson figured that was as worthless at the paper it was printed on.

Dawson ignored the overhead doors which would have been loud to open and visually difficult for a guard to ignore if opened. Besides they were likely locked on the inside. Instead he went to the fire door next to it. He gave it a tentative tug to see if it was locked. It wasn't. He shook his head in disgust and wished in a way that he'd been surprised it wasn't locked.

He slipped inside the building and quickly pulled the door closed. The building was, for the most part as pitch black as the alley had been. The only light he could see was at the far end of the building in what appeared to be an office. He could see two guards standing around a potbelly stove drinking coffee. He doubted anyone would be patrolling the warehouse in the dark.

He pulled a pair of night goggles from his small backpack and put them on. The very low light of the distant lanterns gave him enough light to see and not bump into things but little else. He would need his flashlight for the detailed work he planned. He carefully made his way up and down the rows of steel racks used to store the militia's supplies. Most of it was useless for what he wanted, though he did find some medical supplies he quickly put into his pack. Then he made his way to the basement via the stairway he'd discovered along the back wall.

Once in the basement he knew he'd found what he was looking for. Chain-link fence lockers contained rifles, ammunition and, in the case of one very special locker, explosives. There was a guard sitting at the desk at the end of the room in the light of a lantern. He was as asleep as the first guard had been, except he had his head in his arms resting on the desk in front of him. Dawson killed him as easily as he had the first.

He found the keys to the lockers in a drawer in the desk and opened the explosives locker. He took off the night vision goggles completely and took out his flashlight after setting an alarm on the stairway down. The alarm was a simple thing, a few empty soda pop cans set out of sight under the sill to be tripped by some clear 10 pound test fish line he'd brought with him.

Dawson searched the available explosives. He was surprised by what he found: cases of C-4, grenades, claymores, timers, and dynamite. He'd only known the militia members to carry grenades once, and that was the regular militia who attacked his home. Still he wondered why they were stored away in the armory. It seemed useless to have them but not issue them. He shrugged. More to play with, he reasoned. He took nearly an hour setting things up the way he wanted them set up. He knew he had time and that unless he made noise to attract attention no one was likely come down into the basement until change of watch. That was still a few hours away.

He put as many grenades into his backpack as he thought he could prudently carry and then set a couple of the claymores where he could grab them when he exited. He doubted he would need them, but he wanted to make sure he could cover his escape route and make any pursuers wary and slow. The six pounds of mines wouldn't slow him that much.

Dawson set the timer for fifteen minutes, relocked the locker and then hurried to the stairs. He grabbed the mines and slipped up the stairs as quietly as possible. As quick check of the office from a distance revealed the two guards still standing around in the office only it appeared they were having a rather animated discussion. Suddenly one of them pulled his sidearm and shot the other one in the face. The gunshot shattered the silence of warehouse and the echo grew as the sound waves bounced off the stark walls.

Dawson made a break for the doorway. It wouldn't be long before others would come to investigate the gunshot. He hoped no one would question why the guard from the basement hadn't responded to the emergency. Dawson wasn't too horribly worried they might find the timer and the bomb set up because he'd hidden the timer pretty well. Still, they might if they looked closely.

He slipped out the fire door and placed the body of the dead guard against it to make it more difficult for pursuers to open the door. Then he slipped down the alley as quickly and quietly as possible. He'd gotten as far as the pleasure house when an explosion rocked the night. The primary explosion was followed by several secondary explosions. He didn't need to see it to know that the warehouse and the buildings around it were now leveled or in flames.

The guard at the pleasure house jerked awake at the sound of the explosion and looked upward at the rising plume of smoke and flame.

"Holy shit!!" he yelled and took off running down the street heading toward the warehouse.

Dawson saw his chance. He slipped to the door and opened it. Once inside the pleasure house he was immediately assaulted by the smell of marijuana and incense. It was almost overpowering. Two guards came alert as he entered the building. He killed them with his rifle before they could react to him. His search was going to have to be fast and furious.

He quickly searched the desk for ledgers or any kind of paperwork that might give him a clue about Caroline. Finding one labeled, "Record of Livestock" he stuffed it into his pack. He could hear more commotion in the streets so he went to the door and cracked it open. Militia members were everywhere and he could hear orders being given. Their attention, however, seemed to be focused everywhere but at the pleasure house. He closed the door and made his way to the back of the house through what used to have been the dining room. He opened the window and kicked out a couple of the boards that barred it and slipped out into the shadows of the pleasure house's backyard. Sticking to the back alley he made his way to the chain link fence surrounding the town and followed it to where he'd cut his way through. The body of the guard he'd killed on the way in still lay undiscovered. He took the guard's knife and pinned his 'calling card' to the man's chest. Then he slipped through the hole and set one of the claymores so that anyone coming through after him would get a surprise. He then disappeared into the surrounding hills.

He hadn't gone very far before he topped a hill that gave him a pretty good view of Carrollton. His explosion had done more than he'd hoped. It looked like about a quarter of Carrollton was on fire. The old wood warehouse type structures around the armory were burning wildly and threatening the business district. He smiled. It was unlikely anyone would be following him.

He spent the rest of the night under a deadfall, catching what little sleep he could. He didn't start a fire. Smoke and campfires draw attention so he slept in the early morning chill. When Dawson woke he ate a cold breakfast and got out the ledger he'd stolen from the pleasure house. The records were haphazard and he wasn't sure how reliable they were. There were several "new" women brought into the pleasure house around the time Caroline's family was killed. Coincidentally three of them were written into the record as just "Carolyn" with no last names or initials. The "Stock name" column showed that two of the women named "Carolyn" had been named "Skippy." Apparently the Holderites weren't good with innovative names as numbers of women seemed share the same stock names. Of those two, under the "Disposition" column, one was labeled as "Culled" followed by the date of the public execution Dawson had witnessed. His heart sank. On a whim he found Brandy's record as well. Under disposition the word "escaped/stolen" was written.

Dawson sighed in frustration. He'd counted on that record to let him know for certain about Caroline's fate. Unfortunately the Holderite record keeping was a complete as their security arrangements. However, it was looking more and more like Caroline was dead. He'd been so close, yet as far from saving her as ever that day.

A week later Thompson showed up at the front barricade. Dawson welcomed him warmly and the two conducted their business and then sat on the porch drinking sun tea.

"Big dust up in Carrollton last week." Thompson said genially passing on all the local news and gossip.

"Dust up?" Dawson said.

"Well, official story is that someone was smoking in the powder room and blew the armory up. They also burned up four surrounding warehouses and the barracks too when it went. Killed about twenty or twenty five people, according to the official scoop. Rumor says more like fifty, mostly militia. Between you and me that sounds like something other than a smoking accident. Apparently the dear old Chancellor thinks so too. Ol' Harlan Holder is having a fit and sending in his shock troops to root out any possible rebellion. Life is going to be tense in Carrollton for a while."

"Is that a fact?" Dawson said feigning interest.

"You don't seem too surprised." Thompson said after a moment of looking at Dawson with a questioning eye. "You wouldn't have had a hand in that would you?"

"Me? Heavens no! I have to keep watch on Brandy here. I can't leave her alone for very long at a time. I'm even nervous leaving her for a day long hunt, let alone a week's absence."

"My name is Slu…..Brandy. I think…..my name is….Brandy." she said with great uncertainty.

"That's right!" Dawson said enthusiastically, "Your name is Brandy. Now who named you Brandy?"

"You di….No! My…..parents did?" She seemed to be faint traces of confidence in her voice as she spoke even though she was questioning.

"That is right!" Dawson said triumphantly. "Now, what is my name?"

"I am to call you master."

"No. You should not call me master. I am not your master."

"Daw…son?" she asked fearfully.

"Yes. Dawson. Why do you call me Dawson?"

"Because….You do not own me and…because I love you?" she rushed the last four words out as though afraid they would be heard but not wanted.

Dawson crossed the room to where she stood. He looked into her eyes and saw her looking back at him with both fear and growing adoration in her eyes. There was a spark in her eyes that had not been there before today. He took her in his arms and held her tightly. She did not resist, but embraced him back and seemed to melt into him. Then she started to cry. This time she seemed happy.

The next day Dawson was coming around the corner of the cabin from the garden when he saw Della approaching the front barricade. He waved her on in and then waited for her to approach.

"Didn't bring Ed or one of the boys with you?" he asked in a concerned manner.

"Nope." She said simply.

"That was pretty risky." Dawson said not meaning to be critical.

"Dawson, I have lived on these hills all my life. I know how to handle a bear."

"I wasn't referring to bears." Dawson said with a slight smile.

Thompson nodded his head, but didn't seem too convinced. "Well, someone did a damn professional job on them. That's all I'll say. Even set a claymore by a hole in the fence, or so rumor has it. Killed a couple more militia members who found it."

"Huh." Dawson grunted, "That sounds almost like a SF team to me."

"You did that work din't you? You were U.S. Army as I recall."

"Me? Hell no. I was just a flunky infantryman. I never even got a second stripe. I just couldn't 'adjust' to military life or so the C.O. said. No, whoever did that was beyond my paygrade, if it wasn't actually an accident."

Thompson nodded his head. He wasn't completely convinced, however. That much was clear.

"Well, I've got to get to the Johnson place before nightfall." Thompson said finally after he'd finished his tea. "Much obliged for the tea. Really hit the spot."

Dawson walked with him out to his wagon. Just as Thompson was about to climb up into the seat he turned to Dawson, leaving his foot on the step.

"Dawson, I don't pry into what you do because I know you are a good man. But truth is you seem to have an endless supply of rifles and New Order patrols often don't come back from out here. Just be careful when you do what you do. Harlan Holder is looking for someone to blame and your little rebellious community out here might be just the scapegoat he needs.

They are looking for some terrorist called 'The Wolf' and they may come looking out here. They are scared shitless of him – or her – and they want him bad. He not only blew up the armory but they keep losing patrols all around Carrollton and when they find them they all have that same calling card stuck on one of 'em. Watch yourself. Holder has brought in the wolf hunters." With that he lifted himself up into the driver's seat.

"Take care, Dawson. Catch you next time around."

"Watch yourself out there. I can't afford to lose my news source." Dawson said with a laugh.

"I try." Thompson said, "I truly do try."

Dawson sat on his front porch that evening in his rocking chair. Brandy sat all curled up in the other one.

"What are you thinking about?" Brandy asked suddenly.

"Oh, nothing." Dawson said. "Nothing in particular."

"I know that look, Daw...son." She said still having trouble calling him by his name. "The women used to get it when they were going away."

"I'm not going away." Dawson said with a smile.

She looked at him in a way that let him know she really did want to know what was on his mind. At the same time the look seemed to say that she really didn't feel it was her place to know.

"I was thinking about the first man I killed." Dawson said confessionally. "A kid really. My team was in a part of Syria we weren't supposed to be in, but that was where we needed to go. We'd set up camp. I was just a kid. Not even a year out of the army. The boss hired me to be expendable cannon fodder, I think. He called me "The Red Shirt" for the first year.

"Anyway...we were discovered in the middle of the night: firefight broke out. I came out of my cover in a panic and ran smack dab into this poor Syrian fighter. We literally collided and ended up on our asses on the ground. He fumbled with his rifle for a moment and I shot him with my rifle more by instinct than design. I can still see his face: the surprised look, the shock of what had happened, his life draining out of him as he went down. It was all in slow motion. He was just a kid, probably fresh out of whatever training school they put them through." Dawson's voice trailed off in regret.

Brandy sat quietly for a long time. "You've killed lots of men?" she asked.

"Yeah. I have." Then he sighed. "Looks like there will be lots more before I get to stop again."

"You killed those men in Carrollton and blew up that building didn't you? Mister Thompson was warning you, wasn't he?"

"Yes." he said simply.

"Are you this 'Wolf' he talked about?" There was fear in her voice.

"Yes." he said again.

"Are you used to killing?" she asked quietly.

"Used to killing? I don't think you ever get used to it. I think you just accept that it has to be done even if you hate it."

"**Do** you hate it?"

"Yes." he said simply.

"I'm glad." She said.

"Glad?" Dawson asked.

"No one should be used to killing. No one should enjoy it. But I am glad you did it to save me and that you do it to protect other people."

Brandy got up and stood in front of Dawson. He looked at her inquiringly having no idea what she wanted. She just stood there looking at him for a moment and then sat down on his lap and snuggled up to him. He put his arms around her and held her.

"You make me feel safe." She said.

Chapter 12

"Brandy's infection is pretty much healed up, I am happy to say." Doc Arnie said to Dawson. "After the bout with Ashley, I've always worried about infections and our ability to fight them. Medicine isn't what it used to be."

"That's good." Dawson said. "I was surprised she had it."

"Most of these kinds of infections just crop up. She needs to stop sitting on the floor though. Too much dirt and bacteria. Wearing some clothes would help too if she insists on sitting there."

"You tell her that. I've tried." Dawson grinned.

"If that is what it takes." Doc Arnie said. "Heck, I'll even write her a prescription. Maybe that will do it." He pulled out his pad and wrote on it and tore out the sheet he'd written on. "Here." He said. "Don't take it to the drug store though. I doubt they'd fill it." He then grinned widely.

Dawson took the note paper and put it in his pocket with a laugh. "Whatever you say, Doc. Whatever you say."

"Well, I guess I should head back to the clinic." Doc Arnie said. "I'm sure Della has patients in a holding pattern by now."

He got up and walked out to his horse which he'd tied to the nearest rail fence. Dawson went with him. Doc Arnie easily stepped up into the stirrup and swung up into the saddle.

"Take care, Doc." Dawson said, "If you see Ed and Mike on the way tell them to hurry up. They should have been here by now."

"Will do." Doc Arnie said as he swung the mare around to leave.

Dawson watched him ride down the drive and out onto the two track. They waved a farewell and Doc nudged the mare into a canter and was gone.

Dawson went into the cabin and dug out some shorts and a t-shirt for Brandy while he mentally prepared to fight the clothing battle one more time. He took them out to the fireplace where Brandy sat as usual beside the fire on the floor.

"Brandy, the doctor says you either need to stop sitting on the floor or you have to start wearing clothes. It is your choice. Which do you want to do?"

"A slave goes naked." She said.

"Slaves might, free women don't. You are a free woman." Dawson sighed. Brandy was backsliding into her old slave mentality. That part of her mental healing was taking the longest time. Slavery had been driven deeply into her mind and thinking by trauma and brutality. She had good days and on occasion bad ones.

Brandy looked up at him uncertainly. "Do you want me to wear clothes?" she asked in a tone that Dawson recognized as that of a slave asking direction from her master.

"I think it would be safer for you if you did." He said genuinely.

She nodded her head and reached up for the clothing Dawson held in his hand. Brandy stood and slipped on the shorts and T-shirt and then sat back down.

Dawson sat down next to her close enough that their bodies touched. He didn't say anything right away.

"What do you see when you look into the fire?" he asked gently.

Brandy shrugged. "I see my baby Jessica. I see my husband. They see more real to me every day and I remember more about them.

"I like the fire because I can burn up bad memories when I think of them. I think I have more good memories now than I did when you saved me. Maybe someday I will burn up all the bad ones and only have the good ones left."

She leaned into Dawson a little and Dawson put his arm around her.

"I'm glad you are getting better." He said.

Just then a voice called from the barricade. Dawson got up and waved Ed and Mike in. They soon entered the cabin and nodded a greeting to Brandy that was friendly and warm. Brandy smiled shyly back at them and got up and went into the bedroom.

"At least she doesn't run like a scared rabbit anymore when we come by." Ed said. "She must be getting better."

"She is and she isn't. Most days she is good now, but every now and again for some reason she still calls me master and refers to herself as a slave."

"Well, I guess she's been through hell. It will work out in the end, I'm sure."

"Sit down. I've got something to show you." Dawson said. "I've been wrestling with this since I got back from Carrollton and decided you needed to see it."

Dawson retrieved the ledger and put it on the table in front of Ed. Ed opened it and briefly looked at it, and then he looked up at Dawson.

"When did you get this?" He demanded.

"A little over a week ago."

"You went to Carrollton a week ago? Tanya said you were going hunting."

"I was. I did. Sort of."

"Explain." Ed said, his eyes narrowing and his eyes hardening.

"I raided the armory in Carrollton." Dawson said simply.

"By yourself? You walked in there – into Carrollton - and raided the armory." Ed asked as though making sure he'd heard correctly.

"Yeah." Dawson said.

"Just you? No one else?"

"No. Just me."

"And you raided the pleasure house too, it seems." Ed said indicating the book.

"I wouldn't call it 'raided'. I'd call it intelligence gathering."

"So you are the one who blew up the armory and burned down half the town?" Ed said.

"Yeah. I hadn't planned on burning the town down though. That was just a side benefit."

Ed sat silently staring at Dawson incredulously. "Who the hell are you?" He finally asked in a tone of voice that reflected his incredulity and the realization that Dawson wasn't just the simple man he'd thought he was.

Dawson just shrugged. "Just a guy."

"Just a guy, my ass." Ed said.

"So, what do you think of the book?" Dawson asked.

Ed looked it over again. "Can't tell a damn thing from it." He said. "Other than they've run a lot of women through there and they aren't very original with insulting names."

"It tells me we need to clean it out." Mike said.

"Well, that brings up part of the reason I'm here." Ed said "I've got some guests at the farm right now. They showed up unannounced yesterday about sundown. They are representatives of the Colburn States. Seems they and the AHA have had enough of the both the Holderites and the Ragarians. Those two are the two smallest city states around and they cause most of the problems. The C.S. and the A.H.A. formed a war pact. They want to use my place as a staging area for launching an attack on Carrollton. Once they've settled Carrollton they will move on to Waterford. Once the Holderites are finished they will turn on the Ragarians. If the Holderites and Ragarians should happen to team up in some kind of alliance they can likely only field five to six hundred men between them – and that is pushing it. The Colburn's, AHA and their allies will likely field eighteen hundred.

"They also need you to help them."

"Me? Why me?"

"Tell you what; come on over to the house tomorrow for lunch. Della has a big feed planned anyway, so you might as well be there. They can tell you what they need and you can ask any questions you want direct."

Dawson nodded, "Alright." He said. "I'll be there around noon then."

"Great!" said Ed as he and Mike stood to leave. Dawson escorted them politely to the door and watched them thread their way down the path.

Dawson and Brandy showed up at Ed's door just a little before noon the next day. Della, Ed's wife, immediately latched on to Brandy as a mother hen gathering a lost chick. She swooshed her off into another room leaving her daughter and daughter's-in-law to finish the cooking. They returned just before lunch was served in the huge dining room of the farmhouse. Brandy had been changed out of her sweatshirt and shorts into a very feminine matching blouse and shorts set. Dawson noticed she was also now wearing a bra as well. Most noticeably, though, Della had spent time with her putting on makeup, eyeliner, and mascara and fixing the mess of a haircut the Holderites had given her in what appeared to be an effort to help Brandy start to recover her sense of worth and womanhood. Brandy was beautiful.

Della shot Dawson a glance indicating she needed to talk with him. Dawson nodded. They started to move toward the kitchen when her daughter announced lunch was on the table. Dawson gave her a "later" glance and she nodded uncertainly.

"Well, Councilman Jeffries," Ed said he passed the roast venison to his left after taking a slice "let's talk about your plan while we eat. I told Dawson some of what you told me, but I'm sure he will have questions."

"Councilman?" Brandy interrupted "You are a Councilman? Can you do weddings?"

The Jeffries looked at her with nonplussed expression. Her question was way out of left field.

"Yes. I suppose so." He answered hesitantly as though wondering where she was going.

"I want to marry Dawson! I want to be his wife. Then I won't be his slave." She said excitedly.

"I see." He said even more hesitantly, "and how do you feel about this?" he asked as he turned to Dawson. It was clear he had no idea what was going on and her use of the term 'slave' clearly bothered him.

Dawson gave Della and panicked questioning glance. She returned it with a clear and firm "Say yes! Go on!" type expression. Her eyes flashed as she did so.

"Yeah. I wasn't thinking we would do it quite so soon, but yes." Dawson said hesitantly.

"Have you thought about when you would like to get married?" he asked Brandy more warmly.

"Yes!" Brandy piped up excitedly "Today!"

The Councilman looked inquiringly at Dawson, "Whatever she says. She's in charge" Dawson said throwing his hands up in surrender and attempting to infuse some lightheartedness.

"You'll make a fine husband, Dawson!" Ed's daughter, Ellen, laughed "She already has you trained! Just remember: she is always in charge."

"Well, then. This afternoon perhaps? As soon as we are done here?" Jeffries said with a laugh.

They then turned to business. The Councilman was the main spokesman for the four envoys. The plan was for Colburn to bring five hundred men piecemeal across the border from the various Colburn villages and towns. They hoped to stage them at Ed's farm. Once the entire body was together they would then march on Carrollton. They would arrive at Carrollton from the east. The AHA and her allies numbering around thirteen to fourteen hundred men would arrive at the same time from the south. If things went according to plan they would sweep over the Holderites with minimal bloodshed to the civilians. Once they had consolidated their hold on Carrollton they would move en masse against Waterford. Splitting apart a couple miles out and hitting Waterford with a divided force on two fronts. They expected the fight in Waterford to be slightly harder and more time consuming, but they were certain of their ability to win. Once they had defeated the Holderites they would turn their attention to the Ragarians, hoping they would sue for peace rather than face annihilation as the Holderites had. If not, they would continue the advance against the Ragarians. If they sued for peace, however, our terms will be strict and unbending particularly as regards the question of slavery and territorial acquisition.

"What about the pleasure house slaves and other slaves?" Dawson asked. "What is to be done about them?"

The Councilman paused, "They will be freed, of course. The abhorrent practice of slavery is a major part of the reason for this police action. However, beyond that I am afraid we have little to offer them in the way of assistance."

"Many of these women are damaged mentally by what they have been through. They will need caring for, for a long time." Dawson said.

"Yes. I am sure they will. However we will have to largely leave that to their remaining family members and the larger community to deal with, unfortunately. We will, of course, be dividing the territory between the AHA and Colburn so there will be police and militia protection available to provide a secure environment, but we have few doctors available that can deal with this kind of trauma. We will do what we can, of course, and perhaps we can convince the West Hold Alliance to help, but right now our resources are somewhat limited."

"What do you need me to do?" Dawson asked.

"Yes, well, I am afraid we need you to do some of our more initially dangerous work. You are a woodsman of sorts. Mr. Johnson tells me you trap in the area; hunt its ravines and swales, and so on. In short you know the area like the back of your hand. We would like you to scout on ahead of the Colburn militias and remove any sentries or scouts that appear along the way and alert us to any patrols in our path. It may require very accurate shooting at some distances I'm afraid. Can you do that?"

"Councilman, I've seen Dawson put five .308 rounds in a four inch square at two hundred and fifty yards. Seen it, mind you, not heard about it. I measured the group myself. He can do it."

"Well, then, I guess the question is: will you do it?"

"I will on one condition. That being that when you take Carrollton I am there and I am on the team that busts open the pleasure house. I want to personally escort Caroline Harrison out of there if she is in there and still alive."

"Done!" said the Councilman. "Anything else?"

"No. Nothing."

"Yes!" Brandy piped in excitedly in almost a childlike manner "Can we get married now?" A ripple of laughter ran through the room at her enthusiasm.

The group adjourned to the living room and Dawson and Brandy faced one another in front of the Councilman.

"I am afraid in the Colburn States we do things rather simply, so I hope you weren't hoping for anything elaborate." He said. Hearing no objections he proceeded.

"We are gathered here to witness the marriage of these two people. If anyone can show just cause why they should not marry, speak now or forever hold you peace." He paused only for a moment then continued. "Brandy, do you take Dawson to be your husband?"

"I do." Brandy said beamingly

"And Dawson do you take Brandy to be your wife?"

"I do" Dawson said but with a tinge of uncertainty creeping into his voice.

"Then as a member of the First High Council Colburn States I pronounce you husband and wife." Then he gave a slight shrug as if to say, "That's it."

Brandy excitedly jumped into his arms and kissed him fervently.

"Now I am free!" she beamed happily.

"Your Brandy is still a very damaged woman." Della said to Dawson when they could sneak off alone to talk. "She healing some, but she is still fragile."

"I know." Dawson sighed. "I am not sure about this marriage thing though. I mean I feel for her, and I have a great deal of affection for her, but I don't know that I actually love her."

"I think having you as her husband will give her the security she needs to start to heal. She worships you. You saved her from those beasts and she is still trying to get her head around you being different from all the other men she has experienced over the past two or three years. They worked hard to break her spirit and her mind. They'd nearly succeeded when you happened along. Deep down, she knows that."

Dawson didn't say anything so she continued, "Be gentle with her. Keep teaching her new things so she can grow in confidence about herself and her abilities. Most of all shelter her. She is going to have bad days ahead as she adjusts. Being married will give her moorings to hold on to and she needs that security. I don't know if you really want to be married to her or not, but she is a beautiful, wonderful woman. I've picked up on that already. You could do far worse and the more you get to know her I think you will grow to love her. Besides you are still young and there isn't a lot to choose from as far as potential mates are concerned in this neck of the woods. You need a wife; you should not be alone like you are.

"In the meantime the girls and I will help her as much as we can. I think she has been through a lot of things only another woman can understand. Sooner or later, for example, that forced sterilization will cause her great grief and anguish. Men can't understand what that means to a woman."

Dawson nodded. "I'll do my best."

"D….Dawson?" Brandy asked that night as they sat next to the fireplace, she in her normal spot and he in his chair.

"Yes?" he asked gently.

"Am I really your wife? Was that for real this afternoon?"

"Yes. It was real."

"I am not your slave anymore?"

"Brandy, you never were my slave. Now you are my wife. That is all that matters."

He sat looking at her. She had taken off the clothes Della had given her and put on tank top and shorts as soon as they'd gotten home. Then she went back to her normal spot on the floor, staring into the fire. He assumed that was a reflexive action on her part and worried that she was mentally backsliding a bit.

"Come here." He said softly.

She got up and stood before him. He spread out his arms as though inviting her to sit on his lap. She hesitatingly did so.

"I want to make out with you, Brandy, but you can say no. You have that right. If you say 'no' I won't make you do anything. OK?"

She nodded but said nothing so he kissed her. She kissed back and he wrapped his arms around her and held her tightly as they kissed. Soon his hand found its way onto her left breast and he began to fondle her. She let out a soft moan. After a while of this he picked her up and carried her to the bedroom and laid her on the bed.

"Are you going to fu....Are we going to make love now?" she asked softly but seemingly unafraid.

"Yes. If you are ready."

She held her arms open for him. "You are my husband." She said softly and somewhat triumphantly "I want you!"

He stripped off his clothes and got into bed with her. They kissed some more while he fondled her breasts. They were firm to his touch yet perfectly soft. Her nipples came to attention and he touched her. Then he slid down and started to suck on one. Brandy let out a soft moan and arched her back as though encouraging him to keep going. He ran his hand down between her legs as he continued to suck on her. She spread her legs and gave a slight sudden sharp breath when his finger first gently touched her. It was obvious she had not been gently touched there in a long time. They kissed more passionately. She let out a soft moan followed by a whispered, "Oh God!"

He looked questioningly into her eyes and she nodded her head. He got on top of her and she spread her legs wider to accommodate his presence. He paused and looked into her eyes, worried about what she was thinking.

"Love me!" she begged "Please love me."

He pushed himself slowly into her as he said, "I do love you, Brandy." He stopped for a moment when he had fully penetrated her and kissed her heatedly. She moaned in pleasure. Their lovemaking was heated and passionate. When they were done they laid together in a tangle on the bed

After a long silence she whispered, "I had forgotten."

"Forgot what?"

"How to make love and what it felt like."

He looked at her questioningly.

"All I ever let myself do was fuck. They would come for me I let them use me. I had to shut off my feelings. I just spread my legs and fucked."

Dawson nodded and gently stroked her side and hip without saying anything. He didn't like to think about what she had been through nor how she'd been treated.

"I had forgotten what it was like to make love."

Dawson held her tightly to him and kissed her. "Get used to it." He said softly. She smiled.

"Maybe I'll remember how to have an orgasm someday." She said hopefully.

Dawson kissed her again, "It will happen in time. Trust me."

They fell asleep cuddled together.

They spent the next two weeks in the cabin "on their honeymoon." Dawson made love with Brandy many times and each time she seemed to blossom more. She started to sit in his lap in his chair voluntarily, and in a couple of instances she did so insistently as though claiming her right as his wife to sit there. She slowly began to lose her "slaveness" and became more comfortable with being his wife. They shared normal household chores like doing dished and laundry and gardening and as they did they talked. The more they talked the more she opened up, and she often times cried about things that had been done to her. When she did Dawson just held her silently and let her grieve.

One afternoon Dawson decided they would take a short hike to the river and do some fishing. He wanted to catch some fish for dinner and he also wanted to smoke some to put away for winter. Brandy wore a tank top and some shorts and sandals Della had given her. She chattered away excitedly as they walked along. It was the first time away from the cabin to do something 'different.'

When they got to the river which was about fifty yards wide and several feet deep at this spot they dropped their gear and Dawson quickly got a couple of lines into the water. He didn't have to wait long before he had a fish on the line and he pulled it in after a short fight.

"Nice trout! Dinner tonight!" he happily exclaimed after he'd landed it and held it up for Brandy to see. Brandy just smiled from her spot on the blanket under an old wild apple tree. Dawson put the fish into his basket and went back to fishing. Brandy laid back on the blanket and watched the clouds float by overhead. Her smile never faded.

Dawson concentrated on his fishing for another half hour and landed several more fish, mostly trout, occasionally turning his attention to his wife who just laid quietly on the blanket apparently enjoying nature. After he'd caught the last fish he needed to make enough to warrant starting up the smoker he gathered up his gear off the river bank and started toward Brandy. He stopped short when he realized Brandy was naked and laying quietly on her back on the blanket. He was immediately concerned that perhaps she was having a flashback to her slave days of not all that long ago.

"Brandy?" he asked quietly as he approached her. He didn't want to set off any bad memories.

"You are done fishing?" she asked lazily without opening her eyes.

"Yeah. I think we have enough to eat for a couple of days and to put away for winter both."

"Good!" she said as she broke into a smile and opened her eyes. "Now you can make love to me. This place is so beautiful! I want to make love with my husband and have happy memories of us being here."

Dawson chuckled and dropped to his knees on the blanket next to her. She immediately got up and started to unbuckle his belt and unzip his jeans. As he took off his shirt she pulled his penis out of his pants and took it into her mouth and started to suck on it. He let her pleasure him with her mouth for quite a while but then decided to return the favor. He gently pushed her back onto the blanket and the gently nudged her legs apart.

She spread her legs and looked at him questioningly. He moved between them and put his face into her pussy. The first time his tongue hit her clit she let out a very loud gasp of surprise and then relaxed. As he continued to work it with his tongue and then started to suck on it Brandy began to moan softly at first and then more loudly. She began to buck into his attentions on her clit and to thrash her arms and head around a bit. Suddenly she grabbed his head and held him tightly against her pussy. He started sucking on her clit more vigorously and plunged two fingers into her vagina. "YES!!" she yelled out suddenly "YES!!"

Dawson pulled his head away from her pussy and climbed up on her so he could kiss her. She looked at him with glazed blue eyes that were lit by a fire he'd not seen in her before. He had to have her. He shoved his penis into her body and started to fuck her. She responded almost immediately with very loud grunts and whines as he kept plunging to full depth inside her. He felt her leg muscles tighten against his thighs and he started to plunge into her even harder. Suddenly she picked her head up off the blanket and looked at him with crazed eyes and what looked like a pained expression.

Dawson slammed into her a few more times and then he knew he wouldn't be able to hold it much longer. "I'm going to cum!" he grunted through clenched teeth.

He almost immediately started to cum. It was the most intense orgasm of his life. Then he collapsed down on top of her and she quickly wrapped her arms around him as her vagina continued to gently milk his cock for every drop of semen. After a while he pulled out of her and took her into his arms.

They laid snuggled tightly together and Brandy smiled contentedly as she gazed into his eyes.

"I remembered." She said softly and sexily as she looked at him.

"Remembered what?" he asked gently.

"How to have an orgasm. I came while you filled me."

Dawson smiled at her. As he looked into her eyes he said, "I love you, Brandy." In that very moment he realized he was no longer saying it just to make her feel better and to feel safe. He meant it. Wedding ceremony or no, she was his wife. She had stolen his heart.

The real turning point, as far as Dawson was concerned however, was when they had their first fight. It was over a minor thing, like most arguments are, but still an argument. Brandy started out by slipping into slave mode out of habit when she realized Dawson was angry with her. Dawson then prodded her out of it verbally and purposely trying to make her angry. Finally he succeeded and she lashed out at him clearly drawing the line, marking her personhood, defending herself. Dawson had started laughing in victory and swept her into his arms even though she did not want to be held at that moment.

"I love you!!" he said as he looked into her angry face as she tried to wiggle out of his grasp. "I love you so much!" She stopped and looked at him trying to figure out why he was happy.

"I am happy you are angry with me!" he exclaimed

"Huh?" she said as a weird puzzled look filled her face as she stopped struggling.

"Honey. You are angry because you felt YOU were wronged. YOU felt wronged. You stood up for yourself!! Not all that long ago you would not have done that! I am so proud of you!!"

"You are happy I am mad?" she asked blinking her eyes as though clearing her head and trying to clarify what she'd heard.

"Yes!"

Her look softened and she melted back into his embrace.

"Can we have makeup sex now?"

Brandy looked up in mild interest as Dawson began rummaging through his gun closet. He pulled out one of the AR-15s that he'd gotten from a New Order patrol member who no longer needed it. That patrol had been particularly well armed and seemingly more organized. It was obvious that they were probing more determinedly and purposefully than previous patrols had.

He double checked the action, making sure it was clear, and then checked the rifle's function. He nodded in satisfaction. Next he grabbed a magazine out of the stack of AR mags and double checked to make sure it was a full, and then grabbed a few boxes of extra ammunition. Then he crossed the room and handed the AR to Brandy.

"Here. This is yours."

Brandy recoiled a bit from the rifle and looked at him in dismay.

"There's nothing to be afraid of. It isn't going to bite you. However, you need to know how to use this. Without this, you are just a helpless victim. With it, you may still end up on the losing end, but you will not have been helpless. With it, you could very likely not be the victim at all. You need to be able to defend yourself."

"I don't like them. I'm afraid of them." Brandy said fearfully.

"I know you've had a bad experience with them. But the truth is you had a bad experience with bad men who had them. The rifle is only a tool. It can be a good thing too.

"Now, take it and let's go outside."

Gingerly and reluctantly she took the rifle from his hands and got up. She followed him outside into the yard. Brandy watched as he set up an old bucket on a post about seventy five yards out. Then he came back and took the rifle from her and held it up so she could see it clearly.

"Now, this" he said pointing to a small switch "is the safety. In this position it cannot fire. Having said that, never completely trust it. Never put your finger on the trigger unless you are ready to shoot. The safety is just a backup device.

"Now, this," he said as he pointed to a small paddle like switch, "Closes your bolt. This rifle will lock open on your last shot. When you put a new magazine in, hit this paddle and it will close the bolt and feed the next round."

"This," he said pointing to a t-shaped thing at the back of the receiver, "is the charging handle. Only use this if the bolt didn't feed the next round for some reason. This is the forward assist" he said pointed at another knob. "Only use this if the bolt didn't close all the way for some reason. The rifle will not fire if the bolt isn't closed completely and locked shut. You shouldn't need it very much but it is nice to have."

"This," he said as he pulled the magazine from his pocket, "is the magazine. It holds your ammunition. It goes in here," he said pointing to the bottom of the receiver. "You lock it into place like this." He inserted it, "and then you close the bolt. If you need to drop the magazine you hit this button. The mag will drop on its own. You don't need to pull it out. Gravity is your friend with these."

He removed one of the bullets from the magazine and removed a 308 round from his pocket. "This is your ammunition. It is a 223 cartridge. Sometimes you will find them labeled 5.56. Pretty much the same but they are different. This rifle will fire both. Some won't. Now, this is a 308 round that my rifle shoots. See the difference? You rifle will not shoot my ammunition and my rifle will not shoot yours. So never grab the wrong stuff. If you do you'll be throwing it manually at the bad guys and probably not hurting them."

"I don't know how to shoot." Brandy said. "I've never done it."

"I'm not going to teach you to shoot. Anyone can shoot. All you have to do is pull the trigger to shoot. Most people are content to just shoot and once in a while hit their targets where they wanted to. That won't work if you are trying to defend yourself and stay alive. I'm going to teach you marksmanship. That is a skill set that you need to shoot well and accurately."

Brandy looked at him confusedly.

"Think back on the firefight when I rescued you. How many shots did I fire?"

"I don't remember. Ten, I think."

"Yes. Ten. How many hits?"

"Ten?"

"Yes. Each shot went pretty much where I wanted it to go. Now how many shots did they fire?"

"I don't know. A lot."

"And how many hits?"

"None."

"Exactly. They were just shooting; firing ammunition in my general direction and hoping to hit something. I fired every shot precisely and killed them. That is marksmanship verses just shooting. I'm going to teach you marksmanship.

"Now take your rifle and put the magazine into the receiver…..Good….make sure it is locked in place….good. Now bring the rifle to your shoulder and aim at the bucket. Place the top of the front post in the center of the aperture ring you are looking through. For now we are just going to shoot. I want you to get used to the rifle. Now place your finger on the trigger and when you are ready flip the safety off."

There was a very long pause, almost to the point where Dawson was sure she'd frozen in fear. Then he heard a soft 'click.'

"Now when you are ready, just squeeze the trigger. Don't jerk it, just gently squeeze it. The rifle should surprise you when it goes off."

Another long pause and then the rifle suddenly went off. A hole appeared on the left edge of the bucket.

"I hit it!!" Brandy squealed excitedly and started to swing the muzzle toward Dawson. He quickly caught it and held it forward.

"Yes. You did, but watch your muzzle. Don't swing it around. Safety first and always is the rule. Slip your safety on."

Brandy flipped the safety and Dawson took the rifle from her.

"It didn't kick at all!" she said, "I thought it would hurt!"

"No it really doesn't. The AR is a good girl's gun. It is shorter than an M1A and lighter. It also has softer recoil. It is just as deadly, but easier for girls to handle and easier for soldiers in close quarters. He handed the rifle back to Brandy. "Now, do it again."

Once Brandy was comfortable with just shooting, he got her down on the ground and started to teach her how to properly and accurately aim, how to hold the rifle steadily, and how to lay so that she was completely steady in the prone position. The rest of the afternoon was spent in fine tuning her skills and by the end of the afternoon she was shooting consistent 3 M.O.A. groups at barricade distance. She was able to progress so well, Dawson figured, because she had no bad habits to unlearn. He'd seen it happen before.

"Not bad for a beginner." He said as they went back into the house. "At least now you can defend yourself if you need to when I am not here."

Brandy shot him a panicked look, and he continued. "You know I have to go to Carrollton. I'm taking you to the Johnson's when I go, but you need to be able to defend yourself should something happen. In all likelihood nothing will happen, but you at least need to be prepared."

"I don't like the idea of you going. I don't want anything to happen to you. I want to come too."

"Brandy, I can't do what I need to do if I am worried about your safety. The Johnson men and some of the other community members are all going to be at the farm. They all can defend their property and compound. So can the women. Now you can help if necessary."

"I should stay here in case someone comes here."

"No. If someone comes here while you are at the Johnsons they will find an empty house which they may or may not destroy or rob. They won't find you and they won't take you. If you are here alone, they could and likely would. If they come to the Johnsons they will find a whole world of hurt, and they won't take you. I need that peace of mind."

Brandy nodded. "Alright, but I don't like any of it. I'm your wife and I should have a say in this."

A week later Dawson and Brandy arrived at the compound. Dawson was amazed at what he found. Rows of bivouac tents were set up in the fields around the compound. The thing that caught his eye however was a group of tents set up slightly apart from the others. There was a flag flying overhead on a makeshift flagpole. The flag was dark blue with the British Jack in the corner and a configuration of stars in the blue field.

"My God, the Aussies are here!" he gasped aloud.

"Who?" Brandy said looking where he was pointing.

"The Australians. What the hell?"

They continued on through the gates of the compound and went into the kitchen of the Johnson house. Tanya, carrying Dawson's 'step-grandson,' met him almost as soon as he arrived. She handed the baby off to Dawson.

"He's heavy." She laughingly said. "Good timing on your part."

Kelly, who was about six months pregnant, came in shortly thereafter as did Cassie who was pregnant again and just starting to show.

They chatted excitedly for a while until Ed came into the kitchen from the porch.

"Dawson, they need you in the C.P." Ed said solemnly.

Dawson nodded. "Right. I'll be right there." Brandy looked at him in near panic. He held her tightly and then kissed her. "Don't worry. This is just a planning and strategy meeting. No one is going anywhere right now."

Brandy nodded and they let each other go.

Dawson entered the C.P. to discover a large map spread out on a table which was surrounded by several men in uniform.

"Ah! Dawson! You are here." Councilman Jeffries said enthusiastically. "Let me make introductions. Everyone this is Dawson VanOrder. He is to be your vanguard and guide. He knows this area like the back of his hand and I'm told he can eliminate sentries quite handily in the advance of your troops.

"Now, Dawson, this is Lieutenant General Howard of the Colburn Army. To his left is Major Moltree of the A.H.A. He is here as liaison between our forces and the A.H.A. Next to him are our surprise visitors: Captain Nigel Barrett and Major John Thomas who commands the Royal Tasmania Battalion unit bivouacked with us. It seems they were tasked with tracking down fleeing Iranian troops and decided to throw in with us."

"Only a portion of the unit, actually." Major Thomas said with a smile. "Our battalion was separated into 'chase units' after the Battle of Stockton."

"Battle of Stockton?" Dawson asked.

Major Thomas smiled knowingly. "I'm afraid you yanks were in a bit of a pickle after the bomb went off. Most of the northern hemisphere was actually. You were invaded within weeks of the EMP explosion. We were able to liberate Hawaii with little trouble and then turned our attention to the mainland. We managed to put about 15,000 men on the ground in California and about 4,000 RAAF personnel as well. We would have sent more, except, well,

England was in the same straits as you so...well...you can understand that we made liberating England our priority. Our Navy has managed to keep the Iranians away so rescue or reinforcement was impossible so the fleeing troops went inland after the Battle of Stockton. We, and several others, were sent after them. As near as we can tell, they are now out of ammunition, running out of people, and running out of time. It would seem that the Japanese were wise not to invade your country. I do believe there is a rifle behind every blade of grass here.

"We decided to join your little soiree because, well...justice seems to demand it."

Dawson nodded his head, "Much obliged for your help."

"Now, Dawson, Ed tells me that you have made a couple of trips to Carrollton in recent weeks?" Jeffries said.

"Yes. I did. I did a recon mission and a 'covert operation.'"

"Covert operation?" Captain Barrett asked.

"Well, that is what we used to call it...that and 'wet work.'"

"I see. Special Forces training then?" Thomas asked. It was clear he was assessing assets and liabilities in the coming conflict.

"No, no I was regular army. Just a grunt."

"I see. Then....?"

Dawson sighed. "Have you heard of Angel Logistics?"

"No, I'm afraid I haven't." Thomas said.

"Good. You shouldn't have. Officially we trained security guards and bodyguards for large corporations and security companies. Actually we were government contractors for off book operations as well as training SF forces for specific things related to upcoming covert missions. We even did some training work in Australia just before I 'retired.'"

"I see. Operations were done where?" Thomas asked.

"I've personally been on five continents, in twenty seven countries, and more firefights than I can count including some alongside U.S. Army personnel in Iraq and Afghanistan in the seven years I was with them."

"And you left the company under what circumstances?" he asked.

Dawson chuckled. "Worst of all reasons. I fell in love with a woman who couldn't deal with the fact I could get killed at work."

Thomas smiled. "Yes, well...one cannot blame a man for wanting the joys of domestic tranquility, I suppose."

"Now, then," Chancellor Jeffries interrupted. "We have a map of Carrollton on the table there. Is it still relatively accurate?"

"Well, mostly." Dawson said after examining it for a moment. "From what I understand a chunk of this section of town is now in ruin and ashes."

"From what you understand? You don't know?" General Howard asked.

"Well, when I left it was burning pretty brightly. I was told by a source later they lost most of two blocks to the fire, including their armory and their barracks. I was also told that Holder sent in his shock troops to quell any type of rebellion. I've no way of knowing if they are still there or not. I've not had contact with the underground since that raid."

"Underground?" Howard asked.

"Yeah. There is one. They mostly do sabotage and convenient assassinations."

"And your connection with them is....?" Thomas asked.

"Their leader and I...anyway, she's dead now. I picked up her fight where she left off."

"How do I know you aren't just making this up?" Howard asked. "You seem rather larger than life."

Dawson shrugged. "In my field pack is nine hand grenades and one claymore that used to belong to the New Order Liberation Militia. I took them with me when I left the armory before it blew up. If you want a floor plan drawn out of it, I can do that but it will look like a big box because that was all it was. At home I have fourteen AR-15s, two AR-10s and an assortment of side-arms that until a month ago belonged to a patrol I caught unaware headed toward our little community here. I gave them back a couple of the grenades. I had twelve at one point. The weapons our community uses for defense are ones I gathered up for them. Up to you whether you believe me or not." Dawson's tone of voice clearly showed he wasn't interested in proving himself.

"Now," he continued. "A number of these alleys are blocked off. Defense works, mind you, not with garbage. The streets are fairly clear but there are ambush points along the streets and sniper nests in upstairs windows along the main street. I didn't see any evidence of anything larger than 7.62 but I couldn't see what they have in those upstairs nests. For all I know they have .50 cals or machine guns. Personally, if it was me, I'd use the alleys to my advantage. The militia isn't organized and will likely take off if things get hot. The alleys are a quick way to cut off retreating men and while they will be defended they aren't likely to put their best and brightest in an alley. I would guess a third of the militia will be conscripts and they don't want to fight for Harlan Holder any more than I do. They will take off first chance they get."

"What about Ragarians?" Barrett asked.

"Ragarians? Never saw any. Should I?"

"We don't know. They and the Holderites apparently have decided to put aside their differences and form a mutual defense alliance. If there are Ragarians around...well...it makes things easier and harder at the same time. We'd rather take them on singly but we should still have the advantage should we take them on at the same time." Howard said.

"Westhold should keep them busy on their own frontier. They will be attacking Ragar from the west while we are taking The New Order from the east. That should strain the alliance if it actually exists." Jeffries said.

"Now, Dawson, you asked to command the unit charged with liberating the pleasure house. How to you propose to do that?" Jeffries continued.

"Depends on what I get to work with. I'd prefer a small unit: eight men at most. If I can't get anyone with combat experience I'll take what you can give me and do it differently. If I get the small unit, I'll come in from the north through the fence while you have them fighting to the south and east. We'll take the pleasure house without much resistance that way."

"Through the fence?" Howard asked.

"Yes, through the fence. We'll cut our way in. The fence is 8 foot high but it is standard chain link. I got in that way before.

"Now if I can't get the small group, we'll bust in the same way you do through the gates and then separate from the main body. We'll head down Elm here, the cut down 7th Ave and fight our way to Evergreen. Once there we take the pleasure house. I doubt defending it will be high on their priority list."

"I've got six chaps you can have." Thomas said.

"Done then!" Jeffries announced. "Anything else?"

Everyone just shook their heads.

"Good! You'll move out a 5:00 a.m. tomorrow morning. We expect it will take a little more than two days for you to get to Carrollton so you'll need the early start."

At 5:00 a.m. the next morning Dawson headed out ahead of the advancing Colburn militias. He moved about a mile ahead of the militias and the Australians. The first part of the trip was uneventful and he'd have been surprised if it had been any other way. About 10 miles from Carrollton he began to come across sentries hidden in elevated tree stands. He killed five of them with his suppressed M1A.

When the militias were within 5 miles of Carrollton a Holderite patrol coming from out of nowhere stumbled into the left flank of the Colburn militias. A brief firefight ensued and then the militias moved on leaving the patrol behind unburied.

Two miles out from Carrollton they camped for a second time. Dawson slept lightly. He always did on missions. This was no different even though he had around eight hundred men with him.

At 5:00 he and his team left the camp and started to make their circle to the north. He had brought his complete combat kit with him making him as equally prepared for battle at the Australians accompanying him. The only real difference, equipment wise, between them was that Dawson was carrying Melania's M1 carbine. The militias were supposed to be moving out about an hour later after Dawson's team left camp.

At about 7:00 a.m. he and his team waited patiently in the hills looking down on Carrollton. They would not move until the alarms sounded or shooting started. At about 8:00 a.m. the action started. Dawson had no way of knowing that the combined Colburn, A.H.A., Australian forces hit the gates of Carrollton like a rolling storm. They had approached largely undetected, due to the lazy nature of the New Order guards, until within a quarter mile of the gates. When the alarms started Dawson and his team moved quickly down the hillside to the fence.

The fence was quickly cut and they ducked through and headed in tactical formation toward the pleasure house. There were several guards setting up makeshift defenses around the house when Dawson's team turned the corner on Evergreen. Before the guards could react the team opened fire and the guards dropped like flies.

Once at the pleasure house proper they burst through the door and stormed in. A Holderite who was going up the stairs leading a completely docile naked woman behind him was cut down by Dawson's M1 carbine before he even knew they were there. The squad spread out through the building, half pouring up the stairs and half spreading out through the main floor, quickly hoping to take all the occupants by surprise, kicking open doors and killing any men they found in the rooms, and killing any men in their path who emerged from sex rooms in response to the gunfire. Then as suddenly as it started it was over. The whole raid hadn't taken three minutes. The only thing heard was the frightened crying of the women as they huddled in their rooms.

"Don't touch anyone!" Dawson ordered in a shout. "They think all we are going to do is take them away as our slaves. Just keep them safe, but do not touch them no matter how much you want to comfort them."

He kicked open the basement door and quickly descended the stairs with two of his team following immediately after him. He hadn't seen Caroline yet and he was fearful of what he would find in the basement. The open part of the room right at the bottom of the stairs was a torture chamber. A couple of women dangled nearly lifelessly from overhead wrist manacles. In fact, Dawson thought they were dead until he saw one of them move slightly. They were nearly gone. They had been severely tortured to the point where Dawson wondered if perhaps he should slip a knife between their ribs and end their suffering. One had clearly had her legs and arms broken, yet she hung suspended by her wrists. Her face was battered as though it had been used as a punching bag. The other had been partially flayed, one breast sliced wide open, and from the blood around her mouth he suspected her tongue had been cut out as well. He nodded to the two men with him and they proceeded to take the women down and lay them carefully on the floor.

It was then Dawson kicked open the door that led to the rest of the basement. The door was ominously labeled "Culling Room."

The room was dimly lit and squalid. Dirt and filth were everywhere. Two women in blood covered plastic aprons stood next to two women who'd been hung upside down by their ankles. One hung lifelessly, the last of her life blood dripping off her short cropped hair. The other one of the hung women was still alive, or appeared to be. A pile of hair on the floor indicated they'd just finished crudely chopping her hair off in preparation for cutting her throat. One of the apron clad women was still holding the sheers they'd cut her hair with. The other one held a scalpel in her hand. She quickly knelt next to the living woman and put the scalpel to her neck.

"Drop it or I cut her!" she spat.

It was a useless and desperate threat. Dawson had entered the room with his carbine at the ready and had the women covered almost from the moment he'd charged in. He didn't even have to actually aim. He pulled the trigger twice and the woman with scalpel pitched backward against the wall and then flopped down in a heap into the trough of blood that followed along the wall. She never moved again.

The second woman just knelt where she was and put her hands up behind her head. Dawson stepped aside and his two team members came in and secured her. Then they proceeded to lower the hung woman down to the floor as gently as they could and attend to her.

Dawson could now survey the room. There was an iron barred door and wall that divided the room. One third of the room contained the culling stations and the other two thirds contained five or six women lying on filthy mattresses amid filth he'd never imagined possible. The whole room stunk of sweat, urine, and sickness.

Dawson slipped the latch on the door and went into the cell. Caroline was lying naked on her side, facing the door on one of the mattresses. He rushed to her, knelt down and said softly, "Caroline? It's me! Dawson."

Caroline did not seem register that she knew him. She simply rolled over onto her back and spread her legs for him. To her, he was just another Holderite who had come to rape her again. He picked her head and shoulders up and held her tightly and lovingly against his chest. Her eyes fluttered for a moment and she let out a loud anguished wail. Then she went silent again.

Dawson sighed heavily and reluctantly got up and left the room and went back upstairs. As much as he wanted to stay with Caroline he knew they still needed to secure a perimeter around the house to protect it should the fighting roll their way. An Australian medic team was just arriving as he came through the door to main floor. They headed straight to the basement having been told over the radio why they were needed and where. Dawson and his crew took up positions outside the house and prepared to defend the house. It proved to be unnecessary. The fighting never got to them. The Holderites all fell or surrendered in the face of overwhelming numbers before the fighting got that close. Carrollton was free and would, according to the plan, end up belonging to the Colburn States. Waterford, down the road, would belong to the A.H.A. when it was taken.

"I suppose we will find more of that when we get to Waterford," one of the medics said when he came out of the house a long while later. "Breaks my heart to see what went on in there."

"What about the women in the basement?" Dawson asked.

"The one has so many broken bones I'm not sure she will ever be physically right again, but she should live. The other one died just as we were starting to take her down. That was probably a mercy really." The medic said sadly.

"What about the women in the other room?"

"Most are mentally broken, some are broken physically too. They will need personalized care from now, I think. They will need a quiet place, with nothing but friendly faces around them, and the patience to let them heal if they ever do. That is all we can give them, I think. The shrinks aren't going to be able to help some of them right away if ever. They are pretty much just zombies right now, including your friend.

"I suppose we will find more of the same in Waterford." He said in a pained voice. "Maybe worse."

"I heard they had two pleasure houses there." Dawson said sadly.

The medic nodded, "Yeah. I've heard that too. Supposedly one in Myersville up near the northern border too, I guess. Are you going to lead a squad again for the assault on Waterford?"

"No. That is territory I am not familiar with and I've never been to Waterford or Myersville, so I am pretty useless from here on. I'm going to wait around here for a few days and take Caroline home as soon as she can travel or I can find a way to get her there if she can't walk."

The medic nodded. "Well then, be safe. Be patient with your friend. I don't know if she will ever heal, but even if she doesn't she will need you."

A year later life had changed considerably. The war had been mercifully short though difficult. The Holderites had fallen quickly. Their militias were little more than organized thugs with little training. The Storm Troops had fought hard, but eventually gave it up. The Ragarians were no more but they had been tougher and more disciplined. From what Dawson heard of the conflict it was likely that somewhere down the road the Ragarians would have crushed Harlan Holder's little kingdom on their own anyway and wiped them from the face of the earth.

Harlan Holder had been tried by a military tribunal. The trial had been a public spectacle and once he had been found guilty and when the court heard testimony about the abuses of the pleasure houses, they had let a delegation of women from the houses determine his punishment. The women had demanded public castration and then crucifixion. They wanted his death to be as publically humiliating and prolonged as possible. The tribunal balked at first and then reluctantly agreed to the sentence the women wanted to impose. Most of the community saw it as being just and fair for the mutilations and degradation some of the women present exhibited for the court on their persons and for the pictures of the bodies of mutilated women who had not survived that had been entered into evidence. Holder had screamed like a baby when his manhood was cut away and the wound cauterized. His crucifixion had been done by several of the women from the houses in Waterford that he himself had raped and abused. They vengefully nailed him to his cross in the name of all who'd suffered. He then begged to be shot while on his cross up until the moment he finally died the next day.

The most important news for Dawson and Brandy personally, had been from the doctors at the medical center in Amberton. After a complete examination they had told Brandy that the sterilization procedure performed on her by the Holderites' veterinarian had been so amateurishly done that it was still possible, though more difficult, for her to have children. The effect of that news had been life changing for her. She had more enthusiasm now about everything and seemed to find more joy in life. She was a "whole woman again" as she put it when she heard the news and insisted that they 'officially' try to have a baby. She was getting better each day.

Dawson stood in his doorway looking out into his garden. Caroline was pulling weeds, carefully and painstakingly, stopping to examine each weed after she had pulled it from the ground as though seeing a new thing. It was the first time she had moved from her chair to do anything significant except eat and go to bed since she had arrived. She had been an avid gardener before the world collapsed so maybe this was her first step back into the real world. She still had not spoken yet, but she no longer just rolled over on her bed and spread her legs when Dawson walked by. He did not know if Caroline would ever come back, but he had hope. He missed the woman she used to be. He still loved her very much and wanted her back.

Doc Arnie had examined her and said that physically she was as healthy as she could be given the abuse she'd suffered. Mentally, however, he could not offer an opinion other than to say that the emotional trauma she'd been through might make coming back impossible. He speculated that in addition to the rapes and beatings she'd likely been forced to watch as her children were executed. He based that speculation on things he'd been told by other doctors dealing with other traumatized women from the houses. Brandy had agreed with him. That was what had been done to her by the Ragarians and she knew how effective it was in starting to destroy her mind.

Brandy slipped up next to him and put her arm lovingly around his waist and leaned against him. He could feel her adoration for him radiating off her as she held herself close to his body. She watched Caroline for a few moments.

"She may come back someday." Brandy said.

"I hope so." Dawson said quietly.

"She talked last night." Brandy said.

"She did?" Dawson was surprised.

Brandy nodded. "After you went to bed. I was about to follow after you. She got up from her chair and said she was tired then she got into her bed."

"Well, that is something."

They watched Caroline pull another weed from the ground and examine it closely like she had with the ones previously.

"I was lucky." She said softly after a while. "And so is she."

"Lucky?" Dawson asked as he looked down at her. He could not help but notice she had changed. Her hair had grown out to nearly shoulder length and had begun to show a small bit of a natural wave. Like her hair, Brandy had grown. Every day she seemed to be more and more like the woman he figured she probably had been almost four years ago before everything fell apart. It was like watching a beautiful flower bloom. Granted, there were still occasional days when she would sit and stare into the fire with that lost blank look she'd had the first night she was with him in the cabin, but they were growing fewer and fewer. On rare occasions she would start to hide in a corner when there was a sudden unexpected knock at the door, but not nearly as often as before and when she did she caught herself and didn't hide. She would never completely be over her PTSD, but she was better.

"Yes. Lucky you found me that day; that you killed those men who had me, that you took me in, and that you loved me in spite of the mess I was. I was lucky you married me, and that you saved me. I would have been dead or just like her by now if you hadn't. I was lucky."

"She's lucky because you love her enough to take care of her knowing she may never come back. You'll protect her just as you would me. I think she knows that too. Look at her out there in the garden. She isn't afraid to be there. Down deep something tells her she is safe now."

Dawson put his arm around his wife and hugged her tightly.

"You know who really was lucky?" he asked, "I was the lucky one." Then he turned and embraced her and kissed her lovingly. "I was the lucky one."

Made in the USA
Lexington, KY
18 November 2017